Out of the Dark

Sundae Leighton

Published by Sullen Press, 2021.

Out of the Dark
Available in these formats:
978-1-7376181-2-6 (Paperback)
978-1-7350077-9-3 (eBook AZW)
978-1-7376181-4-0 (eBook EPUB)
Copyright: © 2021 Sullen Press, LLC
All rights reserved.

Beta Reader: Stephanie Cooper
Cover: E Leighton
Editor: Heart Full of Reads

For my husband—

Real love is forever

Playlist

Butterflies— Kacey Musgraves
Alone With You— Jake Owen
You and Tequila— Kenny Chesney
Wildest Dreams—Taylor Swift
Everything I Wanted— Billie Eilish
Knowing You— Kenny Chesney
All I Ask— Adele
'Til Summer Comes Around— Keith Urban
Let You Go— Machine Gun Kelly
Memory I Don't Mess With—Lee Brice
I Should Probably Go To Bed— Dan + Shay
Good 4 U— Olivia Rodrigo
Ya'aburnee— Halsey
When You're Home— Tyler Shaw
Waves—Luke Bryan

Prologue

Hutch

I hurt everywhere. There wasn't a muscle in my body right now that wasn't screaming at me as I made my way back to the cabin that I was currently sharing with three other guys. The coaches at the camp had worked us to the bone today, and even though I loved every single minute of it, the only thing I wanted to do right now was take a shower before I crawled into bed and slept.

I had to admit I wasn't exactly thrilled when my parents suggested going to football camp this summer. Sure, I had dreams of going pro, but I was a fifteen-year-old boy with pretty much on my mind twenty-four hours a day.

Tits, ass, and pussy. The ones that happened to be attached to Mya Lane, my girlfriend, back home in Ocean View. Sure, we hadn't gone past second base, but we were getting really close. I could feel it.

I pushed the door open to the cabin, only to be greeted by the stench of sweat, stinky feet and... Good lord, what was that? I was spoiled rotten not having to share a room with my kid brother, Patrick, and whatever it was smelled like rotten fucking cheese right now. I tried not to dry heave as I grabbed some clean clothes from my bag, a towel, my soap, and then headed down to the showers to wash up.

Maybe I could call Mya later tonight. It had been a few days since we had spoken, but that wasn't for my lack of trying. She was busy working at her parents' grocery store, and like me, was too exhausted most nights when we actually did make contact. I stripped out of my workout clothes and dropped them on the floor before I turned on the water in the shower and stepped beneath it. The water pressure wasn't nearly as good as back home, but right about now, I didn't care. The hot water unknotted the tensed joints and muscles that I didn't even know I had. My coach at Ocean View High worked us vigorously during the school year, so this was saying a lot.

The man never let us slack off, and if someone even tried? Everyone single of us suffered for it.

I was looking forward to getting back to school this fall. I would most likely make starting quarterback this year, and along with the rest of my classmates, and players, we would rule the halls of our school. I would have my beautiful, smart, girlfriend—

Without warning, my arms were yanked behind me as something was dropped over my head, obstructing my vision. I tried to fight, but whoever it was much stronger than I was.

"Don't try to fight this," a masculine voice hissed into my ear. "There are more of us than you can handle on your own, Hutch Kelly." His friends' heavy laughter followed behind his words. It sounded like they were all men.

I didn't recognize the voice. I didn't listen to what he said either and kept struggling as I was yanked onto my back and they began to drag me across the wet concrete floor. "Fuck off." I slammed my head against the floor, which caused bright stars to explode behind my eyes.

Someone clucked their tongue against the roof of their mouth. "Now, now, Hutch, if you fight us, you're only going to make it that much worse for you." I was flipped onto my stomach before my hands were tied behind my back. Then I was pulled up onto my feet. "Walk." Something cold poked me in the back, and I shivered despite the fear that swirled in my belly. I had gone on plenty of hunting trips with my father and uncles to know the feel of a gun.

A hand wrapped around my arm to the left. "If you run, we'll make you wish that you were never born, boy." Then my skin was pierced brutally as he dug his nails straight into my arms.

I wasn't sure how far we walked, but it felt like a million miles. Since I couldn't see with the sack over my head, I stumbled, fell, and had to be helped getting up more than a few times. I never said a word as we moved. Never even peeped, hoping that they would let me go if I played along. Finally, they shoved me down onto my knees and I felt grass and damp leaves against my naked skin from the rain from the night before. One of them clamped a hand down on my shoulder while another spread my legs.

That was right about when I suddenly realized what was about to happen. "No!" I didn't even recognize the sound of my own voice.

Another hand landed on my elbow as I was pushed facedown into the ground. "Relax, Hutch, you might fancy enjoying this," he insisted and laughed when I tried to kick back at him. That just resulted in having my legs pinned down by one of them. I was strong for my age, but whoever it was, was much stronger.

"You should feel honored. You're so much more attractive than the rest of them," another one remarked. Like it was something anyone would even want to be proud of.

I fought like hell as best I could. I screamed and I cried as each of them — I counted six — took turns raping me. They didn't use lubrication, but they did use protection because I heard the sound of the condoms being ripped open in my ear every single time. The sounds of their voices in my ears, their groans, and grunts as they plunged into me from behind would forever stay drilled into my memory as they got off inside me. Tears stung my eyes, poured down my face, and before long, I wished they would kill me. I bit down on my bottom lip so hard I tasted blood because I refused to make any noise. I didn't want them to know how much pain I was in or that right now I wished I was dead.

Then once they were all finished, they left me where they raped me in the middle of the forest, broken and bleeding, with the sack still over my head.

I must have passed out at some point because when I came to it was dark, I was alone and untied. I cried and screamed out into the black forest until I threw up my lunch from this afternoon. My body shook as I got to my feet, my legs threatening to give out from beneath me. This felt like a nightmare that no one, male or female, should ever have to live through. If I thought I had been in pain from practice, I didn't even know what pain was as I weakly tried to navigate my way back to camp.

Each step sent searing pain through my backside, and more than once I had to stop, tears sliding down my face. I didn't want to touch myself. I didn't want to see what I looked like, for fear it would push me completely and totally over the edge. I'm not sure how long it took me to find my way back to camp, but when I did, I stopped at the showers, the same ones that I had been ripped from hours before, and found my bag sitting where I had left it.

I washed off, dressed without looking in the mirrors, and then limped back to my cabin. No one saw me. Not a soul was awake. I crawled into my bed, forever changed.

I would never be the same.

Chapter One

Jillian

I stared up at the ceiling above my bed trying to stop the room from spinning, while focusing on the glow of the dark stars that were stuck above my head. I had returned home yesterday after spending a month at ballet camp and my friends had spared no expense with the party they had thrown for my homecoming. I began to reach for my cell, which I usually kept tucked beneath my pillow, when I heard the faint sound of snoring.

Wait a second. Did I bring someone home with me last night?

I mull over last night's events in my brain. Bella Black had thrown the party at her parents' place since they had been gone for the evening. Claire Meyers, Holly Carver, and my sister, Jo, all had been there. Madison hadn't originally been invited, but because Bella is friendly and kind, she was afraid to tell her Madison wasn't part of crowd once she ran into her picking up things at the store. Jo had left about an hour into the party to go be with her boyfriend, Pat, which was nothing new, but the party had been strictly a clam jam though. No dick allowed.

The snoring started again so I slowly eased myself to the end of the bed before I realized I was on the top of the bunk beds that Jo and I used to share when we were little. Until she decided that she wanted her own room because we weren't babies anymore. When the hell was the last time I slept on the top bunk? I usually kept a pile of crap up here that consisted of my gym clothes that I practiced in, useless junk I didn't know what to do with, and a few other odds and ends. Random dude had begun sounding exactly like a motorcycle now so I peeked my head over the side of the bed to see exactly who was making such a ruckus, and gasped in surprise.

Hutch Kelly snored on the lower bunk before. Older brother to my sister's boyfriend, Patrick, he wasn't exactly a stranger, but not someone I could call a friend either. Not for my lack of trying at least. The way his toned long legs hung off either side of the twin bed might have been comical if I wasn't curious as to why he was here. Hutch was, well, different. Incredibly quiet, known to be a loner, and quick to anger on occasion when provoked; he hardly spoke unless he needed to. Even then, it was usually a word or two that he grunted out, and it always seemed like he was doing it to please the person speaking to him. I had been on the receiving end of that myself more than once, and it was hella awkward. Hutch was the cuter, more beautiful version of Kelly, with his perfect chiseled jaw, flawless cheekbones, and gorgeous blond hair, but there some something danger lurking behind his brown eyes. Something dark and terrible that he wanted to keep hidden from the rest of Ocean View.

He was eight years older than me, which made him twenty-six. I knew that he worked as a mechanic at Zed's Automotive, but we didn't really hang out together despite the fact that he was brothers with Pat. Like I said... a lone wolf. My mother moved us to Ocean View when I was eight, right after Dad died, and according to the gossip mill around town, that was the summer that Hutch started acting the way he is now. No one knew why, and if Patrick did, he never said anything despite the fact that Pat and Jo had been inseparable since the moment we moved here.

I still had no idea why Hutch was in my room right now.

Suddenly his eyes flew open to reveal those deep, milk chocolate browns. They grew wide with surprise when he realized where he was or maybe it was that I was ogling him, before his mouth formed a perfect circle. Hutch tried to jump out of the bed, entangled himself in the sheets, and then simple fell hard on the hardwood floor like a giant sack of potatoes. It might actually have been comical if I wasn't terrified that he had broken a bone.

"Crap, Hutch, are you alright?" I jumped down from the top and landed gracefully onto my feet. *Thank you, years of ballet.* The room spun around me, but I tried to ignore that while silently swearing off booze forever. Hutch held up a hand to stop me with terror in his eyes as I attempted to touch him. He quickly removed the sheets and stood up towering over me. He gripped the nape of his neck with his left hand as he stared me down. I watched as his dark eyes searched my face before they dropped down my body, and I couldn't help but fold my arms over my chest as I felt him take me in. God Almighty, the man was a pure work of art. I was about to speak again when a knock sounded at my door.

"Jillian, are you alright?" Emily Robinson aka my mother asked softly. The woman was always up at the crack of dawn like some sort of bird catching the worm.

I grimaced as I tried to think of something quick. "Uh, sure. Fine, Mom," I tried to assure her. "Just tripped over my gym bag." Hutch's brows dipped at the lie that slipped so easily from my lips.

"You're up early."

Right, because there was a hot man snoring in my bed; I have no idea why or how he got here; and now he looked terrified of me touching him, but it's fucking fine. I glanced over at Hutch to find him staring at the pictures I had of me and my friends against the wall. Or maybe he was just trying to avoid looking at me. "I have breakfast plans at the Egg," I finally answered my mother, hoping she might believe that one. "With Hutch." I watched the way his head swung around to stare at me with surprise written all over his beautiful face.

"Hutch," Mom repeated his name as if she had never heard it before.

I rolled my eyes. "Hutch, Mom. You know, Patrick's older brother. Tall, quiet, and incredibly good-looking." I watched the way his ears turned pink, but he narrowed his eyes as if I had called him a puppy killer instead. "Ran into him last night on the way to Bell's so we thought we would catch up, and if you don't want me to be late, I should really jump in the shower." I was just digging myself into a bigger and deeper hole, but honestly, I should probably blame Hutch for this, since he was in my room.

I heard the sweep of Mom's slippers as she took a step away. "Okay, well, have fun." She sounded confused, but then, her retreating feet told me she had moved down the hallway.

I clamped my hand over my mouth as a laugh threatened to escape, only to notice the way Hutch was scowling at me with dark eyes. "Are you mad at me?" I demanded. "Don't forget you're the one in my room," I pointed out, before he could reprimand me.

He shook his head, but didn't comment further. Instead, he started toward the window, unlocked it, and then pushed it open.

"Wait a damn minute! Are you even going to tell me why you're here?" I placed one hand on his arm, only to have him spin around as he shoved it away. "Shit, I'm sorry. I forgot you don't like to be touched. Have breakfast with me." *What did I just say?*

Hutch simply shook his head as his heated eyes moved over my body again. I guessed he liked what he saw, which made two of us because his biceps were the size of both of my thighs.

"What, don't you eat breakfast?"

He rolled his eyes, apparently annoyed with me, and avoided answering me by yanking the screen up on my window.

I huffed like a spoiled brat. "You're going to blow me off? I invited you to breakfast. The least you can do is—" My stomach clenched when he turned back around to cage me in against the wall. This version of Hutch Kelly was scary as all hell. Sexy, but still scary.

"Nine o'clock," he growled between clenched teeth before he took a step back. Then he somehow managed to squeeze his massive girth through my small window, making sure to pull the screen shut behind him, slipped out onto the roof, and shimmied down the side of my house to sprint across the lawn to his place that was across the street as if it was a normal routine for him.

This officially had to be the weirdest morning of my entire life.

***

This wasn't a date, yet I felt oddly nervous getting ready to meet Hutch for breakfast. I showered, pulled my dark hair up into high ponytail, and then dug around trying to figure out what to wear. I finally decided on a pair of blue jean shorts, along with a t-shirt, decorated with ballet shoes from camp. Comfortable, casual, and something I would normally wear hanging around with my friends.

Friends... Is that what Hutch and I were? I knew nothing about the man, except that he was Patrick's brother. People called him the mute because he hardly ever spoke unless spoken to, and he kept mostly to himself. Usually if you were friends with someone, you knew their middle name, the kind of music they liked, their favorite ice cream flavor, and what kind of movies they enjoyed. I knew none of these things when it came to Hutch Kelly. He probably didn't even like music because that would require you to sing, which would mean you needed to make noise, and he didn't seem to like to do that.

Stop it, Jill, that's rude, I admonished myself before I grabbed my cell phone, slipped my feet into a pair of flip-flops, and made sure my light was off before hurrying out of my bedroom. My mother was on the back porch having her morning tea so I was lucky enough to skip out without having to talk to her. I felt a pang of guilt since I wasn't home long yesterday either before I ran off with my friends, so I made a mental note to make sure to be home for dinner tonight. I hit the sidewalk, wondering if Hutch would actually show up or just blow me off. Shrugging the negative thought away, I focused on enjoying the quiet Sunday morning. Ocean View was a small town—everyone up in everyone's business type of place—but was days like this that I knew I'd miss it when I leave the town at the end of the summer. New York was going to be a completely different place that would take some getting used to.

As I rounded the corner to the Angry Egg, everyone's favorite breakfast place in town, I saw Hutch. He had his hands shoved into the front pockets of his blue jeans as he shifted on the balls of his feet and kept his gaze to the ground. He had put on a baseball cap, maybe to hide his face, but it was hard not to recognize him since he was easily the tallest person in the crowd.

"Ready?" I danced over to where Hutch stood without thinking so I could hook my arm through his, and felt him go stiff next to me. Shit, the touching thing. That was going to be hard for me since I was always a touchy-feely type. I quickly removed myself from him. "Sorry," I mumbled as his ears turned pink.

It was obvious how much Hutch hated this by the way he was looking at me. I should have just let him leave like he had wanted, but I still wanted to know why he was in my room. "I hope you're hungry." I started to open the door, but he surprised me by grabbing it first and holding it for me before following me inside the busy diner.

We were lucky to snag an unoccupied booth by the front. Hutch slid into one side, facing the door, while I took the opposite seat as the waitress came over to leave us with a couple of menus. I glanced up to find Hutch with a petrified look on his face as he looked around the restaurant instead of figuring out what he wanted for breakfast.

"Jo and I come here all the time," I blurted out, trying to break the awkward silence. "I always get chocolate chip pancakes and she orders the blueberry." I grabbed the menu in front of him so I could flip it open to the pancake section and then tapped at it lightly. Hutch still looked like he had seen a ghost. It was obvious he wanted to be anywhere than here at this very moment. Was I that hideous? My ex had always told me I was the prettiest girl he had dated, but I thought he was just trying to get into my pants. *Spoiler alert, he never did.* "That way we can share with one another." He didn't say anything, not a big surprise there, but his eyes roamed around the restaurant, wide and glossy. "Hutch," I said his name softly. "Hutch, honey, are you alright?" I dragged my teeth across my bottom lip.

His brown eyes zeroed in on me for what felt like the first time, and it made my stomach Do all sorts of flips. It wasn't because of all the booze I had consumed last night either. It was because I felt like he could actually see me. Straight into my soul, as if he could read every single thought I was having at this exact moment. "Everyone is staring." His voice was barely a whisper, but I had the feeling he wasn't talking to me. I glanced around, but no one was watching. Okay, maybe there were a couple of blue-haired old ladies, but that was it. "No one is—"

"This was a bad idea." Hutch's hands came up to his hat and he flipped it off so that he could tug and pull on his hair. Jesus, that looked painful. I was almost afraid he was going to start pulling it out in giant chunks.

I was out of my side of the booth before I realized what I was doing and slipped in next to him. "It's fine," I assured him. "Hutch." I rested my hand against his arm, and he instantly jerked out of my grip. "Hey." I pressed my palm against his elbow this time. "You're okay, Hutch. You're safe with me." I kept repeating his name, hoping it would calm him, but I honestly had no idea what I was doing.

He looked at me for a second before his hands fell from his hair into his lap. I felt the way his body turned lax as he twisted his giant frame toward me. My goodness, he was sex on a stick. Hutch's brown eyes softened as he continued to stare at me, and I'd be lying if it didn't make a fluttering feeling in the pit of my stomach. I wondered what it would be like to kiss him. Run my tongue over that plump top lip before I sank it inside his mouth, and just the thought made my core clench with need. His face was perfectly sculpted, his jawline profound, and I suddenly had the urge to reach up to trail the tips of my fingers over the jagged edges.

"Hey, Jill." Molly, one of the servers, came over to our table. "It's good to see you. How was camp?" I watched the way her eyes slid over to Hutch with questions in her eyes. She made no move to speak with him because she knew she wouldn't get an answer.

"Camp was great," I chirped, unaffected. "Although getting up to plier, that's the knee bends that you might have seen ballerina's do, at five in the morning wasn't my favorite thing." I rested my hand on Hutch's thigh without even thinking and felt the tight muscles twitch as he reacted to my touch. At least he didn't push me out of the booth onto the greasy, sticky floor. That would have been super embarrassing.

Molly nodded. "You two ready to order then?"

She had a gleam in her eye that screamed she couldn't wait to spread this gossip. That Hutch Kelly and Jillian Robinson were seen canoodling at the diner this morning. Everyone loves a small town in movies, but try living in one with all the damn tea everyone spilled about you.

I nodded. "I'll have my usual chocolate chip pancakes, and Hutch..." I glanced in his direction.

"Blueberry," he muttered without looking at Molly.

I flashed him a smile before I folded up both menus. "Blueberry for Hutch. Coffee"—I had to look at Hutch again and he gave a quick nod. "Two coffees," I finished.

"Great, I'll put your orders in." Molly headed off to the kitchen leaving us alone, and I started to get up to move back into my original seat when Hutch stopped me with one word.

"Stay."

"Are you sure?" He only nodded. I rested my elbow on the table and then placed my chin in the heel of my palm to look at him. "You're a tough nut to crack," I teased and watched his ears turn a shade of red. "I didn't mean...Sorry." I straightened back up again. "Can you try and tell me why you were in my room this morning?" I changed the subject, only to watch Hutch's eyes narrow.

"No."

I folded my arms over my chest as Molly dropped off our coffees. I thanked her before I reached for the sugar packets to dump two into my cup. "That's not very helpful." I took a sip as Hutch drank his black coffee. "You're going to either have to write it down for me or use your words." I regretted saying that the moment the words slipped from my mouth.

His eyes flashed angrily at me. "No." He shook his head. "Move." The he attempted to stand up.

"You're just going to leave now? Is that it? Because you don't like what I say to you? Newsflash, Hutch, we're adults here, and sometimes people are going to say things that

aren't nice. Time to grow up and get over it," I snapped against my better judgment. I wasn't normally like this to people. What was I doing? Pushing his buttons to purposely upset him? Or just trying to get him to talk?

His nostrils flared. "You...you were drunk, Jillian," he spat out, and popped his jaw. I watched a vein throb in his neck. He was seriously pissed at me right now.

Suddenly a flash from last night came back. I left Belle's house, but instead of taking the long way home, I decided to walk down the beach, even though I knew that I shouldn't. Only, it wasn't just any beach. It was the beach called Biker's Beach, and the one place everyone knew to stay away from at night. The rumors about how the bikers hung out to drink and other nefarious things were actually true. I knew better than to step foot there at night, but I was just in a rush to get home. Molly returned to the table with our food, placing the plates in front of us. I suddenly felt like I had lost my appetite.

"Thanks."

"You are so welcome." Molly flashed a big smile at Hutch before she looked at me. "If you two need anything else, just give me a holler. Enjoy your breakfast." She winked at me and was off again.

I slowly began to cut up my pancakes, wondering if I would be able to eat. I remembered a couple of men weren't looking to walk me home. I took a bite of my breakfast and looked up to find Hutch watching me with venom in his eyes. "You were there," I whispered, but he shook his head. "Then—"

"I saw you." He shook his head before he grabbed his silverware to start aggressively cutting up his pancakes. His jaw was set in a hard line. He growled deep in his chest before he stopped to stare at me. "You could have been hurt, Jillian." He dropped his gaze. "What were you thinking?" He had spoken more to me right here than he probably had in his entire life. Then he began to brutally mutilate his food with his fork.

"Not like that." I went to take the silverware away, but he pulled his hands away. "You cut them up one at a time so that if the other person wants one, they can. What? Why are you are you looking at me like that. Are you mad at me now?"

"Yes."

"You are? Because of last night?"

He just gave a curt nod.

"I'm sorry," I whispered before I picked up my fork to push my pancakes around the plate. I wanted to blame it on the margaritas, but I knew that wasn't the honest truth. I was drunk, tired, and just wanted to get home to my own bed so I took a shortcut that I knew I shouldn't.

"You could have been hurt," Hutch muttered again. "What if—" I looked up to see him staring at his plate with his ears burning bright pink again.

"Thank you." I bumped his shoulder lightly with mine. "Let's eat up before our food gets cold. Maybe we can go for a walk on the beach after," I suggested, effectively ending his train of thoughts.

Chapter Two

Hutch

The first time I noticed Jillian— I mean, really noticed her — was a couple summers back, when she had just grown up into a full-fledged woman on me. It scared me how much I wanted her. She was sixteen at the time, and totally, completely, and absolutely off-fucking-limits, but I still watched her like some creepy dude. Jillian had always been different from the rest of the Ocean View residents. Happier, sweeter, and kinder to me even if we hardly ever spoke.

Thinking about her walking home alone on Biker's Beach last night made me furious. I had been minding my own business, just sitting out on the sand, like I did a lot in the summer, when I spotted her stumbling down the beach. Alone. Everyone knew better than to go there at night, but by the way Jillian was acting, she had forgotten that rule. I hadn't even thought about what I was doing when the first guy had started toward her. I just reacted. I hit him before I grabbed her and ran straight for her place without looking back.

"Hutch, come on!" Jillian cried as she caught me watching her. "How can you be such a slowpoke?" Her laughter was a melody to my ears. "With legs that long, you should be miles ahead of me by now," she teased over her shoulder. Despite everything, despite how I knew this was so fucking wrong, my dick pressed against the zipper of my jeans. Or maybe it was just the sight of Jillian. Her chestnut brown hair, the way her green eyes sparkled with happiness in the sun, and that perfect, dancer's body.

Out of your league, Hutch.

There was my brain, screaming into my ear. Only I found myself hurrying to catch up with her like she wanted. It was the exact reason I had accompanied her to breakfast because she had wanted me to. I would probably eat glass, commit murder, or rob a bank if the girl asked me to. Just to see her smile at me again.

I blinked as I realized she was almost knee-deep in the ocean. She didn't seem to care that the hem of her shorts was starting to get damp or that people were watching as she splashed around in the water like a little kid. No, Jillian was someone who loved life. She caught me watching and waved me over, but I only shook my head.

"Hutch." Christ, the way she said my name like that should be illegal. "You're being a party pooper." She blew a raspberry before she brought her thumb up to her nose and waved the rest of her fingers in the air at me. I had never seen a woman more beautiful.

Jillian was the one that insisted we go up to the beach after breakfast to "walk off our food" as she put it, but she didn't look like she needed to walk off anything. Her body was... hell, her body was perfect. Not like any eighteen-year-old I had ever seen before. I had only agreed because I didn't want the time I was spending with her to end, because I knew once it did? Jillian would simply forget about me. Forget my name, forget this happened, and go on living her charmed life before she disappeared to New York forever at the end of the summer.

"You're no fun." She splashed water in my direction, but it didn't even come close to hitting me. "Jerk," Jillian called before she stuck her tongue out at me. Fuck me right in the taint; that was hot. I could imagine what she could do with that.

I took a couple of steps closer and then nodded in agreement. I hated bringing attention to myself. Going out with her to breakfast today was bad enough, but now, the beach? Hell, everyone would make a big deal out of it, and I just wanted to disappear into the background. Being a person of my size was already hard enough. Everyone would be talking about how Jillian Robinson had gone to the Angry Egg with me and me alone, which was something I was not okay with. People already spoke enough about me behind my back.

Jillian folded her arms over her chest. "Please? For me?" She pouted like a child not getting their way. When I shook my head again, she simply turned to drop into the water and submerged her entire body into the ocean. I watched, mesmerized, as Jillian ducked her head under the water, swam around, and then stood back up, pushing her damp hair from her eyes as a big smile spread across her beautiful face before she began walking back to me.

I was seriously, totally, and completely fucked right now. There was no other way to explain my feelings. When Jillian emerged from the water seconds later, I couldn't help but notice how her shirt clung to her perfect breasts, and the fact that her nipples were rock hard. Kill me now. As she moved closer to where I was standing, Jillian started squeezing the water from her shirt, the one with little ballet slippers all over it, giving me a peek at her toned stomach and abs.

"Tell me you know how to swim. You've lived here your entire life?"

I nodded.

Jillian brushed the water from her arms. "You just didn't want to swim with me?" She tilted her head up at me when she got closer.

My brows dipped as I tried to get out of this. "No trunks." I'm not a big swimmer actually, but I didn't tell her that part. I don't like not being able to see my feet, or the feel of seaweed on my legs, or the thought of getting eaten by a shark. It freaks me the fuck out now, but before *it* happened, I had spent hours upon hours in that water with my friends.

"Sure. I didn't have a bathing suit on, but that didn't stop me." She looked up at me from under her lashes as she continued to brush the access water from her body, and I noticed the goosebumps that had started to break out on her skin. She must be freezing right now.

Without even thinking about it, I yanked my shirt up over my head. "Here." I held it out like an idiot. "You're cold."

Jillian wrapped her slim fingers around the cloth. "How very gentlemanly of you." There was no teasing in her voice. "But now you're going to what? Walk around shirtless?" Her eyes slid over my bare chest, and I suddenly felt incredibly self-conscious. "Thank you, Hutch, but the sun will dry me off." She held her hand out with my shirt in it, which I took and slipped back on.

We started to walk in silence farther down the beach, Jillian carrying her shoes while my boots were filling with sand. It was only a matter of time before I had to stop to remove them. I sat down on one of the many benches that were lined up to empty them out, only to have Jillian sit right next to me.

"Can I ask you a question?" She turned her face up toward the sun and closed her eyes to soak it in, and I had to resist the urge to run my fingers over her flawless skin.

Here we go. "Okay," I answered, emptying out my second boot, and anticipated the question I knew was coming.

Jillian twisted her small body to look at me. "Is this how you thought your life would turn out? I mean, did you always know you wanted to be a mechanic growing up or did you want something more than that? Something bigger in your life?" That was not the question I had expected to come from her plump pink lips.

"No," I answered honestly.

Her brows dipped. "That's all you're going to give me?" Jillian sighed. "Look, Hutch, I know you're a man of few words, but I was hoping for something more." She glanced out to look at the water. The beach was quiet for now, but soon the tourists would arrive, and the sound would be overpowering. I tried to avoid this place as much as possible when that happened. "I've always wanted to be a dancer." I watched as her tongue slid out so she could moisten her lips. Cruel and unusual punishment, but I couldn't drag my gaze away. "But, lately..." She didn't finish her sentence, but I understood what she was getting at.

I squared my shoulders as I tried to prepare myself to answer her. "What I meant, Jillian, was that this was not the life I expected for myself. I had dreams of getting out of this town. Of making a name for myself, but things happened, and well, here I am." Her head swirled around like that little girl in *The Exorcist*. "What?" I saw the way Jillian was watching me with big, wide eyes. God, she was simply stunning beyond words. She must have guys lined up at the door to date her, two feet wide and six feet deep.

"You formed complete sentences, Hutch. Not just a grunt or a word, but actual sentences and everything." She knocked my shoulder. "I'm teasing you, of course." She leaned into me, and I swear I stopped breathing. She smelled like the ocean but mixed with something else too. Something sweeter; a delicacy I wanted to eat with a spoon. "What did you want to do?" Her green eyes had little specks of gold in them that I hadn't noticed before until now. Must have been the way the sun caught them outside right now.

"Hutch?" We both looked up as my brother, Pat, who suddenly seemed to appear out of nowhere. *Cockblocker.* "Jillian." His tone changed when he noticed who I was sitting with. What? He was the only Kelly allowed to be seen with a Robinson girl? "What's going on here?" I didn't like that question. In fact, I didn't like the way he was looking at me right now, like I had been caught with my hand in the cookie jar.

Jillian didn't flinch or made any move to get up. "Where's Jo?" She simply asked because usually those two were connected at the hip at all times.

"At the taco truck." He glanced at me before he looked back at Jillian. "What are you two—?"

I jumped to my feet. "I was just leaving." I shoved my feet back into my boots before I took off. I heard Jillian calling out to me as I hurried down the beach and back up onto the footpath, but it didn't stop me. Patrick was right behind me.

"What are you doing?" he hissed between clenched teeth. "Jillian, Hutch?"

"None of your business." I kept walking, but Pat was hot on my heels. When his hand landed on my arm, I spun around. "Don't touch me," I warned.

He popped his jaw. "I'm not leaving until you tell me what that was." He hooked a thumb over his shoulder back to where I knew Jillian was probably wondering what the hell just happened. Maybe not. She probably didn't even care. Last I heard, she had been dating Knox Carson, so she probably wasn't even interested in me.

"Nothing," I lied.

Patrick looked up at the clear blue sky. "You like her." *Stating the obvious, Sherlock.* "She's eighteen, Hutch, and has her entire life mapped out ahead of her. She's not like you."

I could knock his block off. I could punch him into next Tuesday, and he knew it. Instead, I kept waking because that was who I was. No bark, no bite.

"I didn't...Hutch, wait!" Patrick caught right back up to me again. "I didn't mean that."

I bared my teeth at him. "You meant it." I flipped my middle finger, warning him off. "I'm different. She's not. I'm not stupid, Pat; just mute," I reminded him. "Get out of my way now."

When Pat did what I asked, I kept walking and didn't look back. I made it all the way back to our house where I still lived, even at twenty-six, and into the apartment I had over the garage where I planned to spend the rest of the day drinking and feeling sorry for myself.

Jillian Robinson was going to break my heart.

I should get out while I still could.

She isn't into me like that.

***

I didn't see Jillian again until Friday night. Or at least, I didn't talk to her again. I walked by the ballet studio she had class at every single morning on my way to work, but pretended I didn't see her when she waved to me. I saw her when she was outside with the other girls in her class on their break, laughing and talking about God only knows what, but I acted like I didn't when she turned to look over at the garage.

Patrick was right. Jillian wasn't like me. She was normal, she was good, and she was going to get out of this town. I was the one who'd be stuck here until they buried me six feet in the ground. I thought I had come to terms with my life, but now I wasn't so sure of that.

Friday night rolled around, and I was no longer as pissed off at my brother as I was on Sunday, which meant I let him convince me to go out to a party one of his buddies was having at their house. He made no mention of Jillian so I assumed she wouldn't be there. If I had known, I would have just stayed home like I usually did. He told me it was just going to be a bunch of dudes hanging out. Guys, I could handle, but girls? Girls were something altogether different. Guys didn't care if I sat there drinking a beer, grunting out an answer now and then, but girls? Girls wanted you to talk to them. I didn't do that.

Jillian was there with her friends: Belle, Madison, and, of course, her sister, Jo. I kept to myself like usual, mostly talking with Pat when he could tear himself away from his girlfriend. I sipped on my warm beer by myself and gave a quick smile to whoever might give me a fleeting hello before I decided after an hour that I had had enough. Knox Carson was making my skin crawl with the way he was flirting with Jillian, and I was ready to leave until something made me Jillian's raised voice caused me to change my mind.

"Put me down, Knox!"

I spun around at the sound of Jillian's voice. Sure enough, Knox had Jillian in his arms while he strutted toward the beach as if he was about to dump her in the water. He was laughing as if he was having a great time, but Jillian looked otherwise. I sprinted toward them without a second thought.

"I think the lady asked you to put her down," I growled incessantly.

Knox seemed surprised to either see me or hear me, because he immediately stopped dead in his tracks before he bared his teeth. "Are you serious, mute?" As if I didn't know everyone used that name on me. "I think you're lost." He started toward the water again, but I blocked his path.

"Put her down."

"Hutch, it's okay," Jillian tried to assure me.

I glanced between the two of them. The way Jillian's eyes sparkled with laughter, the way she was gripping his arms; I realized I had read the entire situation wrong. Maybe they were still dating. Crap, where they still together? I was such an idiot. I turned and fled the scene as fast as I could, heading back up to where I had left my shoes so I could make a beeline back to my place. How could I be that stupid? To even think Jillian might be interested in me, when she had Knox Carson in her life.

"Wait, Hutch!" Jillian called out to me as she rushed up the sand. "Are you mad at me again?" she asked.

I turned around slowly to find her standing there in an oversized sweatshirt that fell to her knees. I saw red when I realized it probably belonged to fucking Knox. "No," I assured her. "Not you." I was mad at myself, but of course, I didn't say that aloud.

Jillian searched my face. "I hoped we could finish our conversation from the other day." She took a step forward. Loud, explosive laughter from her friends caused her to look back over her shoulder before she turned to me again.

"You should go back to your friends, Jillian," I muttered.

"Aren't we friends, Hutch?" she inquired softly.

"Are we?"

Jillian moved around to where I had my eyes pinned to my feet. "Yes." Her lips turned up and that was what did me in. A smile so innocent, so perfect, that I had no other choice but to give in to what she wanted. "Stay and walk with me for a second?"

"Okay." I nodded.

Chapter Three

Hutch

We walked a little further away from the crowd of people and the bonfire. I wasn't sure what it was about Jillian that made me feel so relaxed or different, but maybe she made everyone feel that way. Maybe it was just her green eyes or her friendly smile; there was just something much deeper about Jillian that made all my anxieties just fade away. When the first bench came into view, she sat down and patted the spot next to her. I eased myself down without a second thought. I'm not sure how long we sat there in silence before I turned to find Jillian watching me.

"What?" I growled and felt her grow tense. "Sorry." I dropped my gaze to my hands that were in my lap.

Jillian pulled her legs up onto the bench. "You were different before when we were alone," she reminded me. I glanced over to find her hugging her legs against her chest. She had shorts on beneath her sweatshirt, but I caught a peek of her toned thighs, and a glimpse of what I hoped was her bathing suit.

"I'm different."

"Don't do that."

I met Jillian's eyes and quickly looked away. "This is who I am," I reminded her as I dragged my toe around in a circle of sand. She didn't know me or anything about me. I wasn't like her friends, and Jillian needed to realize that. I blinked up in surprise as she suddenly got up to stand in front of me. "What are you doing?" When my gaze met hers, I wondered what would it be like to kiss those luscious lips or hold her in my arms?

"You're not this person you're pretending to be right now, Hutch." Jillian reached out to touch my face with her hand, and I was sure my heart skipped a beat in my chest. Her hand was warm against my cheek, her palm soft over my skin. She slowly tilted my face up to hers.

I gritted my teeth. "What...Jillian—" I couldn't think straight with her touching me like that. It got worse when she pushed my legs open so she could move between them, and my fucking cock grew hard as steel. It had been a very long time since a woman made me feel this way.

"Finish your story," she whispered as the waves washed over the sand. "Tell me what you would do if you left this little shit town without looking back."

I stared up into Jillian's green eyes, her gaze so inviting that all I wanted to do was make her happy. "I wanted to see the world," I confessed truthfully. "I wanted to backpack through Europe, take a safari through Africa, ski in Colorado, and go to a NASCAR race at Daytona. I wanted to work for NASCAR, too, if given the chance. I've always been fascinated by cars, which I guess is how I ended up working on them." I wasn't even sure I was breathing at this point. My lungs hurt from the lack of air, but I didn't care as long as I did what Jillian wanted. She could have a kidney, or all the money I had in the bank right now, if she simply asked me for it.

"Why didn't you?" She didn't move from where she stood. Didn't seem to care that her friends might be watching, or her lame boyfriend was going to be jealous of his girlfriend touching me. That her sister was probably gawking, or my brother was going to fucking kill me when we got home.

The answer to that question...I kept locked in a safe inside my mind that no one would ever open. "I changed my mind," I lied through gritted teeth.

The moment vanished in an instant.

Jillian pulled away. "You could have come up with a better answer, Hutch." She retreated further away from me. "I can hear it in your voice that you're lying." The sounds of laughing caused her to look back toward the fire where everyone seemed to have forgotten about us.

"Go back to your friends." I stood up, but she stayed where she was. I looked down at her, at her small yet alethic frame, and wished that things could be different for me. That what had changed me never happened or that I could have her the way I longed to. Beneath me, above me, and fucking everywhere in-between.

Jillian kept her gaze away from me when she spoke. "Is that what you really want me to do?" Her lashes were so long they brushed the tops of her cheeks.

"No."

"Then I'll stay."

My breath caught in my throat when Jillian turned to look at me again. I noticed the sunburn fading into a tan on her face, the freckles that had started to break out over her nose, and the way she kept chewing on her bottom lip the longer we stared at one another. How long had it been since I had been touched by a female? It felt like forever since I had wanted to be touched by the opposite sex. I had long given up on anyone wanting me, but right now, I wondered if someone might.

A smile tugged at Jillian's plump lips. "You're staring."

"So are you," I answered right back. Shit, was I flirting? I couldn't even remember the last time I had done that. Before everything that had happened to change me.

Jillian broke into a full-fledge smile this time that lit up her entire face. She was the most beautiful woman I had ever seen; and whatever was happening at this moment was wrong. So wrong, but right now, I didn't care.

"Are you going to the carnival tomorrow night?" She tugged on her sweatshirt. "Knox asked me to go, but..." I lost whatever else she was about to utter into a jealous frenzy the moment another guy's name came out of her mouth. *Fucking idiot*. I was stupid to think I stood a chance with Jillian. She was just being normal with me, and now, she was just casually talking like friends do. I suddenly realized I had lost myself in my own thoughts because Jillian was staring at me right now.

Fuck.

"I lost you. Where did you go?" She put her hands into the front pocket of her sweatshirt. When I didn't answer, Jillian shook her head. "I'm sorry, I know asking you to go to the carnival was silly. You're not interested in that sort of thing."

Wait, what? "I'll go." Fuck, what did I just say? I hated that stupid place. Too many people, all those kids running around with sticky cotton candy fingers, and all the people.

"Really?" Jillian clapped her hands together. "Wait, are you sure? I don't want to make you do something you don't want to do." She eyed me carefully as if she could read my mind or something.

Despite knowing this was a terrible idea, that I was going to have anxiety about it up until the moment we got there and after, I assured Jillian I was not doing this to make her happy. That I wanted to go. Only to be closer to her.

"Can I see your phone?" she asked. When I tilted my head at her, she smiled. "I want to put my number in it so I can text you the time. That way, when you come up with a good excuse not to go, you can text me."

I rolled my eyes as I lifted my hip to pull out my cell. I unlocked it before I handed it over and then watched Jillian add her number and she gave it back to me. I looked at the phone for a second before I shot her a text and listened to her phone ding. When Jillian checked her texts, she chuckled.

Hutch: *I'm not going to change my mind.*

"Really?" She looked startled by my text as she looked up at me.

Hutch: *Stuck with me.*

I was so screwed.

***

I spent two hours getting ready for the damn carnival. A carnival that happened every single year at Ocean View, and one that I hadn't been to since I was twelve years old. I took a half an hour shower before I changed into a pair of blue jeans, and a plain t-shirt with Zed's Automotive sprawled across the front, which I decided wasn't good enough, before

I ripped that off to put on a shirt that said *I got it at the View* written in some terrible font. I stared at myself in the mirror. This wasn't going to work either. This wasn't who I was or what I stood for. I was not the guy that cared about what I dressed like. I rummaged around in my dresser before I found a NASCAR shirt I forgot I had buried in the back. It wasn't wrinkled so I yanked it over my head.

I ran my hands through my unruly hair, wondering if I should bother with a hat. It was always windy at the carnival. Probably due to it being on the pier next to the water, and I didn't want to take the chance of losing any of my hats. I glanced at my phone which told me I had five minutes before I would be officially late meeting Jillian so I shoved my feet into my sneakers, slid my cell into my pocket, and made sure my door was locked.

As I hurried down the steps from my apartment that was over the garage at my parents' place, I noticed that Pat was already gone, which meant he and Jo were probably on their way too. I grunted, thinking about running into him. It wasn't that I didn't get along with my brother; it was just that he was probably either going to pretend that everything was normal or give me a side-eye the entire time. I went with the second one as I rounded the corner to the pier. Everything was within walking distance at the View so it didn't take me long to get there, but I stopped dead in my tracks when I saw Jillian.

Dressed in a pair of white lace shorts and a matching tank top, she was staring down at her phone, waiting for me. Did she seriously think I was going to cancel? When Jillian had texted me this morning to confirm the time, I had assured her I would be there. Her dark hair fell in waves around her shoulders, and I caught my breath the moment she looked up to smile at me. Maybe I would have backed out, but it was way too late for that now.

"There you are!" she gushed happily as she slipped her phone in her back pocket. "I kept checking my phone in case you backed out."

I nodded, lost in my own dirty thoughts. Thoughts that included what it would be like to slowly remove those shorts, the panties she had on underneath if she had any on, and then bury my face between her thighs.

Jillian grinned up at me. "Why do you have that weird look on your face right now?" she teased.

Weird look on my face? Oh shit, did I say something about her panties aloud? Damn, this was going to be a bad idea, wasn't it?

"Sorry," I muttered.

Jillian didn't say anything else as we started to walk inside the already crowded carnival. Someone's shoulder hit my arm, followed by a mumbled apology, but I hardly heard it. Shit, there were so many people here. Why did everyone have to come on the opening night? Didn't they know this thing ran all summer long, seven days a week? Jesus, what was I doing here? I felt like maybe it was too much, too soon. I couldn't breathe all of a sudden, and maybe if I went home, I would be okay. That would be better for me than this. Anything would be better than this.

Jillian gripped my wrist. "Hutch." She planted herself in front of me. "Hutch, honey, you're okay," she tried to assure me. "You're with me, Hutch." My eyes slowly focused on her.

"Do you want to sit down for a second?" When I nodded, she eased me into an empty seat, but she stood straight, only to begin tracing my jaw with the pads of her fingers. "Do you need to go home? Is this too much for you, Hutch? We can leave anytime you want," she murmured, moving closer.

"Need a second."

Jillian nodded as she continued to stroke my face with her fingers. Lightly at first, but then the pressure increased enough to make me relax. Why was she not running for the hills right now? She didn't say anything as my breathing gradually began to return to normal as did my heart rate, and suddenly I felt like I might be alright.

When I dared to look up at Jillian again, she had such compassion written all over her face. What had I done to deserve any of this? "Thank you," I stuttered.

She gave a slight nod. "You don't have to thank me, but you're welcome. Are you sure that you don't want to go home?" She tilted her head, then added, "We can leave if it will make you feel better. Watch a movie unless you want to be alone." She removed her hands from her face, and I instantly missed her touch. I wanted it back. I wanted to feel Jillian's hands all over my body. Her lips too, the more I thought about it. How it would sound if she moaned my name. And now, I was fucking hard again.

"I think I'll be alright as long as you're with me." The words escaped my lips before I could stop them.

Jillian searched my face. "You're just full of surprises, Hutch Kelly, aren't you?" She sank her teeth into her bottom lip. "What do you want to do first? Ride the carousel? Throw darts at balloons or take a spin on the roller coaster? Please tell me you're not afraid of heights because I need to go on the Ferris wheel before this night is over." She grabbed my hands as she tried to pull me onto my feet.

"Everything," I assured her as I stood up now that I felt more like myself. "Twice." I let her lead me toward the closest ride which happened to be the swings.

Jillian laughed lightly. "Don't tempt me, giant man, because I might hold you to it!" she teased.

As long as I got to spend time with her, I didn't care what we did. If she wanted to ride the roller coaster all night long...I would do it.

Chapter Four

Jillian

After riding almost every single ride with me, I now watched as Hutch devoured his second candy apple of the night, wondering when his panic attacks started. I had only known him for a short time, but that was the second time he'd had one around me, and the second time I had talked him down. He was a mystery; that was for sure. Jo tried to pump me for information about him the night after the beach party, but one, I didn't have any, and two, I wouldn't have told her if I did. It was simply none of her business.

"You're really going to the carnival with Hutch?" Jo asked as we got ready together tonight. "I thought you and Knox were a thing." She pushed a little further.

Anger flashed through me. "Knox and I are over."

"What? Since when?"

I shook my head. "I think he fucked Madison Rae while I was gone. I don't know; something is going on between the two of them, but neither will tell me. At the beach the other night, I saw them eye-fucking one another when they thought I wasn't looking, but believe me, I was looking." I chewed on my lip. "What has Pat ever told you about Hutch?" I watched the way my sister's eyes narrowed.

She shook her head. "Not much. I mean, he went away one summer to camp, and when he came back?" She shrugged. "He was the way he is now. Quiet, shy, the mute." She used quotes around the nickname Knox had used, which I despised. "Shit, you like him," Jo declared, staring at me.

I blushed as I tried to duck my head. "I don't, not like that." However, that was a lie because I thought he was nice, but more than that, there was something there that I knew I could find if Hutch opened up just a little more. "Do me a favor, Jo?" I looked back up at my sister. "Please don't call him 'the mute' around me. It's not very nice." It was mean, actually, and the more I got to know him, I realized that wasn't who he was at all.

"You really like those, huh?" I asked, pointing at the apple in his hand.

Hutch stopped to look at me for a second. "I like sweets." His ears turned pink before he started eating again.

"Are you having fun tonight?" I watched the way his tongue licked the melted caramel off the apple, and I wondered what else he could do with it.

He nodded, only to raise his eyes to meet mine. "It's not about me." His lips turned up into a slight smile before he looked away again.

It was official. Hutch Kelly was the sweetest man to walk the planet.

"One more ride," I reminded him as I glanced up at the Ferris wheel as it stopped to let on more passengers. There was something about that ride that I loved the most. Maybe it was the fact that you got to go up in the air and look at the stars. It seemed so romantic to me for some reason. Two people cuddled up together without anyone else to bother them.

"Let's go." Hutch wiped off his hands with the napkin he had been provided before he stood up.

It was getting late now. Most of the younger kids had left with their parents so the place was now full of couples as it seemed. We waited in line behind one pair that couldn't seem to keep their hands off one another. I side-eyed Hutch who kept his own eyes pinned to his feet. Again, I wondered what had happened to him to make him the way he was. Was it some sort of PTSD? An accident, maybe?

I nudged his arm so that he had to look at me. "*Awkward*," I mouthed, and he broke into a smile that I had never seen before. Heat curled inside my belly as the concession staff seated us inside the ride, closed the door, and made sure the bar was locked in place against our thighs.

Hutch's leg was pressed against mine inside the tiny car, his hip and broad shoulder even closer, and when I dared look at him again, his back was straighter than an arrow. He looked like he wanted be anywhere than here at this moment. It wasn't until I saw how tightly he was gripping the bar in front of us that I wondered if he might be having another panic attack. Without a word, I placed my hand over his and felt him relax.

When the ride began to move, Hutch let out a slow, easy breath. "You're good, Jills." His voice was raspy as he spoke. "If this ballet thing doesn't work out for you, you might consider psychiatry," he teased. Sometimes he surprised me when he said stuff like that. I wondered what he was like before. Before he changed into the man he was now.

"Jills," I repeated the name he had called me several times tonight. His ears turned pink with embarrassment. "I like it." I assured him so he didn't think that I was making fun of him. I never wanted Hutch to think I was making fun of him. Not ever.

Hutch took his free hand and placed it over mine so that it was now sandwiched between his as our car stopped at the top of the ride. "Sometimes"—he looked up into the clear blue night—"I like to stare up into the sky while I'm home just to look up at the stars. It helps me to relax and sleep when nothing else does." He squeezed my hand lightly. God, when he spoke to me like no one was around, it made me feel so giddy and free.

I turned my gaze up to where he was looking. "It's beautiful," I confessed, taking in the beauty of the stars tinkling in the sky.

"Not the most beautiful."

When I turned to him again, he was watching me with a look I couldn't quite decipher, and I thought my heart might burst from my chest. His eyes were dark, his face smooth, and for a brief second, I thought he might actually kiss me, but then the ride began to move again. Jesus Christ, what was happening right now? I continued to watch Hutch as the ride slowly descended downward, only to stop again. Neither one of us said anything as we continued to stare at one another. I could get lost in those eyes, I wondered.

"Jillian." His deep, throaty voice made my pulse quicken. "We need to get off. The ride is over."

I giggled nervously as Hutch loosened his grip on my hands, but helped me get out of the car safely, then quickly released me the moment I stepped onto the ground. I looked up at him to find him with his eyes angrily narrowed and glaring at something in front us. I turned to find Knox and Madison watching us with amused looks on their faces. I fucking knew it!

"I had a feeling that this is why you broke it off with me, but now, I know for sure," Knox seethed at me. He swung his arm casually over Madison's shoulder. "I was trying to figure out if this was an actual date or not, you know, since I saw you two holding hands before you climbed out from the ride, but I'm not sure." The look on his face was so ugly I couldn't even stand to look at him. Knox was easily the biggest catch at school with his blond hair, blue eyes, and those dimples that he used to make girls drop their panties for him, but right now, he was doing nothing for me. Those dimples never worked on me, which I'm sure pissed him off.

Madison giggled. "Right? I mean, Jill is dressed as if she might be on one, but Hutch? He's wearing some ratty old shirt and jeans. My guess would be no." She pushed her blonde hair behind her shoulder.

"Fuck off," Hutch grunted, and I knew in that instant I was about to lose him again just like that day on the beach. He was quick to embarrass and just as easily angered. He had already stepped a few inches away from me.

I started to reach for Hutch's hand, but he took another step away. It was enough to make me feel like he slapped me even though he didn't touch me. I noticed the smug look on Knox's face when I looked his way again. "What's wrong with you?" I questioned. "Why are you two being so mean right now?"

"I'm not being mean, Jill; I'm just trying to make Hutch realize that this, whatever the heck it is, isn't going to happen. Despite this crazy crush he has on you. You're here"—he raised his hand up above his head—"while Hutch is down here." He dropped his hand back down. "It's actually kind of cute, sure, but think about it. You are going to go off to New York in a couple of months, and Hutch will still be here just like he will be, years later. You'll meet some rich banker, pop out some kids, and Hutch will still be here by himself, living over his parents' garage like the fucking loser that that he is."

Knox wasn't being funny; he was being downright cruel. I turned toward Hutch only to find he had turned his back to us with his shoulders dropped forward. "Jesus Christ, Knox," I hissed. "You are such an asshole. I can't believe I ever dated you." I pointed my finger at him. "Now, just go!" I cried before I moved toward Hutch, despising to the way Knox and Madison laughed as they walked away.

"Hey." I was afraid to touch Hutch because I wasn't sure if he would freak out on me or not. When his head moved at the sound of my voice, I inched closer.

"He's right," Hutch mumbled. "About me still being here years from now."

"Hutch, don't listen to him."

"Jillian, think about it."

I stared at him when he fully turned around. "That's crazy talk," I tried to insist, but I saw it in his eyes. He believed everything Knox had said. "What happened—?"

"Don't." He shook his head, cutting me off. "That's not something I'm going to talk about with you. You should go home." He started walking past me toward the exit of the carnival.

I had to hurry to catch up with him as he ran from me. Did Hutch even tell anyone about what happened to make him like this? He easily maneuvered around the small crowds that were still in the park, and as he rushed down the sidewalk, I wanted to scream at him to wait for me. That I liked him the way he was, and that Knox could go straight to hell, but I knew, deep down, that Hutch wasn't going to listen to me. He had already made up his mind. I followed him all the way home before he noticed me.

"What?" he snapped at me.

"I didn't...I couldn't let it end like this."

Hutch stared at me before he shook his head. "There is no *it*, Jillian. I did you a favor. It's done. Now leave me alone." He started up the grass and then the steps to his apartment while I watched. He stopped when he realized I was still there. "Go home."

Hot tears filled my eyes. "Why are you being like this to me now? I wasn't the one that was mean to you, that was Knox. I thought we were friends." My throat felt tight all of a sudden.

Hutch stared at me from the top of the stairs. "We're not friends, Jillian. We can't be friends. Don't you understand that? We're too different. You don't belong in my world, and I certainly don't belong in yours." He began to unlock the front door to his apartment. When I started up the steps, I thought maybe, when he pushed open the door, he might see that I was upset and hurting. "Go home, Jills. Knox is right," Hutch shouted, and I couldn't help but notice the look on his face. He actually believed the words he was saying.

"Hutch—" He didn't even let me finish. Instead, he slammed the door, and I heard the click of the lock behind it. I stood there, hurt and angry, as tears streamed down my face, unsure of what had just happened. It just felt like Hutch had punched me right in the stomach.

Once I was able to finally move my feet, I managed to walk down the steps, down the driveway, and to my house. I was thankful that my mother was in bed, but wondered if maybe Jo was awake. It was possible she was still out with Pat at his place or sleeping, but I felt soothed when I knocked softly on her door and heard her call out, "Come in."

When I stepped into her room, she was lying on her bed, dressed in red pajama shorts and a matching t-shirt, her face buried in ancient copy of *Harry Potter and the Sorcerer's Stone*[1]. "Yes, I'm reading it again, but you know...what happened?" She turned to look at me and tossed the book onto the bed. "Did he try something or hurt you?" Jo jumped to her feet.

I shook my head as fresh tears began to pour from my eyes. "No, he...Knox was there. He was really horrible, and I think Hutch was more embarrassed than anything." I sniffed.

"Thanks," I said as my sister handed me a tissue. I dabbed at my nose before I went on, "I wish I knew what caused Hutch to act the way he does, Joey, because sometimes?" I

---

1.   *https://www.google.com/search?safe=strict&rlz=1C1NHXL_enUS944US944&sxsrf=ALeKk007BLnHW dIbodvFc_tgGeUwec-w8A:1620238581373&q=Harry+Potter+and+the+Philosopher's+Stone+J.+K.+Rowling&stick=H4sIAAAAAAAAAONgVuLQz9U3SI4vy37EaMwt8PLHPWEp rUlrTl5jVOHiCs7IL3fNK8ksqRQS42KDsnikuLjgmngWsZp5JBYVVSoE5JeUpB YpJOalKJRkpCoEZGTm5BfnF2SkFqkXKwSX5OelKnjpKXjrKQTll-dk5qUDALYoBqh7AAAA*

nibbled on my bottom lip. "Sometimes he says things, does things that confuses me, you know?" I sat down on the edge of her bed.

Jo's brows dipped. "No, I don't, because you haven't told me." She touched my arm in an act of comfort and flashed a tender smile. "Want me to sleep in your room tonight." She flashed a smile. "You know, like when we were kids." I nodded, hating the thought of being alone. "Great, let me grab my phone and I'll be right there."

I watched as my sister gathered her phone, a pillow, and then we moved to my room where we talked, laughed, and stayed up until midnight. I told her about what happened with Hutch, along with the run-in with Knox and Madison, while she talked about Patrick and their future plans. I always knew she planned to marry him, but she wanted to at least graduate college first. By the time we both fell asleep around three in the morning, I felt a little better, although my ego was still bruised.

Chapter Five

Hutch

If I wasn't the worst person on the entire planet, I was pretty damn close. I never should have said those terrible things to Jillian. Those were my insecurities, not hers. In addition, it wasn't her fault that Knox was the biggest asshole I had ever met, yet I couldn't stop the word vomit that slipped from my mouth, and when I saw the tears on her cheeks? It was too late to take the verbal lashing back. It made me hate myself more than I already did.

I didn't sleep much after Jillian left. On Sunday, I walked around, feeling as if I was trapped in my own personal hell, and reminisced what it felt like sitting next to her on the Ferris wheel. How she watched me eating the candy apple with lust in her eyes. How she had been so close to me, her hand sandwiched between mine, and how the moon seemed to sparkle on her skin. She was so sweet, pure, and if she knew me, really knew me, why I was the way I was...It only took Knox to remind me that Jillian had her entire future laid out to pull the rug out from underneath any thoughts I had of a relationship with her.

It still didn't stop me from my picking my cell up every damn five minutes to text her how sorry I was, only to delete the message before I hit send.

Patrick stopped by in the afternoon, trying to get me to talk to him, but he should have known better. I let him into my place and watched as he took off his shoes before he moved to sit down on the sofa.

"Don't ask," I warned, leaning against the wall. "It's done." I waved my hand at him, trying to push his thoughts away.

Pat rolled his eyes. "You sure about that? I saw how you were with her at the beach. Both times. I think you like Jillian more than you're letting on. What happened?" He brought his right foot up to his left knee.

I raised one brow. "You already know." I looked up at the ceiling before I dragged my eyes back down to look at my brother. "What'd she say?" God, I hated how weak my voice sounded.

Pat shook his head. "Sorry, Hutch, I'm not playing that game." He clucked his tongue. "You want me to punch Knox in the mouth for you? Because I would love to have a go at that dude. I never really liked that guy. He sort of weaseled his way into our group of friends."

"I can do that."

"I dare you."

We bullshitted a little more, but Pat never brought up Jillian's name again. We talked about things like college, how he and Jo wanted to get their own place, how they were talking about setting a wedding date, and I told him I was happy for him. It wasn't a lie. Even thought we were opposites in every single way, I loved my brother. I knew he wanted the best for me, and I did for him. When he left, my heart hurt more than I wanted to admit to the point that I drank myself into an early slumber and was in bed before eight o'clock, knowing that I was going to kick myself when my alarm went off for work the next morning. Normally I wasn't a heavy drinker, but I figured it was the only way I could get Jillian off my mind. It worked, but I knew it would come at a price.

***

I literally dragged myself to work. I was an early riser when it came to getting to my job on time. I liked my morning schedule— rise up early, workout, shower, dress, and have a cup of coffee before hitting my workplace. I preferred to get there early, plan my schedule, and make sure I had plenty of time to get things done. I wasn't the kind of guy who walked in with seconds to spare. Today, everything felt off, and Zed knew it the moment I walked into the building, scowling at the world.

"What happened to you?" He chuckled.

"Nothing." I grabbed my timecard to punch in with about a minute to spare. My head felt like it just might pop off today. I had already taken more pain medication than recommended, but what would be worse other than my liver falling out? I slid my clipboard from behind the desk to look at everything he had scheduled for me.

Zed dropped a set of keys down. "Mrs. Donahue cracked up her bumper. It doesn't look too bad, but she asked if you could take a look at it first thing."

"Again?" Someone needed to take her keys away from her. She was in here every other week lately. "I'll see what I can do," I added before I went back inside.

By the time lunch had rolled around, I had finished an oil change on Pat's Jeep, rotated Charlie Vary's tires, and was going to start on Mrs. Donahue's car after I had eaten. My head was still pounding after all the alcohol I had consumed last night, but I had managed to dull the ache with enough Tylenol to kill an elephant. I washed the grease and grime from my hands before I took a swig of my water, only to find Zed grinning at me from the front of the garage stall.

"Got a visitor." His voice sounded way too light. He sounded weird, and I didn't like it.

I narrowed my eyes. "Who?" If it were Patrick, which I doubted, he would have told me. He knew I was planning to bring his Jeep back with me tonight so there was no need for him to come by. No one had texted me all morning, and I had zero friends other than my brother, so who the hell would bother me at work?

Zed's lips turned into a smirk. "Pretty brunette. Dressed in a leotard and pink tights." He chuckled when I scowled harder at him.

I pushed past my boss to find Jillian standing outside the shop, actually dressed in what he said she was. Her chestnut hair piled on top of her head in that tight bun, a pink leotard, a see-through skirt, and matching fucking tights. Jillian had the lean, wiry physique of the dancer from the years of hard work she had put in, and I instantly wanted to put my hands all over her.

Her face lit up the moment she saw me. "I'm sorry for just dropping by unannounced, but I needed to—" Jillian let out a surprised yelp the moment I wrapped my hand around her arm and yanked her inside.

"What the fuck are you doing here?" I grunted, pinning her against the wall. "Didn't I tell you to leave me alone?"

"Yes, but—"

I bared my teeth. "Then let me repeat the question, Jills. What are you doing here?" I grabbed her hair in the palm of my hand and yanked her head up. Fear sparkled in her green eyes. This was not the version of me she was used to, but it was the one she was getting.

"I needed to talk to you about the other night." Her voice shook as she spoke. "I couldn't leave things the way they were. I'm sorry, Hutch, for what Knox said, and if I upset you." Jillian licked her lips nervously as she stared up at me, but as my eyes slowly descended, I noticed how her nipples poked through her leotard, and how she pressed her thighs together. Was this turning her on? Did she actually like being manhandled by me?

"That's the reason you're here? You know you could have texted me." I released Jillian's hair, but slowly dragged the pads of my fingers against her face without even realizing it. "I'm not your boyfriend."

Jillian's face fell and she seethed, "Fuck you, Hutch."

I watched as she ran off without looking back, and once again, my heart felt heavy. The man she just saw, that was who I was before. Before I changed into the mute. I dropped my gaze to my feet when I noticed the brown bag that Jillian must have dropped on the ground in her haste to get away from me. I stopped, picked it up, and opened it to find what looked like two egg salad sandwiches, two apples, and two granola bars inside. She had brought me lunch.

Fuck me.

***

The rest of the week went by in a blur. I would work, go home, and drink myself to sleep. Repeat. All week until the weekend rolled around. Normally I worked on Saturday mornings, but since it was the Fourth of July, the shop was closed, and I was stuck at home, alone with my thoughts. I spent most of the day feeling sorry for myself, avoiding the crowds of tourists that had rolled in for the holiday, but found myself at the beach watching the fireworks around nine o'clock or something—I had been doing that since I was a kid.

I stared up at the exploding colors above me on the beach. I should be home, in my bed, but it was too quiet there. I didn't want to be alone with my own thoughts anymore because Jillian would creep in. She had started to appear now, even with the help of alcohol, and I was hoping that maybe the loud fireworks would drown her out for a while. They had helped with so many other things in the past.

Maybe I could fall asleep on the beach, and the ocean could just take me away. Then I wouldn't have to worry about anything again. The terrible nightmare that my life had become would no longer make me think about putting a bullet into my head. No one would miss me anyway when I was gone.

"I told you to leave me the hell alone! You cheated on me, remember?"

"Come on, you're no fun. You just need to relax a little, Jill."

My back straightened. Did I just hear—?

"We broke up, Knox. I know you slept with Madison while I was gone. Go find her. You two looked super cozy at the carnival anyway." Yep, that was Jillian's voice. I would know it anywhere.

I turned, trying to figure out where the sound was coming from before I realized they were only a few feet away from me. Shit, if they walked any closer, they would trip over me if they weren't careful. I didn't want Jillian or Knox to think that I was stalking her.

Knox barked out a malicious snicker. "You really like that fucking creep, don't you? That's kind of sick if you ask me. He's messed up in the head, but if that's what you're into..."

The sound of Jillian crying out in agony had me on my feet before I could even think about it. "Back off." Both their heads turned toward the sound of my voice. When Knox didn't move, I took a step forward. "I said, back the fuck off," I growled.

"I heard what you said, mute, but I don't have to listen to you." Knox had both of Jillian's arms pinned to her side, and we both knew it wasn't a fair fight. He had to outweigh her by at least a hundred pounds. She was dressed in a black one-piece bathing suit with a pair of shorts pulled on over it, her brown hair pulled back from her face into a ponytail. They must have come from the party I heard at the house next to the beach because there was no one else around.

Tonight might be my opportunity to rearrange Knox's face.

"Are you alright?" I asked Jillian, but when she shook her head, I balled my hands into fists at my side.

"Unless you want to spend the rest of the evening picking your teeth out of the sand, I suggest you let her go." It was probably the most I had ever spoken to Knox, but he had to realize I wasn't scared of him tonight. Not when it came Jillian Robinson.

"You really think that I'm afraid of you?" Knox grinned at me. "Out of all the people in this town, you're at the bottom of my list...Fuck! You bitch!" he cried out, and I watched as he dropped to his knees, cupping his dick in his hand.

Jillian kicked sand in his face. "If you touch me again, ever, I will do more than just knee you in the balls, you piece of shit," she warned him in a deadly tone. Then she took off running down the beach without saying a word to me.

"Jills! Wait!" I took off after her. Even as unsteady on my feet as I was, I was able to catch up to her with my long legs. "I need to talk to you." I touched her arm, but she whirled around as if she might kick me next. "I surrender!" I held up my hands.

Jillian shook her head. "I have nothing to say to you, Hutch. You made it perfectly clear how you feel about me." Her nostrils flared slightly as another round of fireworks began to go off above our heads.

"About that..." I pinched the back of neck nervously before I reached down to cup her face with the palms of my hands. "I was wrong."

"Wrong?"

I nodded.

"What do you mean *wrong*? You told me that we weren't friends, and then the way you acted when I came to visit you at your work...I thought you hated me." Jillian stared at my mouth as she licked her lips.

I leaned forward so that my face was inches from hers. "Negative," I whispered before I slammed my mouth over hers. God, she tasted like fucking heaven on earth. Her taste was sweet, soft, and perfect for me. Her soft, plump lips opened slightly as she wrapped her arms around my waist, and I felt her fingers grip my shirt as the kiss grew longer. "Fuck," I murmured as she let me slide my tongue into the warm concaves of her mouth and swept it around, looking to twirl it around hers. I groaned softly when I made contact, my dick jerking to attention when Jillian's nails clawed into my skin. I wanted, no, I needed more, but this was already getting out of control. When I pulled away, Jillian's face was flushed, her eyes wide, but it was the smile on her face that told me I did something right.

"Where did you learn to kiss like that?" she whispered, reaching for my hand, and laced her fingers through mine. "Because that...that was the most amazing kiss I have ever had in my entire life."

I ran the fingers of my free hand over her lips. "Yeah?" I was sure she was only trying to be nice.

"Jesus Christ, Hutch, yes." Jillian squeezed my hand. "You kiss all the girls like that?"

"Only the ones I like." I had kissed two girls in my life. My first girlfriend, Mya, and now, Jillian. "Listen, about the other day—"

Jillian shook her head. "I already forgot," she assured me. "Why don't you walk me home, Hutch?" She stood up onto her tiptoes and planted a kiss against my chin. "Then you can kiss me goodnight like that again at the front door."

Chapter Six

Jillian

Hutch didn't say much on the walk back to my house. He kept my hand clasped tightly in his as if he was afraid I might disappear or maybe that I might even change my mind, but I liked it. I loved how protective Hutch was, how strong he was, and that even though he was scared, he had finally showed me his true feelings.

Now that the holiday was finally here, the streets of Ocean View were packed with more people, so it took a little longer to get home. We weaved our way through the crowds before we finally started down our street. As our houses came into view, Hutch tugged me closer.

"I know you probably need to get home, but can I show you something?" He sounded nervous, eliciting a smile from me.

"I don't have to get home anytime soon." My mother trusted Jo and me now that we had graduated high school. Not to mention she thought I was at Bella's party. "What did you want to show me?" I squeezed Hutch's hand as he tried to let go of mine.

"It's in my apartment."

"Hutch Kelly, are you trying to have your way with me?" I saw the look of shock on his face and immediately regretted saying that. "You know I'm kidding, right?" I tried to appease him. "It's called flirting."

He chewed nervously on his bottom lip before he brought his free hand up to grip the back of his neck. I noticed he tended to do this when he was nervous or upset. "Yes, I know," Hutch answered.

"So, what did you want to show me?" What happened to the guy on the beach that kissed me until my bathing suit was damp with need. Now it felt like Hutch was disappearing on me again.

Hutch led me across the street to his house, up the stairs to his apartment where he stopped to turn around to face me. "I hope you don't mind the mess." He flashed a quick smile before he unlocked the door and stepped inside.

I followed him inside, thinking I was going to find the place in disarray, but I couldn't find anything out of place. Not a stray piece of clothing, a beer bottle, or an empty dish. Okay, maybe there was a beer can on the counter that shouldn't be, but that was it. "Mess?" I teased as Hutch toed off his shoes. "You're such a slob." I started to walk around, but he stopped.

"Do you, uh, mind taking off your shoes? I worry about sand and stuff getting inside." He gave me a sheepish look.

I shook my head, removing my flip-flops to leave them by his sneakers. "Hutch, this place is amazing." I moved around the small studio apartment. "How long have you been living here?" I liked the open concept. The small kitchen, the oversized couch, and the giant television. I let my eyes move over the slate blue walls until they the landed on the king-sized bed in the back of the apartment. "You do know that this place is anything but messy, right?" I turned to find Hutch staring up at the ceiling with his jaw set in stone. "Hutch? Honey, are you alright?" I took a step toward him, thinking he might be having one of his panic attacks only to have him drop his gaze in my direction.

"I shouldn't have invited you here."

Shame mingled in my throat. Was I reading him all wrong? "I should get going anyway." I started to turn around, but not before Hutch was on me and had me pinned against the kitchen counter.

"I don't want you to leave." His voice came out utterly raspy with desire. "I'm just...afraid of what might happen if you don't." Hutch skated his hand up my arm, over my shoulder, and around my back before he dug his fingers into my skin as he pressed his body against mine.

I felt his body heat seep into mine. "Are you going to hurt me?" My voice shook with fear and desire. I glanced up to find his brown eyes darkened with lust.

"What? No, that's not what I meant," Hutch insisted.

I placed the palms of my hands against his chest before I slid them up and behind his neck so I could hook them together. "Then what? What are you afraid of, Hutch?" I whispered.

He swallowed, and I watched the way his Adam's apple bobbed against his throat. "There are things, things you don't know about me, Jills, and I would hate for you to think less of me when you found out." He dropped his forehead against mine, hiding those gorgeous orbs behind his closed lids.

"I could never."

"Don't say that."

"Prove me wrong."

Hutch gripped my waist as he lifted me up onto the counter. "There are plenty of things I want to tell you, but that isn't one of them." His lips were on mine before I could say anything, and I immediately melted.

I wanted this. The kiss, the man, and everything he was doing right now. The way Hutch took control, how he let his tongue roll over my lips before finally slipping it inside my mouth to dance with mine, was oh-so sexy. His hands roamed my hips then made their way up my stomach and over my already hard nipples, where he grazed over them, making me arch my back and moan softly. Wetness beaded between my legs, causing me to wrap them around Hutch's waist and tug him closer.

"Your mouth tastes like summer on a hot day," he whispered. I groaned as his fingers pulled at my hard peaks. "Fuck, you make me so hard," Hutch groaned.

He wasn't lying. I could feel him jerk against me the longer the kiss went on, so I couldn't help but slip my hand between us to cup his dick in my hands, only to have him pull away and turn his back to me.

"I'm sorry, I just—" I stopped when Hutch held up his hand. There were so many pieces of the puzzle to Hutch Kelly. So many unanswered questions, but I wanted him to trust me with them. I wanted to take the time to get to know him, and I would wait until he was ready.

Hutch slowly turned back around, making sure to keep his eyes on the floor. "I've never...fuck, I've never been with a woman before. Not like that." I watched his ears turn red like they always did when he was embarrassed.

Wait a second. Hutch was a virgin?

I slipped off the counter. "There's nothing to be ashamed of," I assured him. "If you don't want me to touch you and just want to stick to kissing, we can just do that. You're really good at it." Hutch looked up at me shyly, so I touched his hand in comfort.

"You're sure?" Hutch linked our fingers together.

I nodded. "Positive." I didn't want him to think he had to do something he didn't want to. "Didn't you say you wanted to show me something?"

"Right." Hutch started to lead me over to his bed and then released my hand so that he could climb up onto the mattress. He stretched out completely and then patted the spot next to him. "You're going to have to come up here if you want to see it." He pointed up above him at the ceiling.

I followed after Hutch, and once I looked up, I realized what he was looking at. The giant skylight showed off the brilliant moon and you could see bursts of light from the fireworks that were still going off down on the beach. "Whoa," I muttered softly, hoisting myself up onto the mattress next to him.

"I built this place myself," Hutch told me as his hand found mine. "Hey Google, turn off the lights," he called out and the apartment was suddenly dark. "My parents told me I could live here if I built it, so I spent the summer after I graduated high school making it my own after I got home from the shop. It took a lot work, but I think it turned out pretty good." He squeezed my fingers lightly.

I turned to look at Hutch's profile. "Pretty good is putting it lightly," I teased and noticed the smile that spread across his face. "Are you really a virgin?" He turned to stare at me, the firework lights bouncing off his dark eyes.

"Are you?"

"No."

Hutch used the knuckles of his free hand to tilt my face further. "I've never slept with a girl before," he whispered, "but things could change if you play your cards right, Jillybean." Heat flared between my legs. *Also that nickname? Totally a keeper.* "Will you dance for me sometime?" He ran his thumb against my cheek before he dropped his hand.

I gave a brief nod because I needed to get myself together. "Of course," I promised, and we both turned to look back up at the sky.

I found myself snuggling closer to Hutch, my eyes drooping, my breath slowing, and before I knew it, I was fast asleep.

***

I woke up confused and groggy. Staring up at the skylight, I instantly realized I wasn't home. "Shit." I sprang from the bed and dug my phone from my pocket. Sure enough, my mother had texted me as had Jo, and they were both curious where I was.

Mom: *You'd better have a good reason for not coming home last night, Jillian Claire!*

Jo: *Mom is pissed. Where are you?*

Jo: *Did you go home with Hutch last night? Knox said you kicked him in the balls. Bravo, by the way. You know he went* *home with Madison? God, I hate her skanky ass. We're kicking her out of the club.*

Fuck, I was so screwed. I didn't have a curfew, but I still tried to get home at a decent hour or at least give my mother a heads-up if I was planning on staying at a friends' place. I was a decent kid like that.

"Good morning." I glanced up to find Hutch standing shirtless in the kitchen and holding out a cup of coffee. "Sleep okay?"

I took a second to admire the contours of his abs, the muscles that defined his arms and chest, wondering when he had the time to work out because he was in a glorious shape. "Excellent."

"Everything alright?" Hutch jutted his chin at the phone in my hand.

Not exactly, but I didn't want him to worry. "Sure, perfect, amazing." I stood up to slip my phone into my back pocket. "How did you sleep?" I tried to change the subject, but Hutch shook his head.

"No, don't try that with me." He smirked. "Are you in trouble for staying the night? I thought you said your mother wouldn't care?" He tugged on my elbow to bring me closer.

"Uh, I didn't exactly tell her that I wouldn't be coming home."

"Jills." Why was it so sexy when he said my name like that? "You need to tell her you're okay before they think someone kidnapped you. Namely me."

I nodded, and fished out my phone again to text my mother back.

Jillian: *I'm fine, Mom. Sorry I didn't text. Spent the night at a friend's.*

I looked back up at Hutch. "See, all good." My phone immediately dinged back.

Mom: *Would this friend happened to be named Hutch Kelly?*

My sister was dead to me. *RIP, Josephine.* I texted her next. I was now an only child.

Jillian: *You are dead to me, Jo!! *skull emoji**

Jo: *Whatever do you mean? Tell me he's hung like a horse though.*

Jillian: *Ew, gross. He's your future brother-in-law.*

Jo: *You didn't see his dick. I thought I raised you better.*

I shoved my phone back into my pocket, blushing. "All good." I grinned at Hutch as he watched me. "My sister asked if I saw your penis."

Hutch nearly spit coffee from his nose. "What?" He coughed, placing his cup on the counter. "That's kind of awkward. You two talk about stuff like that? Does she talk about Pat's, er, penis?" He blushed and ducked his head.

I giggled. "When they first started dating, she did, but I finally told her I didn't want to hear about it anymore because it was weird to me." I moved to wrap my arms around Hutch's waist. "If and when we ever have sex, I can assure you I won't gossip about it."

Hutch yanked me against his chest. "Not even if I have a giant wang?" he teased. "Like ten inches or whatever?"

"Do you?"

"Maybe."

Hutch pressed his lips to mine. "You want some coffee?" His voice dripped with heat. "Or you want to stand here talking about my dick a little longer?"

"It's so hard to decide. Coffee, dick, coffee, dick. Can we do both?" I laughed when he tickled my ribs until I could hardly breathe, begging him to stop, but secretly praying he didn't. It wasn't until I saw the worried look on his face that I realized something was bothering him. "Hutch?"

He cupped my face in his big hands. "You're really here, Jills? I mean, this isn't some dream that I'm having, only to wake up and find I'm alone?" His browns searched my face worriedly.

"I'm here." I gripped his wrists tightly, and felt him relax in my hold.

He slowly broke into a smile that lighted his entire face. "Are you hungry? I could cook us some breakfast," he offered, pressing a kiss to my forehead. "I'm sure the Egg is packed this morning unless you want to go there instead?"

"Breakfast in sounds perfect." I couldn't imagine anything better.

Chapter Seven

Hutch

Jillian spent the whole day at my apartment. We made breakfast together which was something I absolutely enjoyed doing. I had never had a girl sleep over, never mind cook breakfast with me, so I guess it was many firsts for me. After she went home for a shower and to change, she came back to my place so we watch murder documentaries on Netflix until dinnertime. It was probably the best day I ever had in my entire life. I wanted to ask her to stay, but she said Sunday dinner with her mom and sister was important to her, which meant she needed to be at her place, but she did promise that she would see me tomorrow.

Pat showed up around six with a pizza so at least I didn't have to spend too much time alone. Although I knew that meant he had questions. Ones I didn't want to answer.

"What are you doing?" he asked once I had placed a beer in front of him.

I grunted as I took a bite of the pizza and chewed as slow as humanly possible. "Eating," I answered.

Pat popped his jaw. "You know that's not what I meant, dick." He reached for his beer. "I'm talking about with Jillian." He watched me for a second, and when I didn't answer, he sighed. "Seriously, she's—"

"Too good for me?"

"That's not what I was going to say, and you know it."

I cocked an eyebrow. "Spill it." I leaned back against the chair to stare at my brother. I knew Pat was only trying to be nice. Looking out for me and for Jillian, but this wasn't up to him.

Pat wiped his hands. "Don't get mad at me. I'm your brother, and I love you. She's going to be leaving in a few weeks, and you're only going to end up getting hurt. That doesn't mean you can't do long distance, but Hutch, man, think about it. Do you see yourself going to New York? Visiting her? Living there?" My throat felt like it might close up in shock. "I didn't think so," he said when I didn't answer.

"You're just...you're only saying this because you want me to push her away," I hissed.

Pat shook his head. "I would love nothing more than for you and Jill to fall in love, man. You, of all people, deserve that, but it's not going to happen with her. You've got things locked up in your head that you need to deal with first. Things you won't tell me or Mom or Dad about."

"Don't."

"I'm just being honest!"

I resisted the urge to throw the box of pizza across the room because I knew what a mess that would make. I didn't want to spend all night cleaning the grease from the walls or floors. "Go." I pointed at the door.

"Hutch," Pat objected, "instead of you pushing me away, let's talk about this instead."

I jumped to my feet. "I don't want to fucking talk about it!" I shouted. "I want you to fucking go!" This time, I grabbed my beer and smashed it against the sink. "You don't shit about me or Jillian. She's the only one. Now, just leave," I said again and turned away. Once I heard the sound of the door shutting behind him, I sat back down. I pulled my phone from my pocket and sent a text off before I could stop myself.

Hutch: *You busy?*

Jillian: *Not when it comes to you.*

Shit, what was I supposed to say to her? That Pat just shit all over any thoughts I had for our future. Did we even have a future?

Jillian: *Are you alright? *smiley face emoji* Do you need me to come over when I'm done practicing for tomorrow? Or I could come over now and finish at your place.*

Was she serious?

Hutch: *Really? You don't mind.*

Jillian: *Let me just pack a bag in case I fall asleep again.*

Not even fifteen minutes later, there was a soft knock at my door. When I opened it, Jillian was standing there, dressed in a long-sleeved white shirt, black leggings, and white leg warmers, with her hair up in a tight bun. Just the sight of her, although fully clothed, made my cock stir in my pants. She wore no makeup, but was nonetheless stunning. I reached for the small bag Jillian held her hand as she stepped inside. Her eyes instantly went to the broken bottle and spilled beer on the floor that I hadn't bothered to clean up yet.

"What happened?" She looked concerned.

I shook my head. "Nothing, I just..." I stopped so that I could run my hand down my face and when I met her searching gaze, she had her eyebrows raised. "Pat came over. We argued." I suddenly felt ashamed and couldn't look at her.

"Hutch." Jillian caressed my cheek. "Whatever you fought about doesn't matter in the end. He's your brother, and I'm sure he was just looking out for you."

"He's afraid that I'm going to end up hurt when you leave," I whispered.

Jillian pressed her face into my chest. "What do you think is going to happen?"

"I don't want to think that far ahead."

"Why?"

I pressed my lips together. "Because it hurts," I admitted before I wrapped my arms around Jillian to pull her closer. The truth was I already felt myself falling too fast, too soon, for her, and what Pat said had hit closer to home than I realized. We stood like that for a few minutes, breaking in each other's scents, not saying anything, just holding one another until she pulled back.

"There's this little thing called a cell phone." A smile tugged at Jillian's lips while a sparkle danced in her green eyes. "You can send messages on it or call someone if you miss them. And"—she untangled herself from my arms—"sometimes"—she unzipped her little bag, that I deposited on the floor when she walked in, to dig out her phone—"there's this thing called FaceTime. See?" She winked at me. "Where you can call someone. Watch." Jillian pressed the button that caused mine to start ringing. "You can talk to someone face-to-face if you miss them enough."

"You're making fun of me," I accused.

Jillian shook her head as she hit end on her cell. "I'm not, Hutch, I'm just trying to be realistic." She put her phone on top of her bag. "I'm not sure what's happening between us right now, but what if we don't last until I leave?" I watched her brows dip as her eyes told me a different story. Dared me to defy her.

I took a step closer. "What if we do?" I asked.

"Then we make it work." Jillian's voice caused heat and lust to consume my body and senses. I was seriously fucked.

I was on her before I even realized it; my mouth on hers, telling her without words what I wanted. Jillian kissed away all my doubts and fears away whether she realized it or not, understanding me like no else ever did. Our tongues tangled together as she clutched at my shirt, little whimpers escaping her throat, and when she broke the kiss to nibble at my bottom lip, I knew what she wanted by the look in her eyes.

"It's okay," she whispered. She pressed two fingers to my mouth.

Was it? She had no idea how much I wanted her, how much I yearned to strip her naked, lick every single inch of her skin, and then spread her legs to eat her pussy until she screamed my name. It wasn't just that I was unexperienced; it was that I was scared. Things went on inside my head that no one knew about. I cupped her head in my hands. "I'm sorry."

"You have nothing to be sorry about."

"You deserve to have someone pleasure you."

Jillian smiled. "I'm perfectly capable of pleasuring myself, Hutch." Her words caused liquid fire blaze through me and my cock, which was already rock hard and felt like it might burst through my jeans.

"Is...is that something you do often?" My voice sounded strained.

"Why? Do you want to watch?" Jillian cupped my jaw between her fingers. "I wouldn't mind." Her husked, sultry voice sent my mind into a tailspin.

I growled something that didn't even sound human as I watched her begin to move toward my bed. Holy fuck, was this actually happening right now? I wasn't sure I would be able to control myself. Jillian slowly began to peel her clothes off, first starting with her shirt, followed by her leg warmers, then her leggings, until she was standing naked in front of me.

"Let me know if this is too much for you."

I shook my head.

"Should I put a towel down?"

Again, I just shook my head.

"Are you okay?" Jillian asked.

I swallowed. "Fine," I assured her. Fine was probably not how I would describe myself, but it was the only thing I could think of right now.

Jillian tilted her head and whispered, "Hutch, you can look at me."

"I..." Was I not looking at her? Shit, she was beautiful. Her tits—*breasts*—I corrected myself, were prefect little handfuls with pink little areolas, and her nipples, Jesus, they were hard as diamonds right now. I was pretty sure I groaned when I saw Jillian reach up to pinch them between her forefingers. Her body was a dancer's paradise. Not an inch of fat to be seen, her stomach toned, her legs muscled and long. My eyes darted between her legs. Her pussy, fuck, it was bare of any hair and glistening with desire.

"I really like nipple play," Jillian murmured as she continued to roll and tug at them. "Feels so good and gets me going."

This was torture.

"One time, I swear I nearly came from that alone," she whimpered as she sat down on the bed and dropped her head back to arch her back. "Feels so good. The pleasure goes straight between my legs."

I watched with hooded eyes as Jillian slowly leaned back onto the mattress, her legs spreading further apart, and resisted the urge to adjust my hard-as-nails dick.

"I can't...fuck." Jillian began to slide her right hand down her stomach. "That's it," she moaned when she made contact with her clit. "Fuck, yes," she hissed as her legs spread wider.

Fuck this.

I hadn't even realized I had walked over to the bed until I dropped to my knees. "Tell me what to do," I growled and pushed her hand away.

Jillian pushed herself up onto her elbows. "Hutch you don't—"

I put both hands on her hips. "Tell me," I said again as I looked up at her. Her green eyes were dark with need. "Like this?" I dragged my tongue over her engorged clit, and she cried out. Jillian tasted like pure heaven.

"Play with your nipples while I eat you," I demanded and felt her lean back against the bed.

I let my tongue do all the work. Rolling it repeatedly over her sweet, wet slit, while Jillian pulled on her nipples. Her moans and whimpers filled the room as I worked her over. My cock grew harder in my jeans. I lost myself in making her feel good until Jillian's hands dug into my hair and she cried out my name, her body shaking and quivering as she reached her release. It was the most beautiful experience of my life.

I climbed up onto the bed to pull her against me. "Was...was that okay?" I whispered as she peppered kisses against my mouth.

"That was amazing," she assured me, her eyes hazy. "Thank you."

I blushed. "You're more than welcome." We held one another for a few minutes until she pulled back to look at me again.

"Do you want me to return the favor? I understand if you say no, but I feel like you deserve it after that." Jillian's hands reached for the button on my pants, causing my already painfully hard cock to jerk at the thought of her beautiful, pouty lips wrapping around my dick. Until the moment she popped my jeans open and fear licked at my brain.

"I can't—" I jumped off the bed and shook my head, yanking my hands through my hair. "Trust me, Jills, you're fucking stunning, and I want you, fuck, do I want you, but I just...I can't." I bit my lower lip so hard I tasted blood.

"Hutch." Jillian was suddenly next to me. "Honey, it's okay."

I stared down into her bright eyes as she searched my face. There were so many things I wanted to tell her right now, but I couldn't. I was afraid if I did, Jillian would run screaming from my apartment and never return.

"Why don't we"—Jillian bent down and began to put her clothes back on—"finish watching the documentary we were watching before." I suddenly wished she had something of mine to put on instead. "What, you want to watch something else?" She tilted her head, her gaze searching.

I felt my ear grows red. "That's fine."

"Your mouth says yes, Hutch, but your eyes say something else. What are you thinking?"

"Nothing."

"Hutch." Jillian put her hands on her hips.

I sighed, but didn't say anything. I instead moved over to the dresser to pull out the second drawer and fished out one of my Kenny Chesney shirts. "Here."

"You want me to wear your shirt?" she asked, amusement shining in her features.

I nodded.

Without hesitation, Jillian took the shirt from me, and when I snuck a glance, she had it pulled on over her head before she slid into her leggings. "Good?" She flashed a smile up at me. It hung off her small frame and straight past her knees. "Now, about that documentary." She danced over the sofa on her toes, twirling enough to make me dizzy in the head.

I wasn't sure if it was Jillian's ballet moves or her in general that made me feel that way.

Chapter Eight

Jillian

When I woke up alone in Hutch's bed on Monday morning, I was a little confused at first. We had finished watching the Netflix documentary after he cleaned up the broken beer bottle in his kitchen, and started on another one before we both decided we should get to bed since we had an early morning. I just thought when my alarm went off at six, he would still be sleeping.

I certainly hadn't thought he would end up giving me an orgasm or eating me out last night. That put me off-guard. In a good way of course. Hutch was different from any other guy I had met. I wanted to bring him out of his shell, help him experience things he had never done before, but that was all going to be on his terms. When he was ready.

I also wanted to be the first girl to give him a blowjob.

I smiled to myself thinking about that as I pushed the covers off to climb from the bed. Hutch liked to keep his apartment below zero, and I was freezing now that I was now longer wrapped under the blankets. I made my way toward the bathroom to shower before I had to head off to ballet practice.

The bathroom was small with just a shower stall, a sink, and toilet, but it was clean just like the rest of the apartment. I took a fast shower, washed my hair and body before I wrapped my hair up in a towel. I brushed my teeth, dried my hair off, and secured it in a tight bun for class. I lathered on some of my lotion that I liked to wear, cleaned up anything

I had left behind, and as I was walking back to put on some clean clothes, Hutch was making his way back into the apartment, looking like a girl's wet dream come true.

He must have come from a workout because he was dressed in nothing but a pair of shorts and sneakers, his muscles sweaty and exposed. I let my eyes roam over his perfectly toned body, right down to the V that pointed toward the dick he had yet to let me see before I met his brown eyes. They had a hard look about them. "Good morning." Hutch's voice sounded clipped.

"Good morning," I greeted him back. "I figure by the way you're dressed you were at the gym?" I asked.

"There's one in my parents' basement." He ran his hand through his sweaty hair. "It's not much, but it does the job." Hutch finished off the water he held tightly in his fist. "Sleep alright?" He capped the bottle and placed it gently on the counter.

I clutched at the dirty shirt he let me sleep in last night. "Like a baby. You have the most comfortable bed in America," I teased just to watch his ears turn pink. Cuddling up to Hutch was probably turning into one of my most favorite things, but I left that part out. He seemed a little on edge this morning, but I wasn't sure why. "You okay?" I pushed.

"Fine," he answered quickly. "Just need a shower."

I nodded. "Sure, I'll just get dressed and be on my way." I didn't want to upset him more than he already was. I turned to move back to where my bag was, but I felt Hutch's hand on my elbow. When I looked up, his eyes had softened.

"Come here." He tugged me closer until I was pressed against his chest. Hutch leaned down so that he could press his lips to mine. "Don't think you're leaving without me, Jills." His voice sent shivers throughout my body.

"I wasn't—"

He shook his head. "I'll only be a couple of minutes," Hutch assured me before tilting my head up with his index finger. "Coffee should be ready by now." He dropped a kiss to my forehead before he walked to the bathroom and shut the door behind him.

I could not figure this guy out.

I knew Hutch liked me. It was obvious in the way he looked at me, kissed me, and the way he made me come last night, but this morning? He was acting super strange. I thought about this as I changed into a clean pair of purple tights, a matching leotard and skirt, before I slipped on a pair of white sneakers, making sure my ballet slippers were in my bag before I zipped it up. I carried my bag into the kitchen, placing it on the chair before my gaze moved to two travel mugs sitting on the counter. What time did Hutch get up in the morning? Did he actually sleep at night or was that an act?

I had so many things I wanted to ask him, but knew I couldn't do that. Hutch had to be the one to tell me. It was obvious he had been hurt before. He was scared about the sex thing, but only when it came to be on the receiving end. I knew, from the rumors, that he had once been an outgoing football player, but something had happened to change him, but no one seemed to know what exactly happened. Not even Patrick had any insight on that.

"Ready?"

I jumped at the sound of Hutch's voice, not having heard him walk in. He was already dressed in a tight-fitting white t-shirt, blue jeans, and his work boots. "That has to be the fastest shower in the world," I commented.

"Told you I would be quick." He opened both travel mugs and glanced over his shoulder at me.. "Do you want to take any coffee with you?"

I shook my head. "I'm good, but thank you. Coffee just makes me have to pee a lot during practice." I moved to wrap my arms around Hutch's waist. "You smell good." Like soap and whatever aftershave he had put on. Heaven.

Hutch gripped both my hands in one of his. "Thanks." He squeezed lightly before he turned around to wrap me in his arms. "I enjoyed having you here last night, Jills. Do you...do you have plans tonight?" His voice shook slightly.

I rested my chin against his chest. "Are you asking me out on a date?" I watched as Hutch's ears turned pink. When he gave a quick nod, I stood up on my toes to kiss his chin. "Then no, I don't have any plans," I told him.

"I have." Hutch stopped for a moment, his brown eyes clouding. "I have therapy after work, which is an hour, but if you want to come by around seven?" He shifted his gaze above my head.

I saw the worried look all over his face. He had told me the truth, confided in me, and now he was waiting for my response.

"Of course, that's perfect. It gives me time to wash up after practice." Should I even mention the therapy? Hutch's grip tightened. "I'm not sure—"

"I go three times a week," he whispered. "Have been for years now."

"Hutch—"

"Let me finish." He released me so that he could pace the floor. "It helps, I guess, sometimes or maybe not, but I felt I should tell you. I figured that I was going to tell my therapist about you today, well, I already kind of did, but...fuck." Hutch shook his head. "I hate this."

I did too. When I didn't know what to say or do for him. "You don't have to tell me anything you don't want to." Hutch turned to look at me with uncertainty written all over his face. "I know this is hard for you, but I'm here for you, no matter what," I assured him.

Hutch caged me in against the counter. "You're real, right, Jills?" he whispered. "You're not a figment of my imagination?" His hand came up to pull on my bun, causing heat to pool inside my belly.

"I assure you that I am real," I told him again.

Hutch's mouth came crashing down on mine, and I couldn't help but moan when his obvious erection pressed directly against my core. I dug my nails into his arms as the kiss escalated further, and I felt the urgency behind his kisses as our tongues swirled together.

"We," Hutch murmured, his lips not leaving mine, "need to leave." He finally pulled back.

"Before we're late." His eyes were nearly as dark as the night sky as he stared down at me.

I nodded. "Don't want to be late." I didn't care, but something told me that Hutch was one of those people who stuck to punctuality. I watched as he did a sweep of his apartment. Maybe to make sure everything was in its proper place, or maybe to make sure he had everything; I couldn't be sure.

Once we were outside, Hutch locked the door behind him, and together, we walked to my ballet practice.

***

Hutch kissed me goodbye at the door to the dance studio before he walked the rest of the way to Zed's, which was just down the street, and then I walked inside only to find myself being stared at by the rest of the girls in my class. Madison Rae was the first to speak, and I could see by the way she was smirking at me that she couldn't wait to let her comments fly.

"So, you two are what? Dating now?" She chuckled loudly as she looked around at everyone, encouraging them to join her. "Honestly, Jill, I don't know what you see in him." Everyone snickered in the background.

I shoved my bag in my locker before I spun around. "How is this any of your business?" I eyed Madison. When she didn't answer, I shrugged. "I see how you have nothing to add to that." I walked past her only to have her grab my arm and spin me around. "Are you serious right now?" I exclaimed.

The rest of the girls in class were younger than Madison and myself. We were the only eighteen-year-olds, the ones that had graduated and hoping to become famous dancers if we were lucky enough, but I knew them all. Ocean View was a small town. Jessie Hanson, the blonde on Madison's left, lived a couple houses down from me, and Marley Holly, the brunette with big boobs, across the street from Bella. Both, however, would not want to cross Madison. She was always gunning to be the queen bitch in this town.

"You fucking him yet?" Madison hissed as she pressed her fingers into my skin so tight, I knew she was drawing blood. "Tell me something, Jillian, does he make noise when he comes or does he just open his mouth in a silent scream?"

"You're such a bitch," I snapped at her, disgusted at the angle of her thoughts.

"Girls!" We both spun around at the sound of our teacher, Mistress Dubois, as she clapped her hands together. I felt Madison's hand slip away from my arm. "Starting positions, please." Her heavy French accent floated through the room as we all hurried to get to the barre as she requested.

I shot a look over to Madison as I made sure to get as far away from her as possible, but the sting of her nails in my skin throughout the day never let me forget what she had said to me. I avoided her all day, and when I met Hutch for lunch, he either didn't see the marks, which were now scabbed over, or didn't say anything.

He did make sure our plans were still on for dinner, and by the time I left the dance studio, I couldn't wait to spend the evening with him and forget about everything else.

Chapter Nine

Hutch

I sat down on the oversized couch and looked around my therapist's room. It hadn't changed much since I had started coming here eight years ago. Same white bookshelf in the left corner, with different books, although I suspected they were switched out every couple of months, newer plant because she didn't have much of a green thumb so they all kept dying, and a tired looking painting of fruit on the right wall. It looked like someone at least dusted and cleaned in here every week because this time the painting was not crooked like I had commented on Friday when I was here. Stuff like that bothered me with my OCD issues. There was a beat-up desk shoved in the left corner of the room that I had only seen Megan, that's what she insisted I call her, sit at once or twice, and it was overloaded with folders, notepads, and boxes of Kleenex.

Megan was seated in middle of the room directly in front of me with her tablet, a worn-out coffee table separating us. Her hair had been a rusty orange color eight years ago, but now it had faded into a grayish white. I glanced at the window that looked toward the overgrown lawn and wished I had rescheduled. I wanted to be anywhere but here right now. I didn't want to talk about myself today.

"So, Hutch." I continued to stare outside as Megan spoke. "On Friday you mentioned a girl, but things hadn't gone the way you thought."

I nodded. "Jillian." Just the sound of her name made everything inside my head spin around. The way her lips tasted, the way she tasted, and the way her warm body felt against mine. I glanced over at Megan to find her watching me curiously.

"That's a pretty name."

"She's a pretty girl."

Megan smiled. "Does she know about what happened to you, Hutch?" She crossed her legs and placed her tablet on the arm of her chair.

I shook my head. "No." I dropped my gaze to my legs as the left one jumped up and down.

"You went on a date though. The carnival," Megan went on. "You argued afterward because someone said you were too different. Have you spoken with Jillian since that night? Reached out to her at all even via text?"

"I, uh, ran into her Saturday night. We talked."

"And?"

I could feel my neck and ears burning from embarrassment. "We kissed, held hands, and I sort of gave her an orgasm, orally." At twenty-six, I shouldn't be such a novice about sex, but it wasn't really my fault that I was this way.

Megan must have picked up her tablet again because I could hear her typing. "Did she offer to return the favor?" I nodded. "Did you want her to?" she pried further.

"Of course."

"What happened when you told her no?" she asked.

I shook my head. "I freaked out. I told her I wanted her, but I couldn't." I felt anger burn inside my body. "Jillian is so, fuck, she's perfect. I started to get upset and wanted to hit something, but you know what? She said it was okay." I met Megan's eyes. "I feel like she can see inside me and knows me better than I know myself."

"Maybe she does." Megan uncrossed her legs. "You've talked about having sex then? She knows you're a virgin?" When I nodded my head, she pressed her lips together. "You're going to have to tell her the truth. If you want this relationship to work, tell her what happened to you."

I chewed nervously on my bottom lip. "I'm afraid that she'll push me away," I admitted.

"Hutch," Megan leaned forward, "what would you do if she doesn't?"

I had absolutely no idea.

***

Hutch: *Traffic is not moving.*

Jillian: *I think you're trying to get out of date. Just break it to me easy, honey. You're seeing someone else.*

Hutch: *What? Are you serious right now? I am sitting in the middle of I95 in wall-to-wall traffic, Jills. *Attachment loading**

Jillian: *I was only kidding. When I get hungry sometimes, I say things that I don't mean. *heart emoji* It's called hangry. Ever heard of it?*

Hutch: *I am going to be much later than I had planned.*

Jillian: *Guess the dress I planned to wear will have to wait.*

Hutch: *Dress?*

Jillian: *Nope, you don't get to see it now. You're trying to weasel your way out of it. Might have to finger myself too.*

Hutch: *Wtf, Jillian?*

Jillian: *laughing emoji*

Hutch: *You're not playing fair. Did you not see the picture I sent?*

Jillian: *I did. Doesn't mean I can't pleasure myself thinking about your giant wang.*

Hutch: *You haven't even seen my dick yet.*

Jillian: *Imagination, honey.*

I clutched the steering wheel so tight my knuckles turned white before I dropped my forehead against it. I had been sitting in this traffic for twenty minutes and it had yet to move. Now my cock was hard, my stress was at an all-time high, and Jillian was talking about touching herself while thinking about me. I straightened to text her back.

Hutch: *Can't you wait until I get there?*

Jillian: *You going to eat me out again?*

Hutch: *Yes.*

Jillian: *Then I can wait *water squirting emoji*

She used those emojis too much, but I kind of liked them.

Hutch: *What if it's midnight?*

Jillian: *Don't care.*

Hutch: *Even if it's in your bedroom with your mother in the house?*

Jillian: *Still don't care.*

I brought my attention back to the traffic as I moved half a millimeter, then I texted Jillian again.

Hutch: *Under my mat, you will find a spare key to my place. Go, let yourself into my apartment, and wait for me.*

Jillian: *Are you sure?*

Hutch: *Would I tell you if minded? There are some peanut butter cookies in the cabinet if you get hungry.*

Jillian: *I'll see you soon.*

*****

I was nervous when I pulled my car into the driveway at almost eleven o'clock. Jillian and I texted off and on while she told me she was watching Netflix on my television, waiting for me. When I told her I didn't believe her, she sent me a selfie of herself, smiling, perched on my couch, followed by the open container of cookies. I wished I was there, snuggled up with her. Sure, eating her pussy was what I was thinking about coming home to, but I wanted to hold her. Jillian was the sun, and I was the wilted flower that needed her light.

There wasn't a single light on in my place as I stepped inside my apartment. I toed off my shoes, and I moved closer to my bed to find Jillian lying there in my Kenny Chesney shirt, her big green eyes watching me in the moonlight.

"Welcome home." Her voice sent shivers up my spine and caused my cock to jump to attention. She eased her body onto her side. "Missed me as much as I missed you?" She ran her fingers over the comforter.

I nodded, afraid to speak. Jillian looked more beautiful right here, right now, than any other time I had ever seen her. I watched as she sat up and pulled her dark hair out from the bun she kept it in, causing it to tumble down around her shoulders. Fuck me.

Then she shot a blinding smile at me. "I thought about wearing that dress I told you about, but..." She stood up, causing my shirt to fall to her knees. Desire skidded through my body. No dress could make me feel the way her wearing my shirt did right now. "I figured that could wait for another time." Jillian stood up onto her toes so easily, probably because of all her years of ballet, and hooked her arms around my neck. "You're so fucking handsome, you know that, Hutch?"

"Shit." My cock jerked against my jeans so painfully that I was afraid it might do permanent damage. Jillian's lips fluttered against my jawline, causing me to groan. "Wait." I needed to get myself together. This was too fast, too much, and if I wasn't careful—

She took a step back as she released me. "I'm pushing you, aren't I?" Her eyes were wide. "I'm sorry."

"Jillian, you're beautiful." My hands went to my hair. "I fucking...I want you so badly. I keep imagining being buried inside you would be like being wrapped inside heaven." I bit my lip and copper flooded my mouth.

"Hutch." Jillian gripped my arm. "I wasn't expecting you to have sex with me," she whispered as she used her other hand to touch my chin. "You're not ready for that, honey." She ran her thumb over my bottom lip. "Sit with me." She eased me onto the mattress and sat down next to me.

"I want to tell you something." I reached for Jillian's hand as I turned to look at her. "Something I've only told one other person. The reason I'm the way that I am."

"Hutch, honey, you don't have to do that."

"I want to."

We sat in the dark for what felt like forever as Jillian waited for me to speak. She didn't push me or ask me what it was. She only waited until I was ready.

"Eight years ago, I had everything going for me." My voice shook with anxiety as I spoke. "You might not remember that since you were so young at the time, but I was pretty popular. On the football team, with plans to go pro when I graduated, and of course, seeing the world someday." I stopped to catch my breath. My heart was thumping so loudly in my chest that I felt like it might explode. "The year before my junior year of high school, my father signed me up for football camp. Thought it would be good for me. I thought it sounded like a load of shit because I was already a great player, but hell, why not, right? It would get me out of here for the summer." I needed to get up, move, do anything, as my breathing got difficult.

Jillian watched me as I paced around the apartment. Her eyes were wide when I turned to look at her. She looked so small sitting on my bed with the shirt sliding off her shoulder. She tucked a piece of hair behind her ear as she waited for me to continue. I moved to grab a beer, because I needed to take the edge off, and ended up finishing the entire thing in one gulp.

I made my way to the couch before I spoke again. "It was fun," I told her, which wasn't a lie. "At first. The first week, the second week, but by the third..." I swallowed as bile filled my throat and my beer threatened to come back up. "I wanted to go home." I couldn't look at Jillian now as she stood up to come closer to me. Not when my secret was about to come out. I yanked at my hair and pulled the strands out. Jillian pressed her small frame against my body then while wrapping her arms around my waist. I didn't touch her, afraid of breaking her in half.

"I was in the shower when they came for me. I tried to fight them." I felt my knees give out, and Jillian came crashing to the floor with me. "It was no use of course. They were bigger, there were more of them, and I was tied up. I couldn't see who it was. But I still fought them until I felt the gun on my back." Tears blinded my eyes as I pressed my face into the fabric of the couch. "I was so sore from the workout I had that day that I didn't even have the strength, and I think that was the reason they came for me that day. They took turns on me, all six of them, and when they were done"—I was so ashamed as I spoke the words out loud—"they left me there alone in the dark to stumble back to my cabin. Bleeding and bruised, not caring if I lived or died." I took a shaky breath as the memories came flooding back. "I have no idea if I'm the only person that this happened to because I never spoke to anyone about it. I was so embarrassed." I kept my eyes down, afraid to look at Jillian, not wanting to see the horrified look in her eyes and have her push me away. "I called my parents the next day so that I could beg them to come home. I told them I just wasn't having fun, even though just a few days earlier I had hold them the complete opposite," I whispered.

I felt Jillian's body moved behind me. "Hutch," she murmured my name. "Honey, please look at me." She tugged on me to try to get me to turn around.

"I can't."

"Please, Hutch."

I slowly moved my body around to face hers but kept my gaze down. Jillian cupped my cheeks in her hands to tilt my face up. Her greens were pinched, her eyes full of love, and as she leaned forward, I felt my breath catch in my throat. "None of that was your fault, baby," she whispered, brushing her lips against mine. "I know I can't tell you how to feel or how to act because I've never had anything like that happen to me." Again, her lips were a soft caress on mine. "But I can tell you that you didn't deserve that." She moved to straddle my waist then, and pressed forward, running her tongue over the seam of my lips. "You were a young boy. Those people were supposed to protect you, not hurt you, and they were monsters." She pulled on my bottom lip with her teeth. "I'm so sorry that happened to you."

I planted my palm against the back of Jillian's head so that I could hold it in place before I kissed her. My tongue slipped easily between her lips, and her arms tightened around my neck as our kiss grew rougher, harder, and I realized where this was going. She was already grinding against me in a way that told me she wanted me, but was I ready to take that step tonight?

Jillian pulled back to yank the shirt she had on up over her head. "Touch me," she begged earnestly. "Please, Hutch, I need you." She arched her back and pressed her chest forward.

I groaned at the sight of her hard, dusky nipples before I took one in my mouth. Jillian cried out as I sucked and nibbled softly on it, her body squirming against me. I reached up to roll the right one, the one that wasn't in my mouth, between my fingers, and I swear she was going to come right then.

"More, please, more," she urged. "Suck harder." I was glad Jillian wasn't afraid to tell me what to do. Her hands found my hair so that she could thread her fingers through it, and when I did as she asked, I watched her eyes roll back slightly. "Mark me. Please," she moaned.

I did as Jillian asked—biting, sucking, and pinching her hard enough to leave little pink marks against her skin until I thought I would explode in my pants. There were so many things I wanted to do with her, but most of all? I wanted her to ride my cock until I came inside her tight little pussy.

"Hutch," she moaned my name like a fucking porn star.

I popped my mouth from her nipple. "Yes?" I wanted her. I wanted her more than I had ever wanted anything in my life.

Jillian smiled at me before she touched my cheek. "I want to be the first girl to put her mouth on you, Hutch." She ran her thumb over my cheek, over my bottom lip, and then pressed her mouth against mine. "Will you let me do that?" she asked softly.

Chapter Ten

Hutch

I stared into Jillian's green eyes as her words echoed through my brain. What kind of a man would say no to that? "Yes." I swallowed hard, nodding. "I would...yes."

"Do you want one now?" Jillian asked, licking her lips. "Because now would be good." She grinned.

Fuck, yes. "Now." I nodded again. "What do I need to do?" I asked.

"Just take off your pants, baby, and I'll do the rest."

Baby. That was a new nickname she had just started using on me, but I liked it. I liked it a whole fucking lot.

Jillian stood up so I could lift my hips and slide off my jeans, which I placed on the floor next to me. Then for the heck of it, I tugged my shirt off too, which I tossed right onto my pants. Then I looked up at Jillian, who was watching me, and had to hold back the moan that threatened to escape. She was a goddess.

"So I'm going to just sort of touch you first," she told me as she climbed to her knees. "Stroke you a little, play with your balls." Jillian glanced up at me before she stopped to remove the elastic on her wrist and tied her hair back up. "Tell me if you don't like anything I'm doing or if it feels weird or whatever. Okay?" She leaned forward to plant a kiss against my lips. "Or if you just want me to stop. I don't ever want to do something you aren't comfortable with. All I want is for you to feel good."

"Okay."

Jillian wrapped her hand around my shaft, and I groaned. Her hand was warm as she slowly stroked my dick. Up, down, up, down, I watched as she swiped her thumb over the drop of pre-cum that had leaked out, using it as lube as she continued to work me over. It felt good when I did it, but it felt fantastic with Jillian stroking my dick. She gripped me a little harder, moved her hand a litter faster, and then dropped her head down to swipe her tongue against my head.

"Holy fuck," I blustered out. That was something I couldn't do myself. Jillian's tongue was wet, warm, and perfect as she licked over the head again before she ran it down the length of my dick. "Jesus Christ," I grunted. My hand went to her hair, and she moaned softly. It wasn't until Jillian lifted her head and sucked my entire cock into her mouth that I realized what I had been missing.

I threw my head back as she took me all the way down to the balls, and I couldn't help but want to thrust my hips up into her mouth, but resisted the urge. Jillian's hand wrapped around my balls, rolling and squeezing, as she sucked my dick, never taking her eyes off me. I felt her tongue flatten against my shaft, and it didn't take long before I felt the need to explode build up inside me.

Jillian didn't stop when I tried to pull her off me. She kept going, taking it all when I cried out, and I watched as she wiped her mouth with the back of her hand before she sat back on her ankles while heat flashed in her eyes. "Did you enjoy that?" she asked shyly.

"It was amazing." I kissed her lips softly. I didn't care if she had my cum all over her mouth. My desire for Jillian Robinson was out of control.

"Your turn, Jills," I murmured, wrapping my arms around her waist and lifting her up off the floor. Her legs instantly wrapped around my waist as I walked her over to the bed to place her onto the mattress. "You"—I began to kiss my way down her soft skin—"are"—then ran my tongue over her erect nipples—"the most"—finally clasping Jillian's hips, leaving little wet marks as I slithered down her body—"beautiful woman in the entire world." I stopped to glance up and the look on her face caused my breath to catch in my throat.

Her green eyes were glazed over, her hair spilling out of the makeshift ponytail she had piled it into, and her cheeks pink with excitement. My heart thudded loudly against my chest as I took a moment to realize what was happening. This was more than just a summer fling for me. This was—

"Hutch." Jillian's raspy voice brought my attention back to her. "Are you alright?" She reached out to run her hands through my damp hair. "Do you want to stop?"

"Fuck no," I growled, pushing her thighs apart. I used my fingers to spread her wide and felt my cock spring to attention again. I leaned down to slowly run my tongue over her clit, and the sound Jillian made caused me to groan softly.

I would never tire of this.

Jillian's hands funneled into my hair, pulling and tugging as I teased her, my tongue rolling and licking between her folds. She told me what she wanted, begged me for more, and arched into me as I drew her closer to her climax.

"Fuck, I'm so close," Jillian groaned. "You promised fingers, Hutch. Please fuck me with your fingers like I know you can." She pulled on my hair. "Two, use two," she whispered when I met her heated gaze. I had watched plenty of porn in my lifetime to know the female anatomy. I dropped my hand and slowly slipped my index finger inside. Jillian clenched and pulsed around me. Jesus, that was hot. "More, baby. One more." She released my hair from her grip to attack her nipples. "Fuck, that feels so good."

I groaned as I did as she asked, and when my middle finger slid inside, Jillian cried out with pleasure, her head falling back against the pillow. Fuck, I was going to come again just watching her. I began to fire off short licks against her clit as I moved my fingers in and out.

Jillian screamed out her release, her muscles clenching and her body convulsing as she flooded my mouth before she finally relaxed and stopped to catch her breath. "Hutch," she whispered my name.

I felt my ears burn pink. I don't know why all of a sudden I was embarrassed. I started to get up, but felt her hand on my elbow. "I just...I need to wash up," I assured her before I walked to the bathroom. I turned on the faucet, washed my hands, my cock, and then my face before I tossed the cloth into the hamper. I didn't expect to find Jillian standing behind me with her arms crossed over her chest. "It's an OCD thing, Jills, not you. Please don't make this any weirder for me." I dropped my gaze to my feet.

"Should I do the same?"

"No."

"Are you okay?" She tilted her head to make me look at her.

I nodded.

"Do you want to talk about anything?" Jillian dropped her arms before she took a step closer. "Did you like my mouth on your dick?" My cock stirred at the memory. "Or your fingers in my—"

I clamped my hand over her mouth. "Yes, but if you say it out loud, I'm going to have to do it again." I chuckled, pulling Jillian against me. "Promise me something." I sighed softly as her arms snaked around my waist.

"I promise that I won't tell anyone."

My heart swelled in my chest. I was fucked with a capital F. "Jillian." My voice didn't sound anything like mine, and I couldn't find it in me to form any coherent sentence as she pulled back to look up at me.

She ducked her head slightly. "We should probably go to sleep. It's late." She started to walk back to the bed, but turned to move toward the living room where she grabbed the shirt she was wearing when I came home, and slipped it back on over her head. "Come on, baby." Jillian flashed a quick smile before she moved to stand by the bed. She remembered that I liked to be on the inside by the wall, and this time, my throat felt like it was closing up.

I stopped to pull a pair of clean boxers out of my dresser to wear to sleep before I climbed into the bed where Jillian joined me and snuggled up into my side. She always smelled so good, no matter what. Sometimes it was flowery, but tonight, it reminded me of peppermint. I felt her fingers start to draw circles on my stomach, and I couldn't help but hold her even tighter. Jillian wouldn't be here much longer, so I wanted to enjoy this moment as long as I could.

I stared up at the moon, wondering if things would ever feel as perfect as they did right now.

***

The rest of the week seemed to fly by in the blink of an eye with Jillian and I spending all of our free time together. Tuesday night, she came over after practice, showered, and then gave me another blowjob in the kitchen before I even had the chance to cook dinner. Of course, I had to return the favor by throwing her onto the table, and making her come not once, but twice, before we decided to order takeout instead.

Wednesday, I had therapy. I found Jillian waiting for me in a lace bra and underwear when I got home. Thursday was more of the same. Oral sex was amazing, but what I enjoyed more than that was having Jillian sleeping next to me at night. Her warm, soft body pressed to mine as she slept was probably my favorite part of our relationship. Friday morning, we were getting dressed when Jillian told me her sister had texted her.

"You want to go on a double date?" She hooked her bra behind her back and then pulled the straps up before she glanced up at me. "With your brother and Jo?" She chewed nervously on her bottom lip. "It's weird, right? You don't want to do it?" Jillian turned back around to yank her tights up over her waist.

"Okay."

She spun back around. "Is that okay yes, or okay it's weird?" Her eyes were lit up like starlight.

"Both," I admitted before she threw herself into my arms. "I just want to make you happy, Jills, that's the only thing that matters." I chuckled as she jumped up and down.

Jillian clapped her hands together. "Honestly, Hutch." She spun around on her toes before she jumped up in the air. Fuck, my girl was so graceful. *Shit, my girl.* Was Jillian actually my girl? Could I call her that?

"You make me happy," she blurted out before she spun around with wide eyes. "No, you do. You make me so damn happy I want everyone to know." Jillian grabbed her leotard from her bag to quickly put it on before she dashed across the room, yanked open the door, and was out onto the steps. "Hutch Kelly makes me happy!" she shouted. "Do you hear that, Ocean View?" She giggled hysterically before she sprinted back into the apartment. "What? Why are you looking at me like that?"

Because I love you. The thought flashed through my mind so fast I stumbled. "Because you make me happy too." I managed to answer her just before she jumped up into my arms. I caught her and laughed loud and hard for the first time in so long I couldn't even remember. "You make me so happy, Jillybean, and I feel alive when we're together." Like I used to, but I left that part out.

A wide smile spread across Jillian's face. "Hutch."

"Jesus Christ, what's all that shouting about?" Pat muttered as he whipped my screen door open. "Shit, am I interrupting?" He noticed the way I was holding Jillian in my arms. "Was that you screaming like a lunatic out there, Jill?" She scrambled out of my arms before I could stop her.

"I should go before I'm late." She shoved her dirty clothes into her gym bag before she hooked it over her shoulder. "Hutch, I'll text you after I hear back from Jo." She was red as a tomato right then.

"Jills." I tried to stop her so I could give her a goodbye kiss, but she ducked under my arm. She wiggled her fingers at me before she nudged past Patrick and disappeared out the door. "That's fucking great." I sighed as I glared at my brother, who looked clueless.

Pat's brows dipped. "What?" He popped his jaw.

I rolled my eyes. "Nothing, dude, I'm going to be late."

"Are you two, you know, doing it now?" Pat followed behind me as I locked the door and hurried down the steps.

"Piss off." I scoffed.

"Holy shit," Pat hissed. "You're fucking her."

I spun around once I hit the grass. "I didn't say that." I pointed a finger at my little brother. "Don't talk about Jillian like that either, man, she's not like other girls."

Pat smirked at me. "She sucked your dick though, right? If you're not having sex with her—"

My fist made contact with his stomach before I could stop to think it was wrong and my brother doubled over in pain. "Don't talk about Jillian like that, I fucking warned you." I grabbed the back of Pat's shirt to force him to stand up. "She's different from the other girls." His eyes were wide as I stared down at him. "I love her. Got it?" It was the first time I had admitted it aloud, but now that I had? It was easier to believe it.

The moment I released him, he went running toward the Robinson house. Not our house, the one where his girlfriend was. Which only meant one thing. Jillian would hear about this before I had a chance to explain myself.

Chapter Eleven

Jillian

I stared at my cell phone during one of my first breaks during dance class. I had so many text messages from my sister and Hutch that I wasn't sure where to start. From what I could tell, something had happened between the brothers after I left, and Hutch had tried to get to me first so that he could explain.

Hutch: *I'm sorry.*

Hutch: *Fuck, it's not what you think, Jills.*

Hutch: *Damn, I need to talk to you in person. I hate texting. Which is weird because talking is harder for me.*

Hutch: *Not with you.*

Jo: *Hutch punched Pat this morning.*

Hutch: *I hit my brother this morning.*

Hutch: *He asked me if we were having sex.*

Jo: *WTF, Jill? Why would he do something like that?*

Hutch: *I didn't say anything to him. I swear to God, Jillybean.*

Jo: *What a dick. You need to stop seeing him.*

I closed my eyes. This felt like high school drama all over again. My sister wanted to me to pick sides. Hutch just wanted to tell me the truth.

Jillian: *Baby, it's okay.* *heart emoji*

Hutch: *I thought you hated me.* *heart emoji*

His response surprised me. In the short time we had been seeing one another, not once had Hutch used an emoji. He must have been really worried about what I would think.

Jillian: *I'll see you at lunch.*

"Boy troubles?" Madison's voice drifted into my space.

I slipped my phone back into my bag before I shut and locked the door. "Mind your own business," I warned Madison before I went back to class, but now I was worried. More about Hutch than anything else. I believed him of course, but why would Pat say something that he knew would upset this brother?

When I walked down the street to meet Hutch for lunch, I did not expect to find him the nervous wreck he was when I walked into the shop. His blond hair was standing up, which meant he had been pulling on it all day, his normal clean area was full of parts and tools, while his face had streaks of oil and God knows what else. His face was pinched tight with stress, but when he saw me, his features softened slightly.

"Hey." I smiled when Hutch took a step toward me. I raised my hand to point to my cheek. "Here." I grabbed a napkin and ran it under the water cooler before I brought it up to his face. "You look like you're having a rough day, baby." I wiped the mess from his face.

Hutch nodded. "It's...yes. Let me wash up." He looked like he wanted to say something else, but instead moved back to wash his hands, leaving me to wonder if it was the fight with his brother or something more.

Once Hutch was washed up, we went to sit in the back at the picnic table to eat. I usually sat across from him, but today I made sure to sit next to him. I felt like he needed that. We had our usual egg salad, apple, and granola bars, but when he only picked at his food, I nudged his arm.

"Start talking," I whispered. "Tell me what happened this morning."

Hutch kept his eyes down on his food. "Pat asked me if we were having sex." He tore a piece of bread from his sandwich. "I told him to mind his own business, and then Pat made some comment about you giving me oral." He paused to glance over at me. "So I hit him."

"Hutch."

"I know, I know, but he shouldn't say shit like that."

I swung my right leg over the bench so that I was straddling it. "Hutch, baby, look at me." When he didn't, I tugged on his arm until he twisted himself into the same position I was in.

"That was very honorable. Very alpha of you." I watched his ears turn pink. "You need to fix things with your brother." I held up my hand before he could object. "Not now because tonight it's clearly not going to happen." I slid closer so that our bodies were touching. "Can I tell you something, Hutch Kelly?" He nodded, his Adam's apple bobbing as he swallowed. God, he was so fucking sexy when he got embarrassed. I had a feeling that once I got him out of shell, he was going to be a monster in bed.

I stood up, craving to press my lips against Hutch's ear. "What you did made me so fucking wet," I whispered. "I wish that we were at your apartment right now so you could eat my pussy and make me come all over your tongue." I rolled my tongue against his earlobe before I sat back down. And would you look at that?! The look on his face was priceless.

Heat rolled from Hutch's body while fire burned in his eyes. When I dropped my gaze to his crotch—the bulge in his pants was more than obvious, and I had to stop myself from cupping it with my hand.

"Jesus fucking Christ, Jills." He gritted his teeth before he glanced over his shoulder to make sure Zed wasn't watching.

"My lunch is over. Don't want to be late." I started to stand back up, but not before Hutch grabbed me and slammed his mouth over mine, his tongue plundering my mouth.

This...this is what I loved about him. His control. His dominance over me. His blatant desire for me. Each day, he was showing more and more of himself, and I had a feeling I would meet the real Hutch Kelly soon. Wait, was this love? Did I love Hutch? I gripped his shoulders as the kiss deepened, little moans escaping my throat, and realized I had in fact fallen in love with him.

Hutch pulled back as his hand gripped my bun tightly. "You're a bad girl when you want to be," he growled, "aren't you?" His brown eyes were nearly black with want.

I shrugged. "For you," I teased before Hutch finally let me stand up. "See you tonight?" I knew the double date thing had fallen through, but hoped he still wanted to spend time with me.

"Of course."

"Text me when you get home. I'll come over."

Hutch swung his legs over the bench so that he could stand up. "Right here, Jillybean." He pressed two fingers to his mouth. "One more before you go." He leaned forward, and just as I stood up onto my toes, his arm snaked around my waist so he could yank me against his hard, chiseled chest.

"See you later," Hutch promised as his lips met mine.

***

The rest of the day seemed to move by slower than normal. Something felt different with Hutch when I left him. I don't know if it was the fact that I realized I was in love with him or what, but I couldn't want to see him tonight. Not that that was any different than usual either. We had been spending pretty much all of our free time together since our first kiss. But tonight...tonight just had a special feel to it.

"Jillian, wait!"

I was halfway up our walkway when Pat called out to me. I stopped, folded my arms across my chest, and turned to face him. It wasn't that I was mad at him, well, maybe I was, but I just didn't want to talk to him. I wanted to change out of my ballet clothes, shower, and get ready for my date. Or whatever this was.

Pat came to a stop in front of me as he ran a hand through his short blond hair. "I know you're pissed at me." His shoulders slumped forward. "You have every right to be, but I didn't mean to...fuck." He sighed softly.

I had always noticed the similarities now between Hutch and Pat. The hair, the eye color, but that was about it. Hutch, of course, was more handsome, taller, had the better body, but I didn't know Pat the way I knew Hutch. "It's not me you should apologize to," I pointed out.

"That's true, but I do need to thank you."

My brows shot up. "Thank me? For what?" I had no idea what he was talking about right now.

"Can we sit for a second?" Pat pointed to the chairs on the porch. "My feet are killing me from standing all day." Jo had mentioned he had taken a job at the supermarket. Once we were seated, Pat chewed nervously on his lips. "You've helped Hutch more than you know. He's like the Hutch he was before. He's turning back into the big brother that used to not take my shit, hitting me, pushing me around, and I..." His voice lodged in his throat as he turned away, but not before I saw the tears in his eyes.

I touched his arm. "I haven't done anything," I assured him.

"Jill, you have. Whatever is going on between the two of you, is bringing my brother back to me." Pat glanced down at his hands. "Before he started hiding away, not talking, Hutch was the most popular kid at Ocean View High." He met my surprised gaze. "I'm not even kidding. The girls fucking loved him, he had tons of friends, was never home, and gave me so much shit. Not in a bad way, but in a big brother way. That changed when he came home from camp, but now?" A smile tugged at his lips. "I see pieces of that version of Hutch again." Pat took my hand then, softly caressing it. "Because of you, Jill. I'm just afraid that when you leave, he'll go back to being the mute."

I yanked my hand away. "Don't call him that, Pat," I hissed just as I caught sight of my sister skipping up the sidewalk.

"Shit, I'm sorry."

I sat back in my chair as Jo looked between the two of us. "Everything alright?" She moved closer to her boyfriend like I might claw his eyes out.

"Peachy. I'm going to shower now," I announced as I stood up. "I have plans with my boyfriend." The words tumbled from my mouth so easily. Hutch and I hadn't discussed anything about what we were or weren't, but that didn't matter. I knew what we were. "We're good, Jo, don't worry." I added before she could even ask. I would deal with my sister in private.

Once I had showered, I took my time getting changed. The dress from the other night that I had teased Hutch about still hung on my closet door and as I removed it, I wondered if tonight was the night. I brought it up to my body, admiring the soft fabric, the dark blue color, and thought about what he would think when he saw me in it. The dress was short, hardly coming to my knees, and had tiny thin straps that would require me to wear a strapless bar. I had to have the dress the moment I saw I hanging in the store window. I quickly removed the towel I had wrapped around my body before I found the perfect bra and a matching thong to wear. Then I slipped the dress over my head to stare at myself in the mirror.

Would Hutch like this dress or would he think it was too much or too little? Would he even notice I had it on when he got home? Sometimes when Hutch returned from one of his therapy sessions, he'd be utterly exhausted, moody, and didn't want to do anything other than eat dinner before we made out on the couch and he'd nestle between my legs. Other times, Hutch would be cheerful, tossing me onto the bed and demanding that I eat his cock because that's what he wanted right then. I never knew which version I would get.

As I dug out a pair of sandals to wear, I knew I approved of the dress which was really the only thing that mattered in the end. I knew Hutch found me attractive. He told me all the time, but was that the only connection we had or did he love me like I loved him?

Chapter Twelve

Hutch

Tonight's session with Megan had worn me out. I had told her what had happened with Pat this morning and how I had instantly regretted it. I knew it was about standing up for Jillian, but she had asked me if maybe I was trying to defend myself. Was it? I didn't think so, but now, all I wanted to do was go home, share some peanut butter cookies with Jills, and snuggle on the couch. It wasn't always about the oral. I could just cuddle with my girl.

"I'm home," I announced as I shoved my shoes into the corner of the room. I noticed how she had dimmed the lights as I locked the door behind me. "Jills?" I called out her name as she appeared before me. "Fuck, what are you wearing?" I whispered as my eyes moved over her body.

She tilted her head. "Do you like it?" she asked. "It's the dress I told you about the other night."

"You call that a dress?" I grunted as I took a step forward. It hit her mid-thigh and I wondered if she even had a bra on. My dick stirred inside my jeans as I imagined stripping it off, my hands roaming all over her skin.

"You hate it."

I shook my head. "Fuck, Jillybean, I love it." I cupped her face in my hands. "But no one else is ever going to see you in this because I will have to resist the urge to kill every man that even looks in your direction," I warned before I pressed a kiss to her mouth. "You're so beautiful," I murmured as her tongue found mine and her soft little sighs began to fill the room.

"I want you, Hutch," Jillian whispered. "I want you so bad. I want to feel you inside me, filling me, and I want you to—"

I froze. "Jillian, you know I want that, but I can't." I turned so that my back was to her, pulling at my hair. "You know how much I want to fuck you, feel you wrapped around me, but..." My voice caught in my throat.

Jillian's hand gripped my wrist, her eyes shining with understanding and adoration, before she said, "Baby, it's okay. I'll wait as long as you need me to. Forever if that's what it takes."

God, what had I done to deserve this beautiful woman in my life?

When I just kept staring at her, my eyes blazing with desire, she rasped out, almost begging me, "Kiss me, Hutch."

Whatever ounce of control I had in me, snapped. The strings binding me loosened, almost broke, as I lunged for her mouth.

Before I even realized it, I had picked Jillian up to carry her to the bed, and her dress—so fucking perfect—was bunched up around her waist while she rubbed against my ever-growing erection. Her nails dug into my arms as she nipped and pulled on my lips as my hands tugged on her hair. I flipped her around so that she was straddling me, my fingers finding purchase in pulling her nipples.

"Wait." Jillian's voice came out raspy as she stopped to yank her dress up over her head. "Hutch." She met my eyes with lust in her greens. "Let me...let me feel you." She reached down to pop the button on my pants.

"Jills," I warned with lust in my veins.

She shook her head. "No, just..." She pulled my cock out from my pants, hard and ready just for her. "I want to just feel you." Jillian raised her hips to slip her thong off, something I had completely missed, and glided the head of my dick between her soaking wet lower lips. "Like this." she moaned as she rocked her body against mine.

"Jesus, fuck," I hissed as pleasure rocketed through me. "Stop, right now," I hissed out my warning, already feeling on edge. If she kept that up, I was going to come undone. There was no doubt in my mind.

Jillian leaned forward to run her tongue over my top lip. "Feels so good having you nestled between my legs." Her voice hung with desire. She wasn't telling me something I didn't already know. My hands gripped her waist as she slowly rolled her hips over mine, her clit bouncing over my shaft, soft little mewls escaping her mouth. "Hutch, you're so big," Jillian purred.

I tangled my hand in her hair so I could yank on her bun. "Jillian, I'm going to come, and I don't want to do that. Not yet," I warned as a sexy little smirk slid over her face. "You like teasing me, don't you?

"I do." Her hips rolled again, and this time, she reached up to pinch her nipples between her fingers. That was hot; not going to lie. "Let me come, Hutch. Your dick makes me feel so good, baby," she moaned softly, rocking vigorously against me.

"Jillian."

"Please."

I growled so deep in my chest that I nearly scared myself. "Come all over my cock, Jilly." I watched mesmerized as she milked me. Her pussy sliding over my shaft, her back arched. I pulled her closer to suck one of her nipples into my mouth. I felt that familiar tingle start up my spine, the one I knew meant I was getting close, as Jillian moved above me.

"Oh, Hutch, God, yes!" she cried out as her wetness dripped between us. "Going to come." Jillian's big green eyes stared down into mine just as she locked her lips with mine, and I felt every muscle in my body grow tense as the raging fireball inside me finally burst into flames.

Jillian slumped against me as she started to come down from her high, her body covered in a sheen of sweat. She moved to ease her body onto the mattress, but I held her firmly against me. She raised her head to look at me. "Are you okay? I didn't mean—"

I kissed her, turning her so that her back was pressed against the bed. "That was the most amazing experience of my life." I dropped wet kisses against her mouth, her jaw and neck, before I met her eyes. "Honestly, Jilly, I wouldn't have done it if I didn't want to." I tugged on her bottom lip. "It was hot as fuck. Hearing you talk dirty to me like that..." My dick was already starting to get hard again.

"Yeah?" Jillian's cheeks burned pink.

I grinned. "Going to come," I growled before I buried my face in her hair. "Fuck, I'm so hard right now." I reached down to grip her ass in my hands.

Jillian sighed happily. "Want to do that again?"

"Do you even have to ask me?"

***

I had started to skip my Saturday morning workouts. Mostly because I didn't want to untangle myself from Jillian and leave her alone. I liked waking up with her in my arms. She was so warm, so soft, and just perfect. I stared at her as she slept. Unable to resist the urge, I brushed a piece of hair from her forehead and pressed a kiss to her temple.

If I wasn't in love with Jillian before, I certainly was now.

Last night had been...more than I could have imagined. After the first time we dry humped, we did it again, ordered a pizza from Ocean View Pizza, and did it again while we waited for the delivery guy. I might be addicted to the feeling of her wet pussy gliding over my shaft, but I could only imagine what it might be like to stick my dick inside her for the real deal.

"Is that your dick I feel pressed up against my ass, Hutch?" Jillian giggled as she turned to face me. "I should go brush my teeth." She covered her mouth with her hand just as I reached down to lace our fingers together.

"Why?" I whispered before I slid my mouth against hers. "Your breath smells amazing."

Jillian snorted. "Liar." She tried to get up, but I held her tighter.

"I know you're leaving soon, but I want to make this work."

Her face grew serious. "Hutch, let's not do this now."

"You don't want to make this work?" My stomach dropped. Did she not feel the same way? Were we just casually messing around?

She shook her head. "Wait." Jillian flung the blankets off to hurry from the bed and I heard the door shut as she finished her morning routine.

Shit, she was going to dump my ass. Maybe I should have fucked her like she had wanted. My hands were tugging at my hair without me even realizing it as Jillian walked back out and climbed up next to me.

"We can, you know, fuck if you want," I muttered without looking up.

Her hand came out to swat my arm. "Hutch Kelly." She said my name as if I had gotten in trouble in school. It might have been hot if I wasn't so worried about her leaving me. What my life would be like when she was gone.

"Stop," she said, climbing up onto my lap, and grabbed at my wrists to stop me from pulling out my hair. "Don't do that to yourself, baby." She soothed my hair down around my head. "I want to make this work. I like you so much." Her cheeks flushed pink. "Hutch, I can't imagine my life without you." When she got all flustered like that, it was such a turn-on. It was something that didn't happen a lot.

"You like me."

"Hutch."

"I like you too, Jills, but—"

Jillian cupped my face in her hands. "I don't know why you find that so hard to believe." Her green eyes, flecked with bits of orange and brown pieces, searched my face. "You're so damn amazing. This beautiful human that I want to know everything about." She dragged her teeth across her bottom lip as if she wanted to say something else, but didn't. "I have to go away next weekend for orientation. I leave on Friday night, but I'll be back on Sunday afternoon."

I stared at Jillian as her words began to sink in. She was leaving next weekend. "Going away?"

She nodded. "Just until Sunday though."

I gripped her hips and pressed my forehead against hers. "Jillian, I don't...do you have to?" I felt like I might be having a panic attack as fear burned through me like wildfire.

"Orientation is kind of important. You won't even know I'm gone," she assured me. "We can text and talk on the phone when I'm not busy. I get to meet my teachers, my roommates." I stiffened in her arms at the mention of her meeting others. "Hutch, don't get upset."

I tried to relax, but I couldn't. Jillian was going to be gone for a couple of days. There would be other guys there. Ones that were into the same things she was into, and that could mean she might meet someone else. Someone more suited for her. "Maybe this isn't such a good idea," I lied.

Jillian pulled back. "What?" Her voice shook. "Hutch, it's just an orientation." She tried to make me face her, but I shook my head. "Baby, we're a good idea. We're a damn great idea," she reminded me.

"I should go workout." If I looked at Jillian right now, I would break. I would apologize for being an asshole, which I was, and admit that she's right to go to her school thing. Maybe we were a bad idea like everyone in Ocean View kept trying to tell us.

Jillian climbed from my lap. "You're not being fair."

"Life isn't fair, Jillian."

She sat there while I changed into my workout gear, both of us silent.

"Do you want me to go home?"

It was like a knife to my back. I didn't. I wanted Jillian to stay here forever, because with her, I felt like everything was going to be okay. "Whatever," I muttered before I walked out the door.

I had beaten the living shit out of the heavy bag that was set up in the basement of my parents' house. Hit it over and over again until I knew my knuckles were bleeding, but that was my fault too. Just like everything else. I was so fucking stupid to think that whatever was happening between us was going to continue when Jillian left for New York. When I returned, Jillian was gone, and it made me feel numb all over.

I dragged my hands through my damp, sweaty hair as I paced the apartment. Forgetting about Jillian was the right thing to do...

I shoved the front door open, sprinted down the stairs, and across the front lawn, stopping only to make sure there were no cars before I crossed the street. I climbed up the lattice fencing to her room like I did it every single day to tap on the outside of window with my knuckle, hoping she was alone. Praying she was there.

Jillian appeared at the window with confusion on her face. "We have a door," she muttered, and I saw the tears on her cheeks, in her eyes. Fuck, I did that to her. I made her cry. Why was I such an asshole?

"Let me in."

"Why?"

"Damn it, let me in before I rip this screen off," I growled. Her eyes flashed before she slid the screen up. I climbed into her room while she watched me sternly, her arms folded over her chest. She must have showered because she had changed into a pair of tiny little tan shorts with a matching shirt. "I'm a fucking idiot, Jills." I dropped to my knees, keeping my eyes at her feet. "I'm so damn sorry. You have to—" I stopped when her hands touched my chin and she forced me to look up.

"Don't call yourself an idiot, baby," Jillian whispered. I grabbed her hips, pulling her closer so that I could press my face against her taut stomach. Her scent overtook me and my eyes filled with tears while Jillian ran her hands through my hair. "You stink." She chuckled, and when I looked up, she had a smile on her face. "You didn't even shower before you came to see me?"

"I couldn't wait. I needed to make sure you weren't going to break up with me," I admitted.

Jillian smoothed her fingers against my cheeks. "Hutch." Her voice sent shivers up my spine and straight to my balls. She was it for me. How was that even possible? I had known her my entire life, only as my little brother's girlfriend's sister, and in a matter of weeks, she had changed my life.

"Jillybean, you have made my life worth living again," I blurted out before I lost my nerve. "I don't know what it is about you, but when we're together, I just want to live. I want to be the old me, whether you know it or not..." Her fingers pressed against my lips as she got down to her knees to join me.

"I'm not going anywhere, Hutch," Jillian assured me before she slid her mouth over mine. "I promise you that I'm not breaking up with you." I knew she felt the smile that had broken out over my lips because she pulled back. "You look so happy when you smile, baby."

"It's because of you."

"I'm sorry I left."

I leaned my forehead against hers. "Thanks for letting me in," I whispered.

There was a knock at the door before Jo pushed the door open. "Jill, do you still...oh, hey." She twisted her lips to the side. "Um, I can come back." She looked between the two of us.

I started to get to my feet, but Jillian grabbed my arm, keeping me where I was. "What's up?" Jillian asked her sister.

"You guys want to hang out tonight?" Jo asked. "Pat and I were thinking of having a fire at the beach."

Jillian turned to look at me. It was the last thing I wanted, but her eyes told me it's what she wanted, so I gave a quick nod. The smile on her face told me it was the right answer. "We'll be there."

Chapter Thirteen

I knew that Hutch was only agreeing to go to the bonfire at the beach with Jo and Pat because of me, but I hoped it wouldn't turn into a disaster. I also made Jo promise that no else would be there. I didn't want Knox or Madison to show up and ruin everything when Hutch was finally starting to come out of his shell.

Hutch went home, showered, and told me he would meet me at the beach at six so when I checked my phone to see, it was two minutes after I started to think he was blowing me off. I knew how he was. He didn't like to be late, was always on time, and I wondered if he was even going to text me an excuse. I decided to walk over to his place when I saw him approaching with Patrick.

He looked nervous, but he looked, well, he looked freaking amazing. Hutch was wearing a Kenny Chesney shirt that stretched across his chest like a second skin, and I was beginning to think he had stocked those. He was wearing a pair of swim trunks that fit his muscled thighs perfectly, and sneakers without socks. His hair looked freshly washed, a little damp maybe, and he had a bag hanging off his shoulder that was nearly bursting at the seams.

I swallowed as the butterflies in my stomach fluttered when he flashed me a megawatt smile. Then he stopped in front of me, and I greeted him, "Hi." I felt like I was seeing a completely different man right now. Who was this version of Hutch Kelly, because I wanted to keep him hidden away forever.

"Hi." Hutch's voice caused goosebumps to break out over my arms. "You look beautiful, Jills." His arm suddenly snaked around my waist as he pressed me against his chest. "I really want to kiss you right now," he admitted, and relief washed over me as his ears burned pink. There was the Hutch I knew.

I slid my hand up his impressive chest. "Is this a dream?" I whispered before his lips landed on mine in a soft, wet touch. I bit back the groan that threatened to escape as I felt Hutch's tongue evade my mouth.

"Okay, enough of that." Jo clapped her hands. "You two can make out later," she teased as Hutch pulled away.

I buried my face against Hutch's chest, breathing in his fresh scent. "You smell so good," I whispered as he held me closer.

"Not half as good as you." His fingers gripped my hips. "One day it's peppermint, the next it's flowers. I can't figure you out." His breath was hot against my skin, and heat flared between my legs.

Something was different about Hutch tonight, but I liked it more than I wanted to admit.

I grinned at him. "I have to keep you on your toes," I teased as Pat sat the cooler he had been carrying down in the sand.

"I have burgers, hot dogs, and some beers," he announced. "You girls brought the s'mores for later, right?" Pat glanced at Jo who nodded her head.

I had been on plenty of dates with my sister and Pat before. Knox and I had casually dated for a few months before prom, but it wasn't serious, however the guy I lost my virginity to, who had left the View while we were still juniors, had been close with Pat. Lincoln Matthews was my first real boyfriend, and although I wasn't sure he was the one I would have spent the rest of my life with, he had treated me well, been very sweet, and seemed to care about me. In fact, Pat was the one who had set us up at the insistence of my sister who was more than obnoxious about it when things worked out between us.

"You disappeared on me." Hutch's voice brought me back to the present. "Where'd you go?" He tugged me closer to his warm body.

I smiled up at him. "I was wondering if you had bought stock in Kenny Chesney shirts," I teased, just see that smile break out on his face.

"I happen to like his music." Hutch eased himself down onto one of the logs that was set up around the fire.

"You mean you're obsessed."

"There's a difference, Jilly."

I folded my arms across my chest. "Is there?" I tried to keep a straight face, but the look on Hutch's face was too much, and I burst into a fit of giggles as his eyes grew serious. I laughed even harder as he grabbed me and pulled me down onto his lap, making sure to wrap his arms tightly around my stomach.

"You're teasing me." Hutch chuckled into my ear. "What?" he grunted up at Pat who was staring at us with his mouth hanging open.

Pat shook his head. "Nothing, I just...nothing." He turned to face Jo.

"Say whatever it is you were thinking, Patrick." Hutch went stiff with anger. "Don't fucking hold back, brother," he hissed between clenched teeth.

I turned slightly so that I could reach up to touch his face. "Baby," I whispered softly. "I'm sure that Pat was just glad to see you so happy." Hutch's eyes locked with mine, his face softening, and his body relaxed.

"Is that it?" Hutch glanced up for a second before he met my gaze again. "Jesus, you're sure you don't want to change your mind about being a dancer?" he asked before he dropped a kiss against the top of my head.

"I like seeing you happy, bro, that's all," Pat told him. "Jill's good for you." He threw his arm around Jo's shoulder as I leaned further back against Hutch. Jo popped open a beer and took a sip. "You balance one another out," he added with a wink.

Hutch's arm tightened against my belly. "You hear that, Jillybean? He said you're good for me." His husked voice sent fire through my veins.

I snuggled as close to Hutch as I could as realization began to set in about my future. I knew Hutch had his insecurities about us being apart, but now I was starting to wonder if my leaving was a good thing. Would he be okay? Would he continue to simply go back to living in that shell he had been under before being with me?

Or would he be able to handle the distance that we both knew was coming.

***

"Hutch."

"Mmm."

"I think you're drunk."

He snorted as he swayed with me to the music in the sand. Yep, he was drunk because I don't think he would be dancing with me otherwise. "Not drunk, Jills, just enjoying having you in my arms," Hutch admitted as we moved together.

Totally drunk. "Liar," I teased, but I liked it too. I liked how Hutch kept me as close to him as possible like he was afraid I would disappear if he let me go.

After we had cooked up burgers and hotdogs with Pat and Jo, we had made small talk for a bit until Pat suggested we turn on some music. I had no idea that they both had a thing for country music or that my sister enjoyed it as much as she did for that matter, because before I knew, they had me listening to all sorts of musicians I had never heard of before.

"You and tequila," Hutch murmured as the song played.

God, this man was really doing everything to win me over tonight. "Are you singing to me?" I glanced up at to find Hutch watching me with fire in his eyes. Jesus, he had better be careful with that look.

"You and tequila make me crazy," he whispered before he brought his mouth down to mine. I tasted the booze on his lips, the desire on his tongue, and the way Hutch's hands gripped my hips told me everything he couldn't without words. He was gentle when he had to, but I knew beneath all that, there was a wild man trying to get out, and when he was ready, he would show me just how much he wanted me. "Take me home, baby, I'm drunk." He giggled softly as he stumbled over the sand.

Yep, I knew that already. "Okay, let me just get your things together," I told him. "Be careful and don't hurt yourself." I moved to gather the bag that Hutch had brought which was sitting on the ground. It had a sweatshirt inside, which I was now wearing, a few bottles of beer, and a package of our favorite peanut butter cookies that we hadn't even touched.

Jo looked up from where she was sitting with Pat. "You two taking off?" She flashed a quick smile.

"Hutch is, um, a little intoxicated." I hooked my thumb behind me. "I've never seen him like this before." I turned to watch Hutch look up at the moon and then spin around before landing on his ass. "At least he's a fun drunk."

"He usually doesn't drink this much, but tonight I think he wanted to loosen up a bit. I told you before, Jill, you've helped him so much," Jo reminded me.

"Jills!" Hutch called out my nickname. "Baby, where are you?" He laughed loudly as he tried to stand up.

I glanced at Pat. "You mind helping me? I don't know if I can get him back up onto his feet." I might need his help getting him home at this rate.

Pat was on his feet. "Of course." He walked over to where Hutch was sitting. "Let's go." He bent over and helped Hutch back up. "You going to be trouble here, big guy, or are you going to be good for the little lady?"

Hutch grinned. "I'm going to be good, right, bean?" Where was he coming up with this stuff tonight? Right, the booze had gone straight to his brain. "Jillian will make sure I get home safe and sound." Hutch hiccupped at the last part, which caused him to break out in a fit of giggles.

Pat's brows dipped as he glanced at me skeptically. "Are you sure you got this?"

"I'll be fine," I said, but as Hutch moved to put his arm around my shoulders, reminding me that he outweighed me by more than a hundred pounds, I wondered if maybe I was in way over my head. "Let's get you home." I gritted my teeth, hoping my knees didn't buckle. We made it about halfway before Hutch had to stop and inspect some lilies that were blooming in someone's yard.

He smiled at me as he leaned over. "These...are pretty." He reached down and yanked them up by the root.

Jesus, we're going to get arrested tonight. "Hutch, honey, you can't go doing that," I whispered loudly. "This is someone else's yard," I reminded him.

Hutch grinned at me. "For you." He thrusted out his hand like a five-year-old. His eyes glittered with happiness. "You know how much you mean to me, right, Jills?" I wanted to ask him the same thing. How he had flipped my world upside down and made me question everything I ever knew, but I didn't know how.

"Thank you." I gripped the flowers with one hand before I took his arm to wrap it around my shoulders. "Let's get going before we get into serious trouble."

Luckily, we made it back to Hutch's apartment without any other issues. He grinned at me as he toed off his shoes, threw his shirt onto the couch, and tossed his shorts onto the floor. I made a mental note to never let Hutch have another drop of alcohol again because he was acting like an unsupervised toddler right now.

"Come to bed with me, bean." He wiggled his index finger at me as he began to walk backward.

"My mouth misses your pussy." Hutch stuck his tongue out and wagged it like a dog.

My brows shot up. "Wow, you are really fucking drunk." I grabbed a mug from the cabinet, filled it with water, and placed the flowers he had illegally picked for me inside. "You're going to pass out the minute your head hits the pillow," I insisted.

'Nope." He popped the *p*. "I'm going make you come all over my tongue. Don't you want that?" He moved so that he could cage me in against the wall. "God, you're so fucking gorgeous." Hutch tipped my head up with his finger. "Feel that? It's all because of you," he pressed his erection against my core causing us both to groan in unison.

I reached up to run my hands through his hair. "Because of me?" I cooed as I combed my fingers through his blond strands.

"Fuck, yes, baby."

"Go lie down, I'll be right there."

I quickly rushed to the bathroom, peed, washed up, and removed my clothes before I moved to the bed, where I found Hutch passed out and snoring. Just like I told him he would be. I shook my head. He was going to be sorry in the morning with a terrible hangover. I grabbed the clothes he had been wearing, pulled on the shirt he had tossed on the couch, and threw his shorts in the hamper before I snuggled up to him on the mattress, wondering how I would ever be able to leave this man in a couple of weeks.

Chapter Fourteen

Hutch

Why did my head hurt so much right now? The last thing I remember was Pat handing me that shot of...Oh no. No, no, no, I didn't? I did, didn't? I groaned softly and tried to bury myself under the pillow, but then felt the warm, soft skin next to me. My eyes flew open despite knowing I would regret it. My eyes focused in on the beautiful goddess lying next to me, her dark hair spread out on the pillow, her mouth slightly open, and fuck me, that was the shirt I had on last night.

Why was I naked? Did we mess around? I wasn't drunk enough to have sex with her, was I? I tried to remember.

I picked her flowers.

She brought me home.

I told her that my mouth missed her pussy.

My face flamed with embarrassment. Tequila and I were breaking up for good starting right this moment.

"What?" Jillian rubbed her eyes as she stared up at me. "Did you say something about tequila because you should never touch that stuff again." Her lips turned up into a smile, and I swear my heart was ready to combust.

"Breaking up with it." I grinned. "Did I say anything or do anything that was really stupid?" I dropped back onto my pillow as I felt like my stomach was ready to empty itself.

Jillian wrapped her small hand around my bicep. "You did tell me that your mouth missed my pussy." she giggled softly as she squeezed my muscle.

"That actually happened?" I teased because I remembered that part.

"You totally did, and then you wagged your tongue at me like a dog."

I sat up, not caring that the room was spinning. "Evil woman!" I lunged for her and yanked my shirt she had on up so her beautiful tits were exposed. They were already hard and ready for me. "Fuck," I groaned as I leaned down to suck one into my mouth.

Jillian moaned my name as her hands found their way into my hair, her hips bumping up against mine. "You're a liar, Hutch Kelly," she whimpered as I nipped and teased the hard bud with my teeth. "God, that feels amazing."

I slid my hands underneath Jillian's ass. "I believe I owe you a little something, Jills," I murmured as I kissed my way across her chest. "After I rudely passed out on you last night."

After we orally pleasured one another, showered, and ordered some takeout from Angry Egg, we talked about Jillian's plans for next weekend. She told me that she and her mother were leaving on Friday afternoon for New York, but she would be home by Sunday.

"I'm not going to class." She laced her fingers through mine and brought our hands up to her mouth so she could kiss the top of mine. "You're okay with that, right?"

I nodded. "I'll be fine," I assured her, although my stomach knotted at the thought. We'd been spending every single free minute together lately. I wasn't sure how ready I was to go back to an empty apartment even for a little while.

Jillian twisted her body so that she was facing me. "Hey, maybe you can do something with Patrick. Just him, not

Jo. You guys could hang out, watch a movie, or whatever." She squeezed my knee. "We'll text, FaceTime, of course, but do something with your brother." She smiled at me, but I already knew I wouldn't do that. I would watch a movie alone or a NASCAR race. It's what I always did.

"Maybe." I placed my hand over hers.

"Don't do that."

"I'm not doing anything."

Jillian rolled her eyes. "You are, Hutch." She stood up, but I grabbed her and yanked her onto my lap. "Let go," she insisted.

"Jills." I pushed a piece of her hair behind her ear. "I'll be okay, I promise. Pat and I don't normally hang out like that very much. I'm not going to invade his time with his girlfriend. I want to be available for you." She folded her arms across her chest, but when I pressed my face into her neck, she sighed and relaxed. "Don't go falling for any hot ballet dancers on me."

Jillian spun around so that she was straddling me. "You're the only one for me, Hutch." She dragged her thumb across my bottom lip.

***

Friday night

Jillian: *We're here! This place is huge! So many buildings.*

Hutch: *Pic or didn't happen.*

Jillian: *sends picture of self with skyscraper in background*

Hutch: *I was only kidding, Jills. You looking beautiful. Thanks for the picture.*

Jillian: *blushing emoji*

Hutch: *Having fun?*

Jillian: *Met my roommate. I am not kidding. Her name is Madison.*

Hutch: *I know you said you were not kidding, but seriously?*

Jillian: *Wish I were.*

Hutch: *Besties for life.*

Jillian: *Why do I find it so funny that you used the word bestie?*

Hutch: *Because I'm so manly?*

Jillian: *You're adorable. You know that, right?*

Hutch: *blushing emoji*

Jillian: *Gotta go, but I'll call you later.*

Saturday morning

Jillian: *Sorry about not being able to FaceTime last night. I thought my mom got us separate rooms.*

Hutch: *I totally understand.*

Jillian: *I miss you.*

Hutch: *Yeah?*

Jillian: *incoming picture*

Hutch: *Are you sending me a naked picture? Please tell me that's what you're sending— Shit you look beautiful. Is that my shirt?*

Jillian: *I wanted to have you with me while I was gone. Send me your picture. I don't care if you have bed head or whatever. I just need to see your face.*

Hutch: *incoming picture*

Jillian: *How do you look so good lying on your bed like that?*

Jillian: *Are you naked?*

Hutch: *You're too kind, m'lady. No, I'm not naked. I have on underpants.*

Jillian: *Pic or it didn't happen.* *laughing emoji*

Hutch: *No way! I'm not sending you a picture of me in my boxers!*

Jillian: *incoming picture*

Hutch: *Did you send me a picture of your tits?*

Hutch: *Are you trying to give me a heart attack?*

Jillian: *Something to hold you over until tomorrow.* *kissing emoji*

Jillian: *Talk to you later.*

Saturday night

Jillian: *I'm exhausted. I don't think I ever want to move from this bed. We walked all over New York today after checking out the school. I've never seen anything so big.*

Jillian: *Hutch? Are you sleeping? It's not even eight o'clock.*

Hutch: *incoming picture*

Hutch: *Never seen anything so big?*

Jillian: *I take that back.*

Jillian: *I can't believe you sent me a dick pick. That's total boyfriend material.*

Jillian: *Wait, I mean—*

Hutch: *Did you just call me your boyfriend, Jillybean?*

Hutch: *Because I'm totally digging it.*

Jillian: *Really?*

Hutch: *Really. Does that make you my girlfriend?*

Jillian: *Absolutely.*

Hutch: *Is it crazy how much I miss you?*

Jillian: *Not as much as I miss you. Tomorrow is going to take forever to get here.*

Hutch: *No joke.*

Jillian: *Should I just come over when I get home?*

Hutch: *You don't even have to ask.*

***

Not having Jillian around all weekend was tough, but texting with her had really helped. It made me realize that even though she would be leaving and not coming back soon, I would be able to handle it. Texting wasn't the same as seeing her beautiful face every single day, but maybe, just maybe we would be able to do the long-distance relationship thing after all.

Jillian had called me her boyfriend. I had never had a serious relationship before, not even before everything that had happened, and just thinking about it made me happier than I had ever been in my life. I already knew I was in love with Jillian, but now I wondered if maybe, she felt the same way about me.

I finished sweeping my apartment, emptied out the dustpan, and put the broom away before I took out the Swiffer to pick up any dust that might be on the floor. Since Jillian had entered my life, my OCD hadn't been nearly as bad as it used to, so that meant I had been slacking with my cleaning. I used to do it every single night when I got home from work or therapy, but as I pushed the equipment around the room, I couldn't remember the last time I had cleaned like this.

Once I was done with that, I jumped into the shower to wash up and changed into a pair of clean jeans, along with a fresh button-up shirt just as I spotted Jillian walking up the driveway. My heart soared in my chest at the sight of her, and I somehow managed to resist the urge to run down to grab her. I casually walked over to my kitchen table, leaned against it, and waited for her to get to my door.

"Knock...Hey." Jillian's voice filled my ears as she pulled the screen door open and placed the bag she had on the floor as she kicked off her shoes. Then she closed the gap between us, running straight into my arms, making sure to wrap her arms and legs around my body as she tried to get as close as possible to me.

I cupped her head in my hands. "Missed you," I whispered as I brought my lips down to hers. God, did I miss her more than I could even imagine. I had been stuck in my own head for so fucking long until she came along and saved me. Jillian saved me from the monster I had become. Her mouth opened for my tongue, her soft little moans making me want to carry her into the bedroom.

"Hi." Jillian broke into a smile when she came up for air. Her green eyes twinkled with happiness as she searched my browns. She leaned down to slide her mouth over mine again. "I got you a present." She groaned as I nibbled on her bottom lip.

I turned around to sit her on the kitchen table. "A present? For me?" I dragged my tongue down the soft curve of Jillian's neck. "Is it your gorgeous body all night long?" I stopped to suck on her collarbone.

Jillian swatted playfully at my arm. "I'm starting to think you only like me for my pussy, baby." She let out a full-blown laugh when I lifted the skirt of her dress up to yank her panties down to drop them on the floor.

"My secret has been discovered," I teased before I kissed her again.

Jillian pressed her head to my chest. "I missed you," she murmured softly. "I didn't...fuck." She shook her head. "I need a minute." She tried to get up, but I stopped her.

"Hey." I tucked a finger under Jillian's chin to tip her face up. "Talk to me, Jills." I saw the tears in her eyes. "What's wrong? Why are you crying?" I scooped her up into my arms and carried her over to the couch, making sure she stayed on my lap.

Jillian ran her palms over her cheeks, brushing away her tears. "Nothing, I just...what if I don't leave?" She dragged her teeth along her bottom lip. "I mean, what if I stayed here instead? With you?" Jillian reached up to touch my face, her soft hands gliding over my skin.

"You...you want to stay here?"

"It's stupid, right?"

I gripped Jillian's hips tightly. "Jillybean, what happened while you were in New York?" I felt like I couldn't breathe all of a sudden. If someone touched her or hurt in any way, I would never forgive myself.

"Nothing happened, Hutch," she assured me. "Being away from you was so fucking hard." Hearing her swear was always weird for me. Jillian was well-mannered, feminine, and maybe that was what I liked the most about her. "I just thought we could stay together, but if you don't want that—"

"Fuck, I do, but you are meant for bigger things." I dug my fingers into her skin so hard I knew I was probably leaving bruises. "Jillian, you are the best thing that has ever happened to me. I'm not going anywhere, baby, and you know that. But you...you are going to take the fucking dance world by storm. You're scared?" When she nodded, relief flooded my system. "I don't want you to regret not following your dreams." Her eyes went wide as she opened her mouth. "Don't tell me you won't because ten years from now, you might look back on your life and realize you made the biggest mistake by not following your dreams. I want you to go there and try it out for a month. If you hate it?" I tilted my head. "Come back to me here. I'll be waiting with open arms. Deal?"

Jillian sighed. "Deal." Her lips turned up into a small smile.

I dropped my hands so that I could pull her into a tight hug. "Now, where's that present," I teased.

Chapter Fifteen

Jillian

I panicked. There was no other way to explain what happened. The weekend I spent in New York with my mother, without Hutch, I was so lonely without him, and I panicked. I couldn't imagine what it would be like to go months without seeing his face in person, talking to him, or touching him. I freaked out.

Except Hutch was able to talk me down off the ledge. Like I did to him, Hutch calmed me down and convinced me that I was going to be fine. My plan, since I discovered my love for ballet at the age of six, was to become a professional ballerina. Why now would I change everything?

Because I was in love with Hutch.

Sunday night I couldn't get enough of him, and he of me. I knew we were going to have sex soon. I could feel it deep in my bones by the way he touched me, the way he kissed me, and the way he looked at me. The want in his eyes was there. I wouldn't push Hutch. I knew when he would be ready, he'd tell me. Only our time was running out since I was leaving for New York on Sunday and wouldn't be back until Thanksgiving.

"I have a big weekend planned for us." Hutch winked at me as he grabbed his toothbrush the next morning before I was going to be leaving.

All week, my stomach was in knots. I still wasn't convinced I wanted to go. I had almost told Jo more than once, but realized if I did, she might tell Patrick—or even worse, our mother—and had decided against it. "Oh?" I gazed up at Hutch as he rinsed the toothpaste from his mouth. "What?" I twisted my hair up into a bun before I pinned in place.

"Can't tell you." He grinned before he pinched my chin between two fingers. "Only that it's really special. And you're going to love it." He pressed his mouth against mine, leaving a minty scent behind.

I watched as he walked back into the other room. "Should I dress casually?" I called after him, trying to pry further.

"Casual today, but maybe a dress for tonight."

"Wait, today?"

Hutch was tugging his shirt over his head when I came up behind him. "Don't you have work?" I reached for my leggings. I had considered blowing off class since it was my last one, but wanted to say goodbye to everyone. Well, almost everyone. Maybe I should just stay here and wait for him.

"Nope." He grinned happily at me. "Took the day off to spend with my girl, and Megan let me cancel therapy because it's a special occasion." He was wearing the *I ♥ New York* shirt I picked up for him while I was there. He swore it was his favorite and wore it once a week.

I raised one brow. "Who are you and what have you done with my boyfriend?" I raised my hand to his forehead only to have him laugh.

Hutch was not even close to being the man he was when we first met. He hardly ever avoided eye contact, kept his head up, and was more personable than ever. I only hoped when I left, he would continue to get better. "We need to get moving or we're going to be late." He tugged on my hand to pull me against him before he pressed his mouth against mine.

"Not even a tiny little hint?" I asked as I decided on shorts instead of leggings since I wasn't going to class. I slipped on a bra, followed by a tank top, and found Hutch watching me with a blank face. "You're no fun, Kelly!" I tossed my leggings at him.

He chuckled as he caught them and folded them up to place inside my designated drawer. "I'm loads of fun, baby, just want to surprise you today." He pulled lightly on my bun. "You know how much of a turn-on it is when you wear your hair like this," he rumbled from deep in his chest. "We should leave now or we're going to be late."

***

The carnival was just opening when we walked up. My heart fluttered with happiness when I realized he was taking us back to our first date, and I squeezed his hand tightly in mine as we went inside. It was getting harder and harder thinking about leaving Hutch behind even though I was the one that had convinced him that we could make a long-distance relationship work.

"You okay?" Hutch hooked his arm over my shoulder. "You're quiet. Do you not want to be here, because we can go definitely somewhere else." He looked like a little kid who just lost his balloon.

I shook my head. "No, baby, this is perfect," I assured him. "Let's go there." I pointed to the photo booth. "I want to have it for my dorm room."

"You have plenty of pictures on your phone."

"Not like these."

Hutch was right about my phone. I had been forcing him to take selfies with me lately as well as taking just single shots of him as often as possible. But he didn't really complain and as we climbed into the booth, he pulled me onto his lap, whispering into my ear about how much he enjoyed seeing me smile and making me happy.

"Laugh with me," I urged before I tickled Hutch's side as the flash went off. I planted a wet one on his lips for the second one, we made a silly face for the third, and I bit his chin for the fourth.

Hutch reached out to shove more money into the slot. "Another," he told me before he licked my cheek in time for the camera to go off. Another kiss, another silly photo, and then all smiles for the last and final picture.

Fuck if I didn't love Hutch more now than I did this morning. I planned to tell him before I left, just so he knew what he meant to me.

Hutch helped me from the booth so we could grab our photos. "Jills." He grinned at me as he held out one of the film of pictures. "These are amazing." He searched my face, and when his gaze met mine, the smile vanished from his handsome face. "Baby, what's wrong?"

I shook my head. "Nothing, I just...I'm going to miss this. You know." I waved my hand around in the air. "These are great." I didn't want to upset him after he had gone through all this trouble on my last weekend. Hutch's hand came up to turn my face up to his. "Don't," I pleaded.

"Want to ride the Ferris wheel now? I was going to wait until later, but I think we should do it now."

I took the pictures and made sure they were safe in my purse as we got in line for the ride.

Hutch's hand was tight around mine, our fingers locked together, and I remembered how it felt only a few weeks ago when we did. The nerves, the way Hutch seemed so scared and anxious. He hadn't had a panic attack in such a long time. Once the bar was locked in place, Hutch leaned his arm around my shoulders without saying anything until the ride began to move.

"You're pretty special, Jills." I glanced over at him, only Hutch had his eyes glued straight ahead. "I think I knew that the morning we had breakfast. How easily you calmed me down, assuring me no one was staring at me, but I wanted to tell you now." He swallowed, and his Adam's apple moved up and down his throat. He slid his arm down from around my shoulders, grabbing my hand on the way. "I love you."

My whole body went warm as the ride stopped right at the top. "Hutch..." I hadn't expected that. I had hoped, but he was just the most amazing man, and for him to tell me how he felt was such a big step for him.

Hutch nodded. "I know, I know, but I just wanted to tell you before I chickened out, and before you left for New York."

I kissed him before he could say anything else; my heart beating so loud in my ears. "I love you, too." I felt the smile that spread across his lips upon my admission against mine before he pulled away.

"I had to tell you here, Jillybean, this place is ours."

"I'm glad you did."

As the ride began to move again, I saw the pink in Hutch's ears, the happiness in his eyes, and felt the heaviness in my heart. The more this weekend went on, the harder it was going to be for me to let him go.

"Do you want to get something to eat? How about a caramel apple? Oh, I could really go for one of those right now." Hutch clapped his hands together.

My brows dipped. "It's not even ten in the morning." I pointed out. "Is your stomach made of cement?" I teased, trying to push my feelings aside.

"Possibly." He slipped an arm around my waist. "You're not hungry?" We moved around the crowds that had started to get larger. The tourists would be going home soon, and the carnival would close after Labor Day weekend.

I shook my head. "I'll have a bite of yours."

"Heathen, get your own, because I am not sharing," Hutch teased as we got in line. "I'm not the only one who wants something sweet this early." He grinned. "Jilly, are sure you're alright?" His fingers traced little circles on my hip.

I pressed my lips together. "Perfect," I lied as we stepped up to the counter so Hutch could place his order. I couldn't ruin his day. Not after he told me he loved me.

Once Hutch ordered his food, we found a place to sit. He munched happily on his apple, allowing me a couple of bites, and smiled at me as he ate. I took a couple of pictures because I wanted to remember this day, making sure to add it to my Instagram. Not surprisingly, Hutch didn't have one, and didn't have a Facebook or Instagram at first either, but created accounts when I told him I could tag him in our pictures.

"Did you just tag me in another picture?" he groaned with a hint of a smile when he dragged his phone from his pocket. He rolled his eyes as he unlocked his phone, but broke out into a big grin when he saw the photo I posted. I had posted a picture with both of us biting into the sides of his caramel apple. "You're adorable, you know that?" Hutch twisted his lips into a kiss. "Right here, Jilly," he instructed pointing to his mouth.

I stood up to kiss him as he asked and then eased myself onto his right knee. "You're going to keep that Facebook after I leave, right?" I asked, leaning into him.

"Of course." He placed the half-eaten apple on his napkin. "Why?" He tilted his head. "I'm planning on liking every single picture you post of yourself in your leotard." He chuckled when I swatted at him. "Are you sure you're okay, Jillybean? You're not acting like yourself this morning. Something on your mind?"

I dropped a kiss to his neck. "Nothing is on my mind," I assured him. I knew how Hutch's mind worked. The last thing I needed was for him to think I was going to break up with him today or any day. As he reached for the caramel apple, I felt the lick of desire race through me as he ran his tongue against the fruit. "Can we get out of here?" I felt my core clench. "Take me home," I murmured.

"Home? Are you sure because...Oh. Home." Hutch must have realized what I meant when he pulled back to see the look in my eyes. "Let's go, Jills." He helped me to my feet.

Jillian sighed. "Deal." Her lips turned up into a small smile.

I dropped my hands so that I could pull her into a tight hug. "Now, where's that present," I teased.

Chapter Sixteen

Hutch

We hardly made it into the front door of my apartment before Jillian was tugging on my jeans, yanking my dick from my boxers, and dropping to her knees. "Jesus Christ." I groaned as she sucked the shaft right down to the balls. I pulled on her bun, trying to pry her off, but she held tight, sucking me, and stroking me with her hand where she couldn't reach. "Jillian, we have plenty of time for this," I moaned as she rolled my balls between her fingers.

"Can't stop." She looked up at me from under her lashes. "Want you so bad," she murmured as she sat back up on her feet. "Tell me you want me, Hutch. I love you, please."

There was no doubt in my mind that I wanted Jillian to be the first woman I made love to. "I want you." I watched as she climbed to her feet and began to strip out of her clothes. First the tank top, followed by her shorts, and then her bra, leaving just her barely-there pink thong.

"You're sure?" Jillian pressed her nearly naked body against mine. "I don't want to pressure you into doing something you're not ready for, baby." Her green eyes shimmered with heat and lust. "We can wait as long as you want." She sank her teeth into her fat bottom lip, which would have sealed the deal if it I hadn't already made up my mind about this.

I wrapped my arms around Jillian's slim body. "You taught me how to live again, Jillian," I murmured as I covered her mouth with mine. "I have waited a long time for this moment with you." Her lips were pillow soft as we kissed, so slow and easy like we had done before, but the longer it went on, the more I felt the need to devour her.

"Hutch," Jillian whispered my name as her hands clung to my shirt, her breath hot against mine. She didn't have to say anything else. I knew exactly what she meant.

Slowly without breaking apart, we made our way to the bed where I eased her onto the mattress. I still had my jeans wrapped around my ankles, and I took a step back to remove them before I did the same with my shirt. I stared down at where she laid, my heart beating so loud and so fast, and I felt a smile spread across my face. "I love you." I couldn't stop the words that tumbled from my mouth.

"I love you, too." Jillian leaned up onto her forearms as her eyes dragged over my body.

I dropped to my knees. "Spread your legs for me," I instructed and watched as she did as she was told. I grabbed her hips to pull her to the end of the bed admiring how wet and ready she already was for me. Like she always was. I ran my finger over her clit, and Jillian's hips arched forward, her head fell back, and my cock jerked between my legs.

"Make me come, Hutch, don't tease me," she moaned, bringing her fingers up to her hard nipples. "You know how much I hate that." Her eyes were pinned to mine.

I smirked. "You want me to make you come, Jills?" I leaned forward so that my lips brushed her pussy. I pushed my tongue between her folds and circled her drenched bud, causing her to cry out my name. I curved one finger to slip it inside; never removing my mouth from her core, and Jillian's cries only began to get louder.

"Hutch..." Jillian dropped a hand into my hair. "Fuck, don't stop." I loved how vocal she was, how she was never afraid to tell me what she wanted or exactly what she needed from me. "God, that feels so damn good, baby." Jillian bucked her hips as I continued to bring her closer to her orgasm. "I can't wait to have your cock inside me." She was always so damn dirty when we fooled around too. "Baby, let me suck you off right now."

I sat back on my feet. "What?" I stared up at her.

"I want to suck you off while you eat me out." She gave me a sexy smile as she crawled over to me on the mattress. "Don't be shy now, Hutch, I know you're itching to come as much as I am."

"God, you're filthy today." I climbed up onto the bed only to have Jillian move over my body and plant her crotch in my face. I groaned as she straddled me, and I felt her hand wrap around my cock, her tongue rolling against my shaft before her mouth found its way around the tip of my dick. "Jilly," I whispered as I dragged my tongue against her clit. I was going to come before I had time to finish her off.

Jillian made a soft, sexy giggle sound as she swallowed me whole, and I gripped her hips to keep them in place, digging my fingers into her skin. Fuck, she knew how to make me feel good. Her mouth was so hot, her tongue rolling around my dick, and I felt liquid fire in my veins as we pleasured one another, until I couldn't hold back any longer.

Blood roared in my head as Jillian cradled my balls and coaxed me to climax. I thought I might blackout, I came so hard panting and roaring like an animal, but when Jillian started grinding against my face, I knew she was there with her release. When we were done, she flopped down next to me, trying to catch her breath.

I watched Jillian as she brought her arm up to her forehead, her eyes closed, and her body glittery with sweat. She dragged her teeth across her bottom lip which woke my dick right back up, and then must have realized I was watching because she broke into a beautiful smile, quickly switching her position so her head was next to mine. Jillian intertwined our legs and placed her hand against my chest. "You're so good with that mouth," she teased, bringing hers lips to mine. "I'm going to—"

I didn't let her finish because I knew what she was going to say. I didn't want to hear it. Not now, not today because I was going to miss her more than she could even imagine. Instead I crushed my lips against hers and Jillian's hands slid up my chest, throat, and into my hair. "Don't," I whispered as I pulled back. "Let's not talk about that now." I watched her brows dip. "Deal?" I swung her up onto my lap.

Jillian nodded.

I shook my head and flipped her around until she was beneath me. "Deal?" I asked again as I pressed my rock-hard cock against her stomach.

"Deal." Jillian's voice came out in a soft moan.

I eased her thighs open. "Will I need a condom, Jillybean?" I nipped the soft skin on her neck, loving how easily I could slide between her legs.

"Birth control." Jillian's nails dug into my back, causing pain and pleasure to roll through me. "Hutch, you're doing it again," she warned as I continued to tease us both.

I growled into her neck, "You do realize I'm going to last about ten seconds." I had never known how to pleasure a woman. She knew that, but I still wanted to try to make this enjoyable for both of us.

Jillian pulled my face up to hers. "Baby, we'll do it again. All night long if you want." She kissed the tip of my nose.

I reached down between us and slipped my dick against her entrance, keeping my eyes locked on Jillian's greens. She laced her fingers through my free hand as I slipped the tip in and a delicious shiver raced through my body, right up my spine. "Jilly." I gritted my teeth as she clenched and rippled around me. "Fuck, I can't...it feels too good," I panted.

"Keep going."

I shook my head. "I...give me a second." I felt the beads of sweat that had already begun to break out on my face and back as I stilled. I wasn't even all the way inside, but my balls were tingling, telling me I was going to come.

Jillian pursed her lips. "Hutch," she murmured and arched her hips, trying to get me to move. "I need you inside me."

Fucking hell.

I groaned as I finally pushed all the way in, filling Jillian as she locked her legs around my waist. I pulled out slowly and glanced down to look at the way we were joined together, my eyes rolling slightly as pleasure pulsed through my body. It felt too good to ease back the reins even though I wanted to take the time to enjoy it.

"That's it," Jillian whimpered as she withered below me. "Hutch, God, yes." She tried to let go of my hand, but I held on tight so I could lean down to take one of her nipples between my lips, knowing that's what she needed.

Only it didn't take long before I exploded inside Jillian like I knew I would, and sounds I have never heard myself make were coming from my throat as I buried myself so deep inside her pussy, I was afraid I'll never want to come out. I felt Jillian bite down on my shoulder as she came, and the way she gripped me like a vise made me want to do it again and again. My head dropped down to Jillian's neck and her hands instantly combed my damp hair as I once again tried to catch my breath.

"How was that?" she whispered softly, her legs still wrapped around my waist. "Was it how you always thought it would be?"

I flattened my palms against the bed to look down into her eyes. "You have no idea how amazing that felt, Jillybean." I kissed her soft lips. "But we're not done." I could already feel my length hardening inside her again.

"No?"

I flipped us over so Jillian was now on top. "You promised me all night long." I smirked.

Jillian didn't waste time as she began to rotate her hips. "Feels even better like this," she moaned, and as she threw her head back, I reached up to pull her back down by the nape of her neck, bringing her lips to mine.

She began to ride my dick slowly, taking us both to the brink, stopping, and then repeating again, over and over, for what felt like hours. Jillian murmured sweet nothings into my ear, telling me she loved me, that I'm the only one that ever made her feel like this, and that she'll never love another man the way she loves me, and then finally, when I was practically begging her to let me come, she finally did. I felt Jillian's wetness spread between her legs, watching as her eyes rolled back, and her mouth fell open, but no sound came out as she clenched my cock tightly. Her hands dug into my shoulder as she bounced on my lap, and then a loud scream ripped from her lips as she exploded with a force I'd never seen.

I was happy. In love. All because of Jillian Robinson. She shimmied off my body, leaving my poor dick to flop against my stomach. I pulled her against me so that I could hold her tight. Neither one of us spoke until my stomach rudely interrupted us with its reminder of the fact that all I'd eaten today was a caramel apple.

Jillian snorted. "Hungry?" Her hand slipped against my stomach, and just her touch was enough to make my cock twitch again. "Or something else?" Her eyes gazed up at me with longing. "Both, maybe?" She leaned down to drop a kiss against the tip of my dick. "Why don't we order something in, and then we can shower, fuck, and then fuck again?" she suggested before her hand wrapped around my already hard dick.

The plan was perfect. We ordered pizza for lunch, took a quick shower, ate, had a quickie on the couch, thought about going out, but then I ended up doing Jillian from behind in the kitchen, ended up back in my bed, took another shower because we were sweaty again, and then tried shower sex which was fun too. We ordered Chinese food for dinner, fucked again on the living room floor, again in my bed, and fell asleep, feeling wrapped in one another's arms.

I was the happiest I had ever been in my entire life. I felt like I could do anything and everything as long as Jillian was by my side. Only I wouldn't see or speak to her again for four damn years.

I woke up alone on Saturday morning.

Chapter Seventeen

Jillian

Four years later

I glanced down at my phone. Where the fuck was Jo? She was supposed to have been here half an hour ago to pick me up. My texts had gone unread, unanswered, and now I was starting to get pissed. She knew exactly how I felt about coming back to Ocean View even if it was for her wedding. I glanced around the now deserted airport terminal as a burning rage began to build inside me. My only feasible option was to book an Uber now. I grabbed my suitcase and started toward the exit as I hit my sister's name on my phone. Great! Straight to voicemail.

I hadn't been back here in four years. That was, of course, my own doing. I had fallen for a man I had no right falling for, and then I had up and left him without saying goodbye. I never spoke of him to Jo, and the one time she dared mention his name, I told her if she did again it again, I would disown her. I'm sure Hutch hated me, although I didn't hate him, but I couldn't blame the guy after what I did to him. I told him I loved him, told him we could make our relationship work, and then disappeared without telling him why.

I was an asshole of the biggest kind.

Just as I began to scroll through my phone looking for the Uber app, I heard a soft cough, and glanced up. Standing in front of me was the one person I had hoped not to see for at least a day or two. He had his arms folded across his massive chest, his biceps looking bigger than ever, his blond hair styled to perfection, and his dark brown eyes narrowed into angry slits. The scowl on his face was one I hadn't seen in years, but he had every right to direct it toward me. After all, I had broken his heart when I promised him that I wouldn't.

"Hutch, what are you doing here?"

"Let's go, Jillian."

What the hell? "Why would you be here for me?" I gripped the handle of my suitcase as he reached for it. "Jo was supposed to pick me up." Why did I sound so lame right now?

A growl escaped his chest. "Because she has some dumb idea that we're going to get back together, which"—Hutch ripped the handle from my hand—"is never going to fucking happen because I hate you with every fiber of my being." He sounded so angry, so dark, that I wondered if I had sent him back to where he had been before I had known him. Back to when he was so mad at the world, he wouldn't even look at anyone. "Let's fucking go, or I'll leave your ass here, which honestly, is what you deserve," Hutch warned.

I had to run to keep up with him. His legs were a powerhouse of muscles as he strode out the sliding doors to where a truck was parked. He whipped open the passenger door so he could shove my suitcase behind the seat. "Get in," he grunted, "or you're walking."

I had never seen Hutch this angry before. Not even when Knox taunted him at the carnival or when I came to see him unannounced at the shop. I climbed up into the truck, making sure to hook my seatbelt into place when I shut the door behind me. I glanced over at Hutch to find him white-knuckling the steering wheel and glaring at the windshield like it told him his mother was a whore.

"Don't say a word," he hissed between clenched teeth.

"I wasn't going to."

"Don't stare at me like that either."

I had hoped for more time to prepare for this. Not that I had any idea what I would tell Hutch when the time came because he would never understand. I had never wanted to hurt him. I loved him, I still did, but what I did was wrong, and he didn't deserve to be hurt that way.

"You...you...fuck." Hutch slammed his fist against the steering wheel. "I shouldn't have picked you up." He shook his head as he looked over at me. "This was a fucking bad idea." His nostrils flared. "I should drop you back off, and you can call a taxi." He started to slow down, but then seemed to change his mind. "Someone might hurt you. It's late and dark outside," he argued with himself. I reached my hand out to touch his arm, but Hutch pulled away. "Don't you fucking dare, Jills," he seethed.

The nickname caused my hair to stand up on my neck, and I pulled my legs up to my chest to curl up into a ball. "I'm so fucking sorry." I choked back a sob. I pressed my face into my knees and tried to make it all disappear.

I shouldn't have come. I should have stayed away longer. I pinched my eyes together, wishing I could go back in time and change everything. To not leave Hutch the way I did. To never leave him, but I didn't have a Tardis, and I wasn't the Doctor.

***

When I awoke again, Hutch had pulled his truck in front of my parents' house. Funny how I thought it might look different, but it was still the same slate gray with white shutters. The chairs looked new on the wraparound porch, the grass freshly mowed, but that was the only thing that looked different to me. I started to reach for the handle of the door, but the lock went down, and I turned to find Hutch watching me with questions in his eyes.

"Why?" His voice cracked. "Just tell me why you left without saying goodbye. I've wracked my brain for four damn years, Jills, but I can't figure it out. What did I do wrong? Or what didn't I do? I loved you so damn much. I thought you loved me, and I thought maybe—"

I couldn't do this now. "Don't make me do this now, Hutch." Tears burned my eyes as I caught movement out of the corner of my eye. I turned to see Jo bouncing down the steps toward us.

Hutch sighed. "I deserve an answer."

I managed to unlock the door before Jo got there and nearly fell out of the truck, trying to get away from Hutch. "Thanks," I hissed at my sister as I hurled my suitcase from behind the seat.

"What?" Jo batted her lashes at me innocently.

Hutch managed to get out of the truck, grab my suitcase, and carry up the walkway before I even took a breath, leaving me staring after him. He placed it on the porch and sat down on one of the chairs, like he did it every night. Maybe he did. I never asked about him to keep him as far away from my heart as possible.

"Hutch." Jo hugged him as I got closer, and I'm pretty sure my jaw hit the ground. Was this the same guy? Who was this imposter? "Thanks for picking Jill up tonight. You're the best," she gushed before she turned to wink at me.

"You didn't tell me you cut your hair." She pointed out at me, running her fingers through her own long dark hair.

I shrugged. "It's easier to handle." I had cut it only a couple of weeks ago after I decided I needed a change. It now hung right above my shoulders now.

Hutch stood up. "I should go." He glanced at me again, but didn't say anything. Then he walked back to his truck and drove away without another word.

"Thanks a lot, Jo." I started to open the door.

"I have to warn you about him."

I stopped and turned around. "He hates me. I got that already." Something told me Jo was talking about something else, something bigger.

Jo dragged her teeth across her bottom lip. "I wish that was the only thing, Jill, it's much worse than that." She sighed. "So...it got really bad when you left. I mean, really fucking bad. Hutch talked about killing himself, spent a little time at the Ocean View Institution, you know the one they call 'rehab'?" She used air quotes around rehab.

"Jesus Christ."

"Let me finish." Jo held up her hand. "He met someone."

I think my heart stopped when those words left my sister's mouth. "Like seriously met someone or just fucked around with said someone?" I felt like I might faint. I knew I should have eaten something on the plane. "I...I need to sit down." I closed the front door to move back onto the porch and eased myself into the chair Hutch had just vacated.

Jo twisted her hands together. "I think at first it was more about sex. Just to have a warm body next to him at night because he missed you so much." She squatted down in front of me. "It's Madison."

"What?" I shot up so fast Jo fell onto her ass. "Madison? Fucking Madison? Hutch is with Madison Rae?"

"He knocked her up, Jill, he felt like it was the right thing to do."

I really was going to be sick now. I sat back, feeling fresh tears fall. I deserved this. I deserved all of this because I left him without saying goodbye. I was evil incarnate, and now Hutch had a baby with someone else. "I hate it here." I closed my eyes as Jo wrapped her arms around me.

"They aren't married or anything, hell, I'm not even sure that they live together." I knew she was trying to make me feel better, but it wasn't working.

I choked back a sob. "Madison is a terrible person, Jo. The things she said about Hutch were so awful. She doesn't deserve someone so pure." I wanted to hit something. Madison being that something, but I knew that wouldn't solve my problems. "He proposed? Wait, no, don't tell me. Wait, tell me. No." I shook my head. "Don't tell me. I don't want to know." I did, but I couldn't handle that right now. Learning Hutch had slept with my enemy and had created a child with her was bad enough.

"Sweetie." Jo pulled back and smoothed the hair around my face as she forced me to meet her eyes. "She's going to be super pissed you're here." A smile pulled at her lips at that admission.

My eyes went wide. "You didn't tell her?" You're cruel." I wiped the tears from my face and pulled away from Jo. "Why is this so hard?" I felt empty inside just like I had for the past four years.

"Because you broke the heart of the man you loved?"

"Thanks, bitch."

Jo sighed. "You need to fix this, you know that, right?" She reached down to squeeze my hand. "Despite what you did, despite the time that has gone by, Hutch still loves you. That's why I made him pick you up."

"Which reminds me," I pointed a finger at my sister, "you hugged him. I didn't see him flinch or push you away or anything. What's that about?" I tilted my head.

"Nope." Jo popped the *p* extra hard. "You don't get to ask me anything about his private life unless I feel like talking about it. I told you as much of the tea that I felt like spilling." She dropped my hand as she fake-yawned and covered her mouth. "So sleepy now. I think I should go to bed. See you in the morning?" She gave me a wicked grin.

I nodded before I grabbed my suitcase to follow her into the house. Nothing had changed inside the place either. The kitchen table still had the chairs we all had sat in for breakfast and dinner with the extras stacked in the corner of the kitchen. The bright yellow walls looked like they had been updated, the curtains freshly washed and pressed. As I moved through the hall, I noticed the living room sofa I knew was gone, having been replaced with some hideous faux suede sectional. It was bigger than what was there before, but it fit perfectly even if it was ugly as all hell.

"Mom's been redecorating." Jo caught me looking and shrugged when I turned to face her. "I think it's an empty nester thing," she added.

The stairs still creaked when I stepped on them, but my mother had always been a heavy sleeper so I didn't worry I would wake her. I flipped on the light of my old room, but wasn't prepared for the loneliness that hit me when I stepped inside. The bunkbeds were gone, replaced by a large bed that was now covered in what I figured were brand-new white sheets and comforters, but everything else was still the same. Pink walls covered with ballet posters, photos of me with my friends, and...shit. I moved over to the window seat to pull the last photo I had stuck there before I left, removing a chunk of paint with it.

Hutch stared back at me with a lopsided grin and his arm was around my shoulders. It was taken the night we had gone to the beach with Jo and Pat. His eyes were glossy from all the alcohol, but he looked so happy, the way I always liked to remember him. My hair was a mess, my bun falling apart, and I had that summer tan I always seemed to get every year growing up here.

I was so in love with him.

I jumped at the knock on my window and immediately dropped the photo onto the floor when I saw Hutch crouched on the roof watching me. He made a motion for me to let me in, and as I stepped forward to unlock it, I wondered why he was here and not with Madison. "What?"

I hissed as I pushed up the screen to watch him climb inside my room.

"I need answers, bean, this can't wait." He shoved the window down so hard I waited for the glass to shatter into pieces. Hutch looked around the room with wide eyes. "Christ, this place hasn't changed, has it?" he muttered before his browns landed back on me.

I shook my head. "No, forget it, leave." I pointed back to where he had just came from.

"What the hell!" I exclaimed when he slammed me back against the wall and stared at up at him, wide eyed.

Hutch's nostrils flared as he popped his jaw. "Don't fucking test me, Jillian, because you won't like me when I get angry," he seethed.

"Okay, Bruce Banner."

"Why? Why did you fucking leave without saying goodbye?" he asked that question again, the one I had been dreading for four damn years.

Chapter Eighteen

Hutch

I stared down at Jillian, waiting for her to answer me. To give me anything that would make some damn sense about why she ruined my life four years ago. Her green eyes filled with tears and her mouth parted, but then I watched her face crumble. Even though it hurt me to see her cry, I wasn't going to break down. I planted both my hands on either side of her body against the wall to cage her in and waited.

"Shouldn't you be with your child?" Her voice shook. "With your girlfriend?" Jillian raised her chin. "What does it matter why I left, Hutch? You have more important things to worry about now." She ducked under my arm.

I spun around. "What? You expected me to wait for you to come back here? What if that was never?" I watched as Jillian lifted her suitcase up onto a chair and unzipped it. "I should be alone forever?"

"You slept with the devil."

"I fail to understand how that is your concern."

Jillian started yanking clothes out, tossing them onto the floor until she found what she was looking for and then pulled her shirt off. What was she doing? Getting naked now? The shirt hit the floor with everything else, but then she grabbed another one from the suitcase and pulled it on. It fell to her knees as she spun around to face me, tugging her shorts off and removing those next. "I want you to leave," she said again.

Without even caring, I let my eyes roam over Jillian's body. She was thinner than I remembered, but I suppose dancing full time would do that to you. Her legs were still toned, but the shirt she had on covered the rest of her body. Speaking of that shirt.

"That's mine," I insisted. "You took that." I knew I sounded childish as hell.

Jillian rolled her eyes. "Sue me. At least I didn't breed with Satan." She started toward the bed to pull back the covers before she climbed in.

"I want it back."

"Not happening."

Why was Jillian acting like this? She used to be nice. She was sweet. She was...turning off the light and now it was dark. "What the fuck, Jills," I growled as the room went black.

"I'm tired, Hutch, and I'm not doing this now," she whispered. "I'm sure you can find your way out the same way you came in. Please leave."

I stood there and let my eyes adjust to the dark, knowing I should leave. I had Madison to worry about, our daughter, Hazel, and Patrick's wedding. I shouldn't be here, in my ex-girlfriend's room, who was currently wearing nothing but my t-shirt and a pair of panties. Without even thinking about it, I strode across the room to her bed, ripped back the covers and climbed into the bed.

"What the hell do you think you're doing?"

"Shut up."

Jillian stared at me, and with the moonlight that filled the room, I could see her green eyes filled with fear. I realized that's what I was doing to her. Scaring her. I didn't want Jillian to be afraid of me because that's not what this was about. It was about getting answers, finding out what happened, and maybe, just maybe, getting the closure I so desperately needed in my life.

I stretched out onto my back. "I didn't mean that." I sighed and tucked my arms behind my head.

"Are you seriously going to just lie in my bed?" Jillian moved onto her side, but I could feel her watching me. I wondered if she still felt the same way she did just a few years ago.

I grunted, which wasn't really an answer of any sort. I had dreamed of this moment for years. What I would do or say and what might happen, but now that Jillian was actually here? I didn't want to let her go again.

I could feel her gaze boring into me. "You're not staying here," she whispered. "I told you before, Hutch, and I'm going to say it again, you need to leave before...what the hell!" she exclaimed as I flipped her onto her back in a flash.

"You think you know me, baby?" I smirked. I moved so that my body now flanked Jillian's, my hard muscles against hers, and her legs dropped open. "You don't know shit." I ran my nose down her cheek, toward her ear, and licked my lips before I spoke again. "You're going to have to tell me one way or another, Jills, so why not now? Save us both the trouble of making me fucking wait any longer." I knew she felt my tongue against her skin because she trembled beneath me.

"Hutch." Her breath came out in a hoarse whisper. "Don't."

What the fuck was I doing? I leaped from the bed, gripping my hair, and when Jillian turned on the light, I spun back around. "Shit, I'm sorry. I shouldn't have done that." I stared down into her frightened eyes. "You know I would never hurt you, right? I'm just...just so fucked up over you," I admitted.

Jillian patted the bed, and I didn't have to think twice about climbing back in with her. "I can leave the light on," she offered.

"It's okay," I assured her, and when the room plunged back into darkness, I reached for her hand even though I knew it was wrong, expecting her to fight me, but she didn't. I stared up at the ceiling, at the colored glow in the dark stars that were still stuck there, and listened to the sound of my own heart and felt the tears that burned my eyes. It wasn't supposed to be like this. Jillian was supposed to be my forever; only now, we were acting like two people who hated one another. My stomach clenched at the thought, because as much as I tried? I could never hate her.

Jillian took a shaky breath, causing me to turn my head toward her. "I missed you, Hutch." Her sweet, soft voice caused an ache in my heart that I thought I had buried. "I know that's not what you wanted me to say or what you wanted to hear, but it's all I can tell you right now." A tear slipped from her eye, and I reached up to catch it with my finger. "I know you're with Madison now, and I can respect that. Maybe."

My lips were on hers before I realized it. Soft, plump and so damn kissable, Jillian didn't even try to stop me, but instead brought her hand up to grip my neck while funneling the other through my hair as our tongues twisted and tangled together. When I pulled back, I thought I would be racked with guilt, but that never came. I brushed a piece of hair from her face before I buried my face into her neck and wrapped my arms around her small frame to pull her close.

I don't think either one of us meant to fall asleep like that, but it was always easier for me when Jillian was next to me. Sleep was hard for me before she came into my life. I often overmedicated with sleeping pills or even alcohol, but not when Jillian was in my bed.

I heard the birds first, chirping and making God-awful happy sounds. Who was that excited to be awake? I still had my arms wrapped tightly around Jillian like I was afraid she would disappear again, and my arms were stiff when I started to move them. The alarm clock across the room blinked 12:00am, which meant it was wrong, and when I rolled onto my back and reached for my phone, I had several missed calls and way too many unopened texts from Madison.

Fuck.

"Sweetheart, are you awake?" Ellen Robinson knocked on the door, and I froze where I was lying. The handle jiggled, but Jillian must have locked it because the door never opened. "Jill, why is this door locked?"

I glanced over at Jillian whose eyes were focused on me. "*Seriously*?" she mouthed before she rolled her greens over to the door. "Mom, I'm twenty-two now. I can lock the door if I need to. Besides, since when do I have rules?" She hadn't cracked a smile yet. "Give me a minute to wake up, huh?"

"I need to fit your dress. I know you've lost weight so we need to make sure it fits, sweetie," Ellen told her. "I haven't seen you in four years."

Jillian shook her head. "Can I shower first?" She pulled the covers back, and I tried not to notice the shirt had risen up enough to give me a glimpse of her flat stomach.

Ellen let out a breath. "Alright." Her footsteps disappeared down the hall, leaving us alone again.

Jillian gave me a quick, shy smile that didn't meet her eyes. "You heard the woman." She stood up. "I'm assuming you have work or whatever?" She was fishing for information that I wasn't going to give her. Last night was something I shouldn't have let happen—a fluke—and I'd be damned if I would give her shit.

"Don't do that."

"Do what?"

I stretched my arms over my head to crack and pop the sore muscles and bones. "Act like we're friends or something. We're not." I pointed my index finger at her. "You fucking broke my heart, Jills," I reminded her and watched the way her face fell.

"You think I don't know that?" Her voice came out in a rush. "Every single day for the past four years?" She closed her eyes. "I thought about what I did to you. How you trusted me..." Her voice broke before she could form a complete sentence.

"Then why did you do it?" I roared so loud I expected the windows to break. "You won't even tell me why? Did I mean that little to you? Was I some sort of game for you on your way out of this town?"

Jillian flinched. "I loved you," she whispered.

"Bullshit."

Jillian stared at me. "I'm not the one that hopped into bed with the town slut and knocked her up," she spat.

"At least I know that Madison won't disappear on me," I growled.

"I want you to leave."

"Isn't that what *you* do, Jills?"

Her chin trembled as she stared up at me before she turned and sat down on the bed with her back to me. "I deserve everything you've said, but I honestly have no fight left in me this morning, Hutch. Please leave before I say something else that I don't mean." She dropped her head as her shoulders slumped.

"Jilly—"

"Please, Hutch."

I wanted to tell her I was sorry for the things I said. That I didn't mean to hurt her, but honestly, I did. I wanted Jillian to hurt the way I did when she left me without saying goodbye. I had plans to go visit her every weekend. I had plans to maybe move there if she wanted me to. I had plans to ask her to marry me. I wanted Jillian to be my forever, only she hadn't felt the same way.

I didn't say another word as I opened the window, the screen, and then climbed out, making sure to shut them both behind me before jumping back onto the lawn. Only to come face to face with Jo sitting on the porch with a cup of coffee in her hand.

"Gee, if I had known I'd see you this morning, Hutch, I'd have brought you a cup too." She smirked as she brought the mug to her mouth.

"It's not what you think," I assured her.

Jo's brows dipped. "No? Then why is Madison blowing up my phone like it's a pandemic?" She leaned forward. "Seems you told her you were going to visit your brother, but never came home."

"I did, I mean I was." Fuck, I was a dead man.

"But here you are, leaving my sister's room with guilt written all over your face."

I pinched my lips together. "Nothing happened." Why was I acting as if I was nine instead of thirty?

"I know that, but Mads doesn't." Jo pointed out.

"What do you want?" I blurted out. "Because I don't like blackmail, Jo."

She chuckled and crossed her right leg over her left. "Fix whatever the hell happened between you and my sister." She acted like it was so simple.

"Jillian needs to do that," I reminded her.

Jo took another sip of her coffee. "You still love her."

"Not having that discussion with you about my private life."

"I'll take that as a yes." Jo winked. "Pat will cover for you. You tell Mads you were there, and we'll get the two of you back together. Dump that bitch something fierce when the time comes because she really is no good for you. I thought you were going to shit yourself, bro." She stood up and raised her hand for a fist bump, which I returned.

"Thanks, I think?"

"You love me." Jo waved as she went back inside.

Sorry, but you are not the Robinson sister I'm in love with.

Chapter Nineteen

Jillian

"Jillian, stop fidgeting," Emily hissed into my ear as she put a hand on my shoulder. "I'm going to stick you with this pin if you don't." Her brows dipped as she looked me in the eyes. "Just let me finish and then you can take the dress off." That was like music to my ears.

This maid-of-honor dress was hideous. I swear, Jo was doing it on purpose. The mint green was God-awful, and I hated every single minute I had it on. I had been fitted at a shop in New York before they sent my measurements to the bridal shop back here, but I had yet to actually put the finished product on. I made a mental note to burn it when the wedding was over.

Jo was watching me from across the room with a cup of coffee in her hands. She was wearing our mother's wedding gown, which Emily had taken in for her measurements, but the rest of the bridal party was stuck wearing these terrible gowns that Jo had picked out for us. That included me, and our other friends—Claire and Holly. "You look better than you did this morning, Jill." Jo walked around me with a smile creeping up her face. "Did you sleep well last night?"

"I slept fine, thanks. Ouch, Mom, watch it!" I felt a pinch where the pin stuck into me.

"I warned you." Mom shook her head. "Josephine, dear, don't you have something else you can do besides bothering your sister? Where's your dress?"

Jo gave me a wicked grin. "My dress is hanging up in my room." Wait, did she know that Hutch slept in my room last night? What was the gleam I saw in her eye? She looked like she might say something else when the loud male voices came booming from the kitchen.

"Good morning, beautiful Robinson women!" Patrick's voice bounced off the walls from the kitchen. "I hope you all are decent."

"Pat, really?" Hutch sounded horrified, but he stopped short when he saw me standing there.

Patrick appeared in the doorway. "Jill, look at you. I don't remember ever seeing you in a dress before." He hugged Jo tight against his chest.

I rolled my eyes. "Thanks, Pat, but I've worn plenty in lifetime. Ballet dancer, remember?" I tried to ignore the way Hutch was staring at me, but it was as if he was seeing me for the first time all over again.

"What are you two up to?" Jo asked, trying to change the subject.

"Man stuff," Pat answered as if that was a normal thing to say.

I wrinkled my nose. "Man stuff? What exactly is man stuff or do I even want to know?" I stole a glance at Hutch who was leaning against the wall, looking like he wanted to be anywhere but in this house right now. He had changed into a pair of blue jeans and a polo shirt that was so tight across his chest that I thought it might rip in two. He clearly hit the workouts harder these days.

"Sure, bachelor party stuff," Hutch answered. Wait, was he actually holding a conversation in front of my mother? I had so many questions right now.

"Jillian." My mother's voice brought me back to the real world. "You need to eat more." I knew she was trying to keep her voice down, but everyone could her here in the room. "You're so thin. I'm going to have to bring this dress down almost half a size before the wedding."

My face blazed with embarrassment. I wasn't not eating if that's what she thought, and I didn't exactly make a lot of money. I ate two meals a day and the little I had left went to pay the bills I had. "Are you done?" I wanted to die right now. She could have at least waited until we were alone to say something or maybe not said anything at all. I had lost a little weight, but nothing to be concerned about.

Hutch coughed softly. "Hey, Jills, when you're done, you want to go grab something to eat at the Egg? My treat." I brought my gaze back to him. He gave a brief smile before he looked back at his feet. He saved me. He saved me from my mother, and I wanted to kiss him so hard right now. Even if he hated me or wanted nothing to do with me.

Mom patted my arm. "Go on, sweetheart. You can change, but make sure you hang this up in my room before you go." She tucked a piece of hair behind her ear.

I looked over at Hutch. "Don't you have *man stuff* to do?" I made air quotes at him, and he broke into a smile.

"Not if it means I can spend time with you, Jills." Hutch tilted his head. "You look beautiful
in that dress by the way," he added.

"Let me change." I lifted up the dress so I didn't trip over it. "We're getting pancakes," I called to him as I headed upstairs to change.

***

After I changed into a clean pair of jean shorts and a baggy t-shirt, I found Hutch waiting for me on the porch. Gone was the happy face he shared when my mother had been around, and I realized that had been just for show, for my family, and probably Pat too. He hardly even glanced at me when I closed the screen door behind me, but I noticed the way his body stiffened. For a second my brain flashed back to the morning after I left his apartment.

I don't understand why you left without saying goodbye, Jills. What did I do? Why won't you answer my calls or texts? I can't do this without you. I love you. I thought you loved me, but clearly that isn't the case. Your Instagram is private now, you deleted me from your Facebook, and Jo won't tell me anything. This is my last attempt at trying to get in touch with you, and after this? I'm not going to bother you anymore.

"Let's go," he grunted, practically stomping down the front steps which brought me back to the present. He was halfway down the walk before he noticed I wasn't following him. "Jillian?" Hutch stopped to look at me over his shoulder.

I put my hands on my hips as I walked down the steps. "Is this how you're going to talk to me? How you're going to act at the restaurant? Like a complete and total dick? You said you wanted to spend time with me," I reminded him.

"I think I have the right to act however I want, considering what you did to me."

Point to Gryffindor. "I don't want to be around if you're going to be mean." Hot tears blinded me before I could stop them, and I turned my face so he couldn't see me cry.

"Don't do that." Hutch sounded closer now. "Don't try to make me feel guilty for being mad or hurt with you. You broke my heart, remember?" He placed a finger under my chin to force me to look at him. "Don't cry, Jilly." Hutch used his thumb to wipe the tears from my cheek before he took a step back from me. "I said I'd treat you to breakfast, and that's what I intend to do. I promise I won't be mean," he whispered, his brown eyes searching my face.

We walked in silence down to the Angry Egg, and even though Hutch walked next to me, I could feel the wall between us. I was thankful for the tourists that kept us from speaking, happy that my sister had decided to get married on the week of Fourth of July. As we approached the popular restaurant, there was already a line of people waiting to get inside to be seated.

"It won't be long," Hutch assured me. "They have seating outside now." He ran his hand through his hair and leaned toward the right to see past the line into the diner.

I wanted to touch Hutch. I wanted to hold his hand and wrap my arms around his thick frame to get closer, despite the hot sun that beat down onto our skin. I wanted to smell his scent, the soap he used, the aftershave he wore, and get lost in him all over again. I missed the way he said my name when he came in my mouth, the way he kissed me, and the way he looked first thing in the morning. How his muscles felt above me when we made love, and how he always made me feel like I was the most important person in the world. I missed Hutch. That's what I missed most of all.

"Jilly?"

I blinked up at him, shading my eyes from the sun. "Wh-what?" I hadn't even realized he was speaking to me.

A smile tugged at his lips even though I could tell he was fighting to hold back. "I asked how ballet was going." He tilted his head. "Jo mentioned you had gotten a part in *A Midsummer Night's Dream*? That's pretty exciting, right?" He rolled on the balls of his feet.

The line moved so we stepped with it. "Uh, yeah." I glanced around, trying not to meet Hutch's eyes. "It's great." Lie. "I'm only playing the part of a butterfly, but it's just great to even be able to be out there with the New York City Ballet." Another lie.

Hutch looked like he might call me out, but the line moved again, and we were suddenly inside. All the memories came flooding back. The place hadn't changed at all. The paint on the walls was still faded, the grease stains on the pictures and floors were still there, and the smell of food hung in the air.

"Welcome to the Angry Egg—Jillian?" Madison's voice was like nails on a chalkboard, and any happy thoughts I had about Hutch went up in smoke. "What are you doing back at the View? With Hutch?" Her voice changed the moment she realized I was standing with her boyfriend. "Seriously?" she hissed trying to keep her cool, but her eyes narrowed into angry slits.

I waved my hand in the air. "Don't worry," I assured her. "He's all yours. I'm just here for the wedding." I gritted my teeth, trying not to knock Madison out. "You know, I'm not really that hungry." I began to turn around, only to have Hutch's arm snake around my waist to keep me in place.

"Table for two, Mads, please." Just hearing Hutch call her by that nickname made me sick to my stomach. His grip on me tightened when I tried to untangle myself. "Stop fighting me because you're doing this whether you want to or not," he growled into my ear.

Madison led us over to an empty both, dropped the menus on the table, and walked off without saying another word. How she kept her job with that attitude, I'll never know, but I suppose seeing her boyfriend with his ex, who she didn't even know was back in town, might do that to a person. I sat down with a huff while I pouted like a five-year-old throwing a tantrum.

"Mature." Hutch smirked as he sat down across from me. "Stop it," he muttered loud enough for me to hear. He grabbed the menu, flipped through it, and then stopped to stare at me. "I'm not kidding, Jills, you're acting like a spoiled brat."

That only made me cross my arms over my chest. "Because you could have given me a heads-up." I popped my jaw.

"Coffee?" Madison interrupted, batting her lashes as she turned to look at me with the fakest smile on her face. "You know, Jillian, I should actually thank you."

"For?"

"Leaving, silly. I got this job because you didn't take it after you said you would." She flashed me a shit-eating grin. "Because of you, Hutch and I were able to meet here, fall in love, and well"—Madison placed her hand on his shoulder—"the rest is a perfect romance novel ending." She turned to look at her boyfriend, but his wrath-filled eyes were glued to me.

A cold sweat broke out over my skin. Madison hadn't told Hutch that until right now. It was like she had been waiting until this exact moment to do it. I watched the way his brown eyes flashed with confusion. "What?" He turned to look at her. "What are you talking about?"

A smile that could rival the joker's spread across Madison's face. "Oh, did you not know?" She tried to act surprised, but it wasn't working. "Babe, you want blueberry pancakes, right?" No, no, he fucking didn't share that with her. "What about you, Jill?" She turned back to me with a gleam in her eyes.

"Don't try to change the subject, Mads." Hutch's nostrils flared.

"I'm not hungry." I shot out of the booth before I could stop myself. "I...I have to go." I pushed passed the patrons waiting to get inside, running as fast as I could into the warm sun and down onto the beach across the street, praying Hutch didn't try to follow me because right now, I didn't have the strength to fight him anymore.

I stumbled once I hit the sand and put my hands out to save myself from face planting. Luckily, I didn't hurt anything, but figured since I was down, I might as well just stay there. I felt like a horrible, terrible person, and didn't even care that the beach was crowded. I began sobbing as I thought about what I did. I thought that I was doing us both a favor, but in the end, I hurt us both. I wasn't sure how long I sat there on the beach; only that once I was done, I felt exhausted. I was starving, and my head hurt from crying. I stood up, brushed the sand from my body, and figured I should head back home to get myself together. That's when I felt a light tap on my shoulder and when I turned around, I came face to face with Knox Carson.

He gave me a shy smile. "Hey." He ducked his head almost as if he was nervous. "I wasn't sure if I should come over." He looked good, tanned, and like maybe he, too, had been working out a lot. "Are you okay?" Knox's brows dipped. "I saw you come running from the Egg, and you were crying…" His voice trailed off. "Shit, I'm sorry."

I shook my head. "No, don't be sorry. I fucked this one up all on my own." I tried to laugh it off, but it sounded weird. "You look good." I tried to change the subject.

"You look like shit, Jill, are you eating in New York?" Leave it to Knox to be brutally honest. "Let me buy you a taco." He pointed to the one and only Ocean View taco truck. "I won't take no for an answer either because you can't forget how amazing those bad boys are." He flashed a smile and those dimples that first got me in high school appeared on his handsome face.

I nodded. "Alright, but just one," I answered and followed him toward the food truck.

Chapter Twenty

I finished off my second taco—I was starving, sue me—and wiped my mouth as I felt Knox's blue eyes burning into me. "Say it." I placed the napkin under my plate. "I know you want to, and you've never been one to hold back," I reminded him.

Knox sipped his water, recapped it, and then leaned his elbow on the table we were lucky to snag. "You're not acting like yourself." He placed his chin onto his hand. "What's going on, and it's not just this whole Hutch, Madison, and baby shit that's got you fucked up either." He raised his brows.

"Damn, just stab me in the heart." I tossed my empty straw wrapper at him. "It's that, plus a whole lot more that I don't want to talk about."

"New York?"

I scrunched my nose and made a face. "New York, dancing, my shitty life, the fact that I left the love of my life behind—" I stopped to look at him. "Sorry, Knox, I'm not talking about you," I teased.

"Ouch, babe, you hurt me." He held his hand up to his heart. "I never thought we were endgame, Jill, but we had fun for a little while, right?" Knox gave me a small smile.

"Sure, until you started fucking Madison," I reminded him, then held up my hand. "Sorry, we're not here to talk about that." I sighed and let my gaze drift over to the water. "I never should have left," I murmured. "I had plans to stay here with Hutch," I admitted aloud for the first time, and I had to admit, it felt good. The look of shock on Knox's face was priceless.

His blue eyes were wide. "You, what?" He leaned forward. "He asked you to stay and give up your dreams? Jill, that's fucking selfish."

"You think Hutch would actually do that? Hutch is anything but selfish. He's the kindest, nicest man I have ever met." I swallowed the lump in my throat. "No, Knox, I wanted to stay because I couldn't imagine being away from him. I just..." I felt my phone buzzing in my pocket. "Shit, hold on."

Jo: *What happened? Hutch is here freaking out!*

Jo: *He said something about you taking a job at the Egg?*

"Knox, this has been great, but I have to go defuse death con five back at my mother's place." I stood up from the table. "Thanks for lunch. It really hit the spot."

"Can I walk with you?" he asked. "As friends of course."

"Sure, Chandler," I teased just to watch his dimples pop. We used to watch that show together all the time.

We dropped our garbage in the trash and began to head back to my mother's house, which only took a few minutes. I wasn't surprised to find Hutch standing on the front porch, but the second he spotted me with Knox, he looked mad enough to spit nails. Maybe having Knox walk me wasn't the best idea.

"This is fucking perfect." He threw his hands up in the air. "You run off from me and right back to him? Is this why you left me in the first place?" He glared at Knox like he was Lucifer himself.

Knox pushed me behind him. "I happened to be at the beach, so cool your jets, bro."

Hutch got right into his face. "Was I fucking talking to you, *bro*?" he roared. "No, I was talking to Jillian." I watched as he clenched and unclenched his hands at his side. I guess, he really had changed because the Hutch I knew wasn't always so ready to hit someone, but then again, he never really liked Knox much.

"Hutch." I peered around Knox. "You need to tone it down just a little bit," I admitted. "Knox is just a friend, you're with someone else, and I can hang out with whoever I want," I reminded him.

"A friend." His brows dipped as he looked at me. I nodded. "Well, that's fucking great. Does he know why you left?" he demanded.

Knox shook his head. "I have no fucking clue, man."

I moved between the two men. "Maybe you should go," I suggested to Knox. "I'm sure I'll see you before the wedding. It's a small town." I didn't want Hutch to start a fight or get arrested over this either.

"You're sure?" Knox's eyes went behind me.

"Yes," Hutch answered for me.

I rolled my eyes. "I'll be fine." I patted Knox's arm and waited until he was out of vicinity before I faced Hutch again. "What the fuck was that?" I folded my arms over my chest. "You're acting all alpha asshole which is not the Hutch I know." My brows dipped as his browns flashed angrily.

"Knox Carson, Jilly? Really?"

"You have the balls to question me when you're with Madison?"

His jaw clenched. "She was here when I needed you," Hutch reminded me. "You left. She helped mend my broken heart, and now—" He shook his head. "It doesn't matter, does it? You're never going to tell me the truth." His hate boiled over like an open wound. "What did Mads mean when she said you took a job at the Egg?"

I was not doing this now. Not outside with my sister and the neighbors gawking. "I can't."

"Of fucking course, you can!" Hutch exclaimed. "Jesus fucking Christ! Who even are you?" He spun around, yanking his hands through his hair. "God, I haven't done that." He pulled his hands through his hair again. "You show up again, and guess what? The mute is back!" He glanced up into the sky as I winced at the nickname he used on himself. "Damn, I really thought you were it for me, Jillian." Hutch bit down on his bottom lip. "Guess I really am as stupid as everyone though I was back then. Do me a favor?" he asked. "Don't talk to me the rest of the time you're here, and I'll do the same."

It felt like my heart was breaking all over again just hearing Hutch say those words, and my knees threatened to give out from under me. "I..."

"I know. The wedding! But I think if we just continue to hate one another?" Hutch shrugged. "We'll be just fine." He squared his shoulders. "Have a nice life, Jill." Then he turned and walked across the street to his apartment.

I managed to walk up to the house on shaky legs, but sat down on the chair next to Jo. Hutch had just told me goodbye in a not-so-subtle way, and I hadn't even told him anything. I hadn't been able to give him the reason for leaving or why I didn't say anything. Once again, I didn't even tell him goodbye. I was the worst human on the entire planet.

"I know you look like your best friend just died, but now might be the time to tell me what the fuck happened." Jo squeezed my arm. "I don't mean just now, but back when you deserted the man who stole your heart four years ago."

Only I couldn't do that. It wouldn't be fair to Hutch to tell my sister without him knowing the truth first. "You know I can't do that. Hutch doesn't even know," I reminded her and leaned back in the chair. "I hate my life," I whispered.

"Starting to realize that, Jill, and I'm worried about you. What is going on with you?"

"How much time do you have before our Jack and Jill tonight?"

***

"You know Hutch is going to fucking probably murder me, right?" Knox placed my vodka and cranberry down on the table in front of me before he sat down. "He hasn't stopped staring daggers at me since he showed up."

Maybe inviting Knox to be my date to the Jack and Jill wasn't the best idea, but whatever. I didn't want to go alone, and I knew Hutch was going to show up with Madison, so what other choice did I have? I took a sip of my drink, wiggled my fingers at Hutch in a little wave who scowled even more at me, and then shrugged my shoulders.

"Don't care," I answered.

Knox raised one eyebrow. "You're using me, Jill, and honestly?" He chuckled softly. "I kind of dig it." He peeled the label of his beer. "I have to say I was a bit surprised when you texted me."

"I was shocked that you had the same number." I picked up my glass, swallowed the rest of my drink, and placed it back down. "I think I'm going to get wasted tonight," I admitted.

Knox grabbed my elbow before I could get up. "Not that it's any of my business, but why?" His fingers squeezed lightly. "Are you trying to make your ex a little jealous because I know he wants to beat the shit out of me already," he teased before he dropped his hand.

"You're right." I stood up. "It's not any of your business." I walked over to the bar, leaving Knox alone at the table.

"You and Knox, huh?" Madison appeared to my right with a smile on her face. "Can't go wrong there." Her fake *customer service* voice made me sick. "I mean he was fun when we were kids, but..." She shrugged and rolled her eyes as if we were two friends sharing a secret. Two friends who had slept with the same two guys, and I wanted to break her nose for it. She did me a favor by taking Knox from me, but Hutch was a whole other ballgame.

I resisted the urge to poke her eyes out. "I'm not having your sloppy seconds, Madison, like you're having mine." I shot back and turned my back to wait for my drink.

"No need to be rude, Jills." She did *not* just call me that.

I spun back around. "Don't you ever call me that, do you understand me?" I warned.

Hutch dropped his hands on Madison's shoulders. "You said you were going to the bathroom." He glanced over at me for a brief second. "Go sit the fuck down," he ordered and waited for her to leave before he spoke to me again. "Jilly, I'm sorry for whatever she just said."

I smiled at the bartender as he handed me my drink. "You don't need to apologize, babe." I mimicked the endearment Madison had used on him early. "But the next time that cunt calls me Jills?" I brought the glass to my lips to take a drink. "I'm going to knock her into next fucking week." I smiled innocently before I walked back to my date.

Knox spun around to face me from his seat. "I thought Mortal Kombat was going to go down. I was fully prepared to shout 'finish her' when you punched Madison for whatever she was saying to you, Jill. I never really...never mind." I must have had the look of death in my eyes because he clamped his mouth shut. "I'm hungry. Are you hungry? That food smells amazing." He quickly changed the subject.

"Starving." I smirked into my glass. "You're actually not the giant douche canoe I thought you were, Knoxy." I reached over to run my finger up his arm and squeezed his bicep. "How come you're single?" I teased.

Knox stared at me for a second. "Is that a compliment, Jill, because it sure doesn't feel like one." He looked at where my hand was still wrapped around his arm. "I'm single because I haven't found the right girl, and if you don't let go of me, I think I'm going to probably end up six feet under." He reached over to remove my hand himself. "Jesus, are you drunk already?"

"Maybe." I stood up and smoothed my dress down around my hips. "How about we go get something to eat?" I noticed my sister waving me over while Pat stared at Knox with surprise written all over his face. "Since I'm in the wedding party, we get to eat first."

Knox held out his arm. "To make sure you don't fall over," he assured me. "Even though you two aren't together, Hutch clearly wants to figure out new and exciting ways to plot out my murder."

"Hutch can go pound sand."

"Don't talk about my brother like that," Pat warned as we approached the buffet. "Doesn't matter who I'm marrying, I'm always going to be Team Hutch forever." He wiggled his brows at me. "By the way, did you really bring Knox to my Jack and Jill?" He rolled his eyes.

Knox tightened his grip on my arm. "Standing right here, man, and weren't we friends once or is that all a fever dream I made up in my mind?" he asked. I was sure he had no idea how Pat only put up with him because his parents were rich and sort of owned most of the town, but I kept that to myself.

"Were we?" Pat asked as he piled chicken onto his plate. "The way I remember it, you sort of weaseled your way in when you started dating Jillian, but maybe that's my version."

Jo pressed a palm against her soon-to-be husband's chest. "This is our party, sweetie, so please no fighting. Knox was our friend, so he's welcome here." She smiled innocently. "It's nice to see you, Knox," she added, but I saw the warning flash in her eyes.

"You, too, Jo, thanks." Knox's voice sounded off, and I wondered if he was remembering things better now. He held out a plate for me before he took one for himself, and I almost felt bad for him until I remembered the reason we broke up. He put his dick in another girl. That same girl who was now currently digging her claws in the man I loved. I turned briefly to see Madison glaring in our direction, but she raised her glass in my direction anyway with an evil smile on her face.

"Hey." Jo nudged my side as she brought her face closer to mine. "Don't let her win, Jill, because she wants you to have a meltdown," she whispered. "Also, I would hate for you to ruin that dress you're wearing, because Hutch and Knox probably have boners the size of downtown Chicago."

I snorted. "You're disgusting." I tried not to laugh as I grabbed the tongs to drop some chicken onto my plate. I had picked my dress out back in New York because I had fallen in love with it hanging in the window of a second-hand store. It was a blue maxi dress with white flowers, and it fell straight to the floor. I love how it clung to me, showing off the little curves that I had, and for once, I actually liked how I looked. "We all know Madison has hated my guts since we were in high school, and now she's trying to put the final nail in my coffin." I was happy to have something in my hands so I couldn't flip her the bird while I spoke.

I pretended not to notice the way she fawned all over Hutch. The way she looked at him with big doe eyes. Or the way she slid her hands up his chest and pressed a kiss against his mouth, leaving her lipstick behind just when she thought I might see.

Knox pressed a hand to my back. "Jill." His voice was calm, but he wasn't the one that I wanted or needed right now. No, the man that I loved was too busy whispering sweet nothings to my arch nemesis because I had been stupid enough to let him get away in the first place.

Chapter Twenty-One

Hutch

The urge to rip Knox's arms from his body and then beat him with them was strong tonight. The moment I saw him walking down the sidewalk with Jillian this afternoon, I had to actually talk myself out of breaking his face with my fist and that was only because I had Hazel to worry about. Then, Jillian brought him as her fucking date tonight? Did she forget what he did to her or the things he said to me the night we went to the carnival?

Having a child was never high on my list of things I wanted in my life. I was beginning to have my doubts about Madison since she dropped that bomb at the Angry Egg this morning. Clearly, she had held on to that, waiting for the exact moment to release it.

I stayed when I knew it wasn't right. I might have been a lot of things, but I was a decent human being. I stepped in, told Mads I would be there if she wanted me, and now? Well, here we were. Did I love her? Love was a strong word. I cared for her, wanted to make sure she and Hazel had a roof over their heads and food in their bellies. I didn't see us getting married, although Madison dropped hints all the time. I wasn't the white picket fence kind of dude and probably never would be even if I was with Jillian. Madison and I lived in an apartment over Zed's Automotive, which I now owned, and even though it wasn't as nice as the place I put together living at my parents, with a little work and a lot of love, it was home. Or at least, a place to rest my head at night.

"I'm going to call my parents to check in on Hazel." Madison tried to be a good mother. The moment she found out she was pregnant, she stopped smoking, drinking, and anything else that might hurt our unborn child. "I'll be right back." She stood up, making sure to press a kiss to my temple. "You okay? I know this can't be easy for you." Madison knew nothing about my past. That was something I had only told to Jillian, my therapist, and my family, but only after Jills left. It had helped in my healing and to finally turn my life around. I was thankful I never told Madison because there was no doubt she would find a way to hang it over my head. My trust in her was dwindling by the second the more I thought about this morning.

I shrugged. "How do you think I am, Mads?" I drained the last of my beer.

"Do you want to leave now?"

"Not a chance."

Madison's eyes darkened. "Because she's here with Knox?" She pursed her lips as jealousy ripped through my veins. "Baby—"

"You should check up on Hazel. Tell her I love her," I reminded her. I wanted to tell her to leave and not come back, but I bit my tongue. I slid my eyes to hers. "I'll be fine."

Madison nodded, dropped another kiss against my cheek, and as I leaned back into my seat, I saw Knox leading Jillian out onto the dancefloor. Fuck my life, could this night get worse? I cursed myself for thinking that because Kenny Chesney's "You and Tequila" began playing. Fuck. There was no way I was letting Knox Carson dance with my girl now. Wait, she wasn't my girl anymore. Had Jillian ever really been mine in the first place?

Before I even realized what I was doing, I was out of my seat, striding across the room, and tapped Knox on the shoulder, probably a little harder than I needed to. "I'm cutting in," I growled. "Don't fight me."

Knox glanced down at her. "Are you okay with that?" he asked.

"This is our song, Jilly."

Her green eyes flew up to mine to give me a quick nod as Knox moved away to let me step in. As I wrapped my arms around Jillian's small body, I felt her tremble against me. She smelled perfect. Sweet and feminine, with a touch of perfection like always. Her skin was warm under my fingers as I gripped her arms, but I didn't like how thin she had become. We didn't speak, only swayed to the music, and I couldn't resist whispering the lyrics against her ear.

"When it comes to you, oh, the damage I could do."

Jillian stiffened against me before she pulled back to look up at me. "Don't do that," she pleaded.

I ran the back of my hand over her cheek. "What's wrong, Jilly, afraid you might finally tell me the truth this time?" I teased. She struggled against me, causing me to hold her tighter.

"This isn't the time or place."

"Then when?" Jillian's face had drained of blood when I finally looked down at her. "You and tequila," I reminded her, daring to lift a hand to tuck a loose piece of hair behind her ear. "I told you my deepest, darkest secret, Jillybean, and you can't even tell me why you broke my heart. Doesn't seem like a fair trade to me."

She sank her teeth into her bottom lip. "Hutch, I—"

"Don't you dare tell me you can't, Jillian, because I swear to God, I will tear this place apart if I hear those words come out of your mouth again. It nearly broke me when you left. You ignored all my calls, my texts, and I thought it was me you running from." I snarled. "You know what? I give up." I released her from my arms. "I realize now that you couldn't have possibly cared about me the way I did for you. I'm done." I took a step back, after declaring my final admission.

"Wait."

I shook my head. "No, you fucking wait." I pointed my index finger at her, horrified to see that it was shaking. "I know you're mad that I'm involved with your arch nemesis now." That sounded ridiculous coming out of my mouth. "But we're all adults here. In case you forgot, you left me first. You dropped out of my life without explanation or reason, after you told me you loved me, by the way. After you told me you couldn't imagine not being together. That is fucked up. I'm sorry you can't deal with that, but I. Am. Done." I turned to storm off the dance floor, knowing Patrick and Jo were probably horrified right now.

When Knox tried to stop me, I shoved him. "Fuck off, man, this has nothing to do with you. She's all yours now. Have at it." I noticed Madison standing by the door and wondered just how much she had witnessed. "I'm not talking about this with you," I warned her when I shoved the door, only to have her follow me outside.

"Hutch, what was that about?" Madison was struggling to keep up with me on with the heels she had on even though I had warned her not to wear them.

I gritted my teeth. "Did I not just say I was not going to talk about this?" I glanced over my shoulder at her.

"You were dancing with Jillian?" she pushed.

"Mads." I stopped to stare at her.

"No, you don't get to just blow that off. We're together, Hutch. I don't care if she was your first love or whatever the fuck Jill means to you. We're a family now. You can't just drop that because she blows back into your life." Madison planted her hands on her slim hips. Her blue eyes were furious as she glared at me.

"Do not say another word about Jillian. Do you hear me?" My voice was cold when I spoke. "I need to be alone." I started walking again. I thought for sure that Madison would follow me, but when she didn't, I let out a sigh of relief. I had no clue where I was going; only that I needed to think.

***

I walked around for what felt like hours before I finally went back to my apartment over my parents' garage. I went there sometimes when I needed to be alone and just think. I considered going to Jillian's, but what good would that do? She was never going to tell me the truth. She was never going to tell me why she left me and broke my heart. I sighed as I climbed the stairs with heavy legs. That morning was still fresh in my mind. The crushing blow that I never saw coming.

I felt a smile spread over my face as I thought about my last night and reached for Jillian, only to find the spot where she should be on the bed, empty. I sat up.

"Jills?" My voice echoed off the walls as I flung the blankets back from my legs. The apartment was eerily silent. "Jillian?" I sprang from the bed, grabbed a clean pair of boxers from the dresser, and rushed to the bathroom hoping she was there.

Nothing.

My entire apartment was empty except for me. Her bag was gone. The drawer Jillian had been using to store her clothes? Empty. My heart cracked, and I dropped to the floor by the bed. What the fuck was going on? I felt sick, as bile filled my throat, and pressed my forehead against the cool floor.

Jillian had left. She had left without saying goodbye after she told me she loved me. Why would she do that unless...no. I shook my head. She told me she wanted to be with me and wanted to make things work.

I slammed my fist against the hardwood to feel the pain race through my muscles and then jumped to my feet. I grabbed my phone from the charger.

Hutch: *Where are you?*

Hutch: *Jills, what the fuck is going on?*

Hutch: *You're scaring me.*

My texts went unanswered that day or any other time I tried to reach out to her. Any calls I made were sent straight to voicemail. When I finally went to Patrick the next day, who then brought Jo over, they had no idea Jillian left me the way she did. She had told them she left a day early because she wanted to get settled. Get more comfortable with her roommate and life at school. They were as clueless as I was.

Jillian had lied to them too.

I had removed her number from my phone after a year of trying to reach out to her, but that was only after I ended up in the hospital. I stopped asking Jo about her and tried to move on with my life. That was right around the same time I told my parents about what had happened at camp.

My life changed dramatically after that. I started to feel like my old self, stopped hiding and staying away from things. I had breakfast with Pat one morning at the Angry Egg, and that's when I ran into Madison. She asked me out, and I figured it wouldn't hurt since I was lonely. I never expected to sleep with her, never mind have a baby.

I stripped off my clothes, making sure to dump them in the hamper before I climbed into the bed. I stared up at the moon under the skylight. I hated this place after Jillian left. Every single memory of her was here, and I had resisted the urge to burn it to the ground many times.

My phone blinked on the table next to me.

Unknown: *I need to talk to you.*

Unknown: *It's Jillian.*

Unknown: *I have Jo's bachelorette party tomorrow night, but can we get together after?*

I stared at her messages in shock.

Hutch: *I want to tell you to lose my number.*

Lie.

Jillian: *You have every right.*

Hutch: *I have the bachelor party, but I can bail early.*

Jillian: *You don't have to.*

Hutch: *For you, I will.*
Jillian: *I am so sorry.*
Hutch: *Don't do that.*
Jillian: *I want to tell you the truth this time.*
Hutch: *Promise?*
Jillian: *Pinky promise.*

I laid back to stare up at the window again. Was this actually going to happen or was she leading me on again? My heart rattled against my ribs as fear clenched my mind. Would I be able to handle the truth from her?

Hutch: *I want to believe you, Jilly, but I can't trust you right now.*
Jillian: *Can't say I blame you.*
Hutch: *What time?*
Jillian: *Nine?*
Hutch: *You don't plan on hanging with the girls that long, huh?*
Jillian: *Naked dancing dudes is not my thing.*
Hutch: *I agree with you on that one.*
Hutch: *Nine sounds good.*
Jillian: *You want me to come to you?*
Hutch: *Sure. I'll see you then.*

It took me a long time to fall asleep. I had waited a long four years to get the answer to why she left me. Now I only had few hours to find out.

Chapter Twenty-Two

I knocked back another shot as I watched Magic Mike gyrate his hips in Jo's face while Belle, Holly, and Claire urged him on. I was happy that she was having such a great time, but honestly, ew, no, thank you. I tilted my head back to get a better look at him. Strong jawline, handsome face, with a nice body; only he wasn't really my type of guy. Hutch was my type of guy.

I reached for another fruity pink shot and winced as the liquid burned going down my throat. I rolled my eyes as Belle eagerly shoved folded dollar bills down the stripper's pants. Yikes, maybe that was my cue to leave.

"Whoa, whoa, where are you going, sis?" Jo grabbed my arm as I got to my feet. "You're dressed to kill, it's not even ten o'clock, and you think you're just going to waltz out of here the night of my bachelorette party?" She slurred her words just enough for me to realize she was already half in the bag. Fabulous.

Jo was right about the dressed to kill part. She had convinced me to wear the sheer black top with a black bra underneath, and a pair of black dress pants that made me feel like a million bucks tonight. The last time I remembered feeling this sexy was when I wore that blue dress that Hutch...I shook my head. No, I had to stop thinking about him. This night was about my sister, not about Hutch.

"I was going to get some fresh air," I lied. "It's really hot in here."

Jo nodded. "That's the sweaty man meat." She grinned. "You're not going to go home and feel sorry about yourself because Hutch is with lame-assed Madison," she drawled on. "Not tonight anyway." She stirred me back to my chair. "Hey, Channing!" Jo snapped her fingers. "My sister needs a little one-on-one to get over her ex."

"How drunk are you?" I hissed between clenched teeth.

My sister only giggled. "Well, we had the champagne at the house before we got here." Jo ticked off one finger. "Then we had a few drinks at the restaurant, followed by more shots and drinks here." She stuck out her tongue at me. "So I'm really, really, really fucking drunk." Jo stumbled slightly when she turned toward Claire, who threw her head back and laughed.

"Jesus fucking Christ." I rolled my eyes. "Okay, enough." I planted my palms against the burly chest dude in front of me who clearly didn't get the hint I wasn't interested. When he didn't move, I let out a huff. "Hey, guy, get a hint. You're cute and all, but I'm not the bride. Also?" I slid away from his sweaty body. "You're totally not my type." I went rushing after my sister who was reaching for one of the shots still left on the table. "Maybe not a good idea, Jo, what do you think?" I'd had my share of booze, but not as much as my dear sister had.

Jo waved her hand. "I'm fine, what happened to Mister Hot Pants?" She giggled again before she threw her shot back and then adjusted the crown on her head that read *Bride*. "You two would look super cute together." She smirked.

"You know how hungover you're going to be tomorrow?"

"Don't care."

My brows dipped. "You're going to care when you wake up tomorrow with the worst headache in America, hugging the porcelain God." I pointed out. "Maybe take a moment to breathe a little." I suggested.

Jo rolled her eyes. "Don't be so boring, Jill, live a little. I'm going to be married in two short days to the love of my life. Can't I have a little fun tonight?" She threw her hands up in the air. "If you're so bored or don't want to be here, just leave because we all know that's what you want to do anyway. You've been staring at your phone the moment we left the house, like you couldn't wait to fucking not be around us."

I knew that it wasn't my sister talking right now but the booze that was currently running through her veins. "Fine." I placed the glass I had just picked up back on the table. "If that's the way you really feel." I squared my shoulders. "Sorry to ruin everyone's fun." I turned to head out of the club.

"Jill, wait, don't go." I heard Holly calling after me, but I didn't stop. I knew when I wasn't wanted, and I was already late for my meeting with Hutch. I had promised him that I would be at his place at nine tonight to finally tell him why I had left him without saying goodbye. I had dragged my feet long enough. It was time to face the music.

***

All the lights were off at Hutch's apartment when I arrived at nearly eleven o'clock. The front door was open, the screen door shut, and that was odd to me considering how he felt about safety. I tightened my grip on the six-pack of beer I had picked up on my way before I headed up the stairs, noticing the light from the television inside. How long had he been inside waiting? Did he blow off Pat's party for me? The screen door slapped shut behind me, and I saw Hutch's bulky figure on the couch, but he never moved. I toed off my shoes and walked barefoot toward him.

"I've been waiting for you." Hutch's voice was low when he finally spoke, and I realized he had the sound off on the television. "What happened, Jilly? Couldn't decide if you wanted to show up or not? Got cold feet or something?"

I took a shaky breath. "It's not that simple." I hated how I sounded. "I tried to leave earlier, but Jo was drunk, and..." My voice trailed off as I stared at him when he finally glanced over his shoulder at me with a completely blank face.

"Is one of those beers for me?" Hutch's husked voice sent heat throughout my body. I placed the alcohol on the end table next to the sofa. Hutch reached for one, popped it open, and took a long sip without saying anything. I finally reached for a bottle, but didn't open it right away.

I knew I hurt Hutch. He told me his darkest secret, we fell in love, and then I left him without saying goodbye. It hurt me just as much, but I did it because I had no other choice. I was here tonight to finally confess everything, and wish him the best because I wanted him to be happy. He deserved nothing less. I suddenly had the urge to touch him, but kept my hands to myself.

He finally glanced over his shoulder to look at me, his brown eyes shining from the light of the television. He didn't say a word as he stood up, placing the now empty bottle of beer on the table, and began to move toward me. I hadn't even realized I had backed up until I felt the wall behind me. Hutch's hands cupped my face as he slowly brought his lips against mine. They were warm, and I eagerly opened my mouth for his tongue to evade my space. Hutch growled deep in his chest, causing desire to pool deep inside my belly, and I clung to his shoulders as he pushed me further against the wall.

Hutch's tongue swept through my mouth from top to bottom and back to meet mine again as my nipples hardened inside my bra. They ached to be touched, needed to be licked and sucked as Hutch's teeth grazed my lips. When he stopped to look at me, I felt like I might burn up into a million pieces with the way his gaze made me melt. How could I have left this man? Why did I think that I would be okay without him in my life? When I opened my mouth to speak, he placed a finger over my lips and simply shook his head, his lids heavy with lust.

Hutch ran his hands down my arms, over my hips, and then my ass, causing a pounding need to begin to build inside me. He peppered little kisses against my mouth and down my neck as his hands moved around my back to remove my shirt. He took a step back to help me slip off my top, and then he moved in to unhook my bra, making sure to drop it onto the floor. He easily removed my pants next, his hands brushing over my nipples, and then he hooked two fingers into my panties, ripping them off.

I reached up to grab Hutch's face, kissing him hard on the mouth, the sound of his zipper somewhere in my mind, and then he slammed me back against the wall, thrusting into me in one move. I screamed out his name, pleasure pulsing through my body. I wrapped my legs around his waist as he lifted one leg, and then the other, his cock searing into me over and over again. "More," I demanded. "Please, baby, more." I needed him to make me forget the past four years before I came apart.

Hutch's hips smacked against mine as he dove into me, his lips never leaving mine. His eyes flashed between lust, desire, love, and need as he fucked me with something I had never felt before. "I missed you, Jilly," he murmured as he moved together like a well-oiled machine.

"Fuck, you feel so good," he groaned as we moved together. "I've been dreaming about this since the day you left," His voice caught in his throat as he thrusted harder, and when he pressed his hand down to my clit, I dragged my nails across his back, seeing stars behind my eyes as I exploded around him. He buried his face in my neck just as all his muscles went stiff and he followed me over the edge.

I clung to Hutch for only a moment before he helped me back onto my feet. He took a step back from me before he turned and rushed to the bathroom, the sound of water filling my ears. I followed him, hoping I could ease whatever was going on inside his head right now, only to have him meet me halfway. "Whatever you're thinking right now, I want you to tell me."

"I was getting a cloth to clean you up." Hutch held out his hand. "Please." I couldn't see his ears in the dark apartment, but something told me they were probably bright pink.

Once I was washed up and clad in another one of Hutch's shirts, we sat down on the couch, with the lights on and the television off, facing one another.

"You've changed." I traced his palm with my finger. "I think I like this alpha male version of you," I teased just to see him blush.

"This isn't about me, Jills." Hutch took his free hand and tilted my face up, this thumb dragging along my jaw. "Tell me." His voice sounded sad. "Tell me what I did." I saw the way his baby browns filled with tears, and I was in his lap before I could stop myself.

"It was never you, baby, I can promise you that."

"Prove it, bean, because you made me feel like I wasn't the man you wanted."

I cupped his face with my hands. "You're the only man I wanted in my life, Hutch Kelly. Always and forever. There has never been anyone after you." I slid my lips over his.

Hutch flashed a brief smile. "Please tell me," he begged again.

Chapter Twenty-Three

Jillian

"I had plans to stay," I admitted before I got up to sit on the couch. I held up a hand before Hutch could interrupt me. "Remember how I came back from visiting New York, meeting my roommate, and going to check out my school? How I wanted to stay here with you instead?"

Hutch nodded.

I swallowed hard as I twisted my fingers together in my lap. "Before I came here, after I got home on that Sunday, I went to the Angry Egg and applied for a waitress job." I glanced up to find Hutch staring at me with total surprise all over his handsome face. "I...I...I had decided that I was going to stay in Ocean View with you. Work at the Egg, and hopefully, you would let me move in here with you."

Hutch narrowed his eyes. "Jillian, what the fuck?" he snarled. It looked like the wind was completely knocked out of him.

"Let me get this all out, Hutch, or I'll never finish." I pinched the back of my neck. "I had it all planned until you told me I would end up hating myself or you for not following my dreams. Maybe not right away, but five or ten years down the line." I felt tears beginning to fill my eyes, but I let them. I was an asshole for leaving him behind. A pussy for not having the guts to tell him in the first place. "Which I realized I would. I would hate myself for not at least going to New York like I had wanted since I was five years old and trying to make it." The tears began to fall now. "I should have said goodbye, but I knew that if I waited, I would chicken out and stay here with you. I couldn't bear to see the look on your face when I left. I couldn't deal with saying goodbye to you. I thought that it would be easier." My voice cracked. "I hated it. I hated living there, but at that point?" I sobbed. "I was there. I had left you, and I had nothing. I wanted to come home, but what was I going to say?" I buried my face in my hands as my body shook angrily.

Hutch moved closer so that he could pull me against him. He didn't say a word as I cried; he just held me until everything was out, and I felt like I had nothing left in me. When I was done, he smoothed the wetness from my cheeks and stared into my eyes. "I wish you would have told me, Jills." He pressed a kiss to my forehead. "If you had just..." He shook his head. "You're here now though," he whispered.

"You still want me? Why?" I dared asked.

"I will always want you."

Another sob threatened to escape my chest. "I hate it there so much, Hutch. I'm a great dancer here, but just an okay dancer in New York. I'm so fucking tired all the time and—" His lips descended on mine before I could finish my sentence.

"Stay here. With me," he murmured. "Get a job at the Egg." A smile tugged at the corners of his lips. God, he was so fucking handsome.

"You're with Madison."

His nostrils flared. "I'm not with Madison. Not the way you think," he told me. "We have a daughter who I love with all my heart, but that's all we share." Sincerity shone from his eyes. "I never stopped loving you, Jillian." His lips brushed mine before he pulled back. "You could buy the ballet studio. It's for sale."

"What?" I blinked at him.

"Yeah, I saw the other day that there was a For Sale sign on it. You could teach ballet to the kids in Ocean View. We could get married, start a family, and have a life together here."

"You...you want to marry me?"

Hutch dragged his thumb along my bottom lip. "You find that so hard to believe, beautiful girl?" God, he had changed so much since I last saw him. Or maybe, this was the Hutch he had always been.

"You're different," I whispered, reaching up to touch the light-colored scruff that covered his jaw.

A smile appeared on Hutch's face. "Therapy," he answered, like that was the answer to everything. "I'm not different, Jilly, I'm me." He kissed the tip of my nose lightly. "I love you." He grabbed my waist and lifted me up onto his lap. "First thing on my to-do list," he murmured as he dropped little kisses against my mouth, chin, and neck. "I want to get some meat on these bones."

I moaned softly as he licked along my collarbone. Hutch's touch had always been gentle, but now it felt a little more dangerous. A little more feral. "Then what?" I sighed softly.

"What do you want?" Hutch stopped to cup my face with his big, calloused hands.

"You." Not that he ever doubted that, but I wanted him to know that now. More than ever, I wanted Hutch. "Make love to me." I lifted my hips so he could pull down his boxers.

My panties were still in a crumpled heap on the floor. "Right here, right now."

His darkened gaze was enough to tell me he'll devour me. "Your wish is my command."

***

I forgot how much I loved Hutch's bed. It was so soft and comfortable. Not to mention he was lying next to me with his arms wrapped tightly around my body like he was afraid I would disappear again. Not that I blamed the man. He not only made love to me like I had requested last night, but then he proceeded to eat me out until I screamed his name, afterward fucking me again right here in this bed. God, I missed him.

He stirred next to me, his face still buried in my neck as he started to wake up. "Good morning." He gave me a sleepy smile and ran his hand through his messy blond hair. "Fuck, you're really here," he whispered.

"I am." I caught my phone lighting up out of the corner of my eye as it sat on the table, but I ignored it. I just wanted to stay here all day, but I knew that was impossible. "Feels like a dream though," I admitted.

Hutch tilted his head. "How so?" He moved his hand up to my head. "You miss me that much, bean?" He grinned as he started to drag the blanket down. "Wait, do you have a tattoo? When did you get that?" His finger traced the small, pink ballet slipper on my hip. "Sexy," he whistled.

I pretended to slap his hand away. "I got it last year with Madison. My roommate. We're actually like besties." I giggled as his fingers tickled my ribs.

"So I was right?"

"Smart man."

Hutch dropped wet kisses all over my stomach. "You really hate it there, huh?" He dragged his gaze up to mine. "You don't really like to talk much about it." He glanced over where my phone sat. "Someone is really trying to get your attention this morning."

I twisted around to grab my phone. "For someone who said they weren't going to be bridezilla...shit." I sat up to unlock my phone to reveal dozens of texts from Jo.

"Everything okay?" Hutch asked. "You look upset."

Jo: *Where are you?*

Jo: *The wedding is off!*

Jo: *I need you!*

Jo: *I'm serious, Jill!*

Jo: *Pat cheated on me!*

I glanced back at Hutch. "I have to go." I flung the rest of the covers off to jump from the bed. "Something happened last night." I found my bra and my ruined panties in the living room where Hutch had left them.

"I guess so." Hutch had his phone in his hand. "What an idiot," he groaned as he shook his head. "Damn it, Patrick." He began to shove his jeans on. "I guess I need to go talk to my brother." He met my gaze just as the front door flew open to reveal Madison.

"Is this why you didn't come home last night?" she exclaimed. "I thought you were done with her, Hutch?"

I found my pants, pulled them on—sans underwear—and quickly yanked my shirt on. "I'll let you deal with this." I had my sister who needed my help right now.

"Deal with?" Madison roared as she turned to me.

"Mads, don't," Hutch warned.

Madison shook her head. "You can't have us both, Hutch, that's not how this is going to work." She stuck out her left hand. "Did he bother to tell you we got married yesterday?" It was like a kick to the stomach when I saw the gold band wrapped around her finger. "I didn't think so." Madison dropped her hand. "Nothing fancy; I'm afraid. Just down to the courthouse, but it's official. I'm Mrs. Hutch Kelly, and you're not."

Everything Hutch had said to me last night was a lie. Was that his way of getting revenge? "I have to go," I muttered before I shot out the front door with my shoes in my right hand and hurried down the steps, trying to keep myself from exploding into tears.

Hutch was married.

Not just married; Hutch was married to Madison Rae.

Jo was sitting on the front porch as I made my way across the street. I tried not to let my feelings show as I dropped onto the steps next to her and pulled her into my arms. Now it was my turn to comfort my sister after she had helped me so many times before.

"I didn't think he would actually go through with it." She sobbed into my chest.

Wait a second. I pulled back to look at Jo. "What does that mean?" I searched her face. "Back up and tell me the entire story."

Jo pressed her lips together as she sat up. "Okay, so we always had this agreement." She squared her shoulders.

"What kind of an agreement?"

"Pat and I had never been with anyone else. I mean I lost my V-card to him, and he lost his to me. We both knew that we wanted to spend the rest of our lives with one another—"

I jumped to my feet. "Are you telling me that you told Pat he could fuck around last night?" I was so not emotionally stable to handle this right now. I had my own shit that I was going through.

"No, well, kind of." Jo's eyes filled with tears again, and I dropped down next to her.

"Wait, did you come from Hutch's place?" She let her gaze roam over me. "Did you sleep with him?"

I narrowed my eyes. "Not the topic at hand," I reminded her. "Back to you and Pat." I felt my throat close up when I remembered the fact that Hutch was now married to Madison. "Fuck," I whispered as tears burned my eyes.

"Holy shit, you did." Jo touched my arm. "Sweetie, maybe you need to talk to me instead?" Her brows furrowed together.

"You have two seconds to tell me what happened with Patrick before I go inside," I hissed.

Jo held up her hands. "Fine, fine. He just got a blowie from a stripper." She rolled her eyes. "I might have blown it out of proportion. The wedding is not off." She shrugged her shoulders.

I closed my eyes, trying not to freak out on my sister. "I'm going to go inside, take a shower, and wash last night off my body," I said calmly.

"Can I ask you another question?"

"Fine."

"Why is Madison coming over here?" My eyes flew open to see Madison marching up the front walk like a woman on a mission. Probably to sever my head off and hang it on her wall so she could stare at her every morning to remind herself she won.

Jo and I both stood up before she even made it to the steps. "That's far enough," I grunted and folded my arms across my chest. "You won, you got Hutch. Happy?" I watched her nostrils flare.

"No, bitch, I'm not. Are you clean?" Madison seethed, and I heard Jo gasp next to me. "I know that Hutch only goes bareback so I hope you don't have any STDs from the guys you slept with in New York." I was going to smack her into next year, but before I had a chance, Jo stepped forward.

She slapped Madison right across the face. "How dare you!" she cried. "You come here, to our house, and accuse my sister of carrying a disease when Jillian is the one that should be running down to the clinic after sleeping with Hutch. You're a whore, Mads, and you're always going to be. Doesn't matter if you end up with him, doesn't matter if you don't. You've never been equal to us." She watched the expression on Madison's face change from shock, to angry, to glee.

"Jilly, you didn't tell her?" She smirked. "I won, Jo, fair and square. So, yes, I might be a whore, but I'm Hutch's whore wife." She waved her hand in the air. The one with her damn wedding band on it.

I grabbed my sister before she could jump onto Madison. "Leave," I growled. "Now, Madison, before I let her go, and trust me, she'll do much worse than just slap you this time." I turned away as Madison turned and walked back toward Hutch's apartment.

"Jesus." Jo sighed. "So, that's it, huh?" She hugged me.

I hugged her back. "That's it," I whispered.

Chapter Twenty-Four

Hutch

Marrying Madison had been a spur of the moment idea. It had been something I had suggested because I was furious with Jillian for not talking to me, for showing up at Patrick's party with fucking Knox, and I wanted to prove once and for all that I was over her. I knew it was a lie. Fuck, the entire town of Ocean View knew it was a lie. I felt like the world's biggest asshole. Jillian finally told me the truth, spilled her guts out, told me she loved me, and then Madison had come crashing through everything to ruin any chance at a future we might have together.

"You in here?" Patrick's voice carried through my open screen door. "I can see you, so don't try and pretend you're not." The sound of the door slapping shut behind him had me sitting up. I had managed to shower, put on clean jeans and a shirt, but that was about it before I dropped onto my bed. "Jesus, you look like shit," he commented.

I flipped him the bird. "If you're here to give me hell, I don't want to hear it." I swung my legs over the side of my bed.

"For?" Pat tilted his head.

Did he not know? "Why are you here?" I tried to change the subject, but I could already tell by the look in my brother's eyes he wasn't having it.

"What's your deal?" He glanced around my small apartment. "You don't even live here anymore—You fucked her!" Pat exclaimed before he slapped me on the back.

I grunted, "Don't talk about Jillian like that. Remember what happened the last time, Pat? She's your soon to be your sister-in-law," I reminded him.

He chuckled. "You're not denying it." Pat dropped onto my couch making himself comfortable. "Hey, I got a blowjob from one of the strippers last night." He puffed out his chest as if it was something to be proud of. "Which you would have known if you hadn't left my bachelor party early."

"I got your text."

"Bet your night was better."

"Not talking about my sex life with you." Christ, that was more than I wanted to share with him.

"Ha! So you did sleep with Jillian?" Pat grinned. "Are you two back together? You can ditch Mads now?" He lifted his right leg to rest his foot on his knee. "Because honestly, she's a drag, dude. Jo hates her, and I'm not really fond of her myself. She was always hanging off me when we hung out even though she knew I was with Jo. Pretty sure she slept with Knox while he was still dating Jillian and that's why they broke up." He stopped to stare at me.

I ran my hand through my hair yanking on the ends. "Thirsty? I have water," I mumbled, making my way to the kitchen to pull out two cold bottles from the fridge. I handed Pat one as I sat down next to him.

Pat narrowed his eyes at me. "I thought you would be doing cartwheels or something. You've been pretty hung up about Jillian for years. You love her, right?" When I nodded, he opened his bottle to take a swig. "What aren't you telling me?"

"I fucked up," I answered.

"How bad?"

I let out a loud sigh. "Really fucking bad." I dropped my eyes down to the floor. "I married Madison yesterday," I confessed.

Patrick shot up so fast I expected him to trip over the coffee table. "Wait, you did what?" he exclaimed. "You just told me you loved Jillian, bro, how can you go and marry that sea creature?" His eyes were wide when I looked back up.

"She's not that bad." She was pretty, but not nearly as beautiful as Jillian.

"What the fuck is wrong with you?"

"You can leave if you're going to act like an asshole." I pointed toward the door and for a second, I thought Pat was going to do just that, but instead, he sat back down. "What?" I asked as my brother stared at me.

Pat shook his head. "I don't know what to say."

I snorted. "That makes two of us." I leaned back against the couch. "I love Jillian. With all my heart and soul. She is it for me, man, but—"

"She left," Pat finished my sentence. "I know. I saw what happened when Jill was in your life. You became my brother again. The Hutch you were before...then when she left?" He shrugged as he took another swig of his water. "You lost your ever-loving mind on us." Pat glanced up at the ceiling. "You have to get rid of the trash."

"Watch it. Mads is the mother of my daughter," I growled.

"Jo slapped her this morning."

Water nearly sprang from my nostrils and it took a good sixty seconds to gather myself together. "That must have been something to see." I chuckled. "How exactly did that go down?" I asked.

"I missed it, but from what Jo told me, Madison went over to gloat about marrying you." Pat paused. "You're bringing her as your plus one tonight to rehearsal and to the wedding, right? I don't want her to start any drama, bro, I'm serious. This is my damn wedding day, and Jo doesn't deserve that. I want her to have the best day ever. I will personally remove Madison myself if she starts anything."

I felt my stomach clench. "Don't worry. I'll make sure she doesn't do anything stupid," I promised.

***

Madison had gone all out for the rehearsal dinner tonight, making sure that she was dressed to the nines. I'll admit the dress she had looked good on her, with the tight waist, and the perfect blue that brought out the color in her eyes, but I knew she would never compare to whatever Jillian was wearing. The dress was sleeveless, Madison's arms were toned and tanned, her legs looked long and lean, but I couldn't help feeling well, nothing when I saw her. I had made a huge mistake marrying her, but that was my own fault, and I couldn't back out now.

"Well?" Madison placed her hands firmly on her hips. "What do you think, baby?" She twirled around to give me the full effect. "It's perfect, right?" She batted her over coated lashes at me.

"Perfect," I echoed Madison's words, even though I didn't feel the same.

She pouted. "Come on, I spent a lot on this for you." She touched the skirt. "It's special," Madison murmured as she fingered the fabric.

"You're right." I didn't want to upset her tonight. I needed her on her best behavior for my brother and for his future wife. "You look beautiful." I dropped a kiss against the top of her head, knowing she wouldn't want me to wrinkle her outfit or makeup. "It will look even better on the floor later when I take it off you," I added to make her smile.

Madison beamed happily at me. "You look great, too, babe." She let her eyes wander down my body at the green dress shirt and black slacks I had on. "Too bad we don't have time for a quickie before we go." She dragged her teeth across her bottom lip.

Fat chance. "Tonight," I assured her, lying through my teeth. "Before we go"—I stopped Madison as she was about to open the front door—"promise me something." I pushed a piece of blonde hair behind her ear.

Her brows dipped. "What?" Her voice dropped. "If this is about Jillian or Jo, please spare me."

"This is Pat and Jo's wedding rehearsal." I ignored the look on her face. "I don't want to ruin this for them. For my brother and future sister-in-law. Your brother-in-law," I reminded her. I cupped her face with my hands. "Let's just play nice with everyone for the next couple of days so everybody is happy." I slid my lips over Madison's as she sighed.

"Fine, but only because I love you."

The rehearsal dinner was being held at the same location as the Jack and Jill, and was only a few minutes away from the apartment we shared over Zed's Automotive. When we arrived a few minutes later, Madison chuckled softly under her breath as she turned to face me with a smirk on her pretty face.

"Remember what you were saying to me back at the apartment?" Her smile told me something big was about to hit me in a not-so-good way. "I think you might want to remember that when you see who Jillian brought as her date, again, tonight." I swear she might be enjoying this.

At first, all I could see was Jillian. She looked so beautiful I could hardly breathe. Her dress had thin straps that clung to her shoulders, and the dress itself fell right above her knees with some sort of sheer lace hanging from the trim. The color, fuck me, it was a beautiful maroon that just seemed perfect for her, and it was designed to make her legs look like they were a mile long. It wasn't until she turned to her right to speak to whoever was standing next to her that I realized just exactly what Madison had been talking about.

Fucking Knox. Again.

I couldn't tear my gaze away as rage tore through my body while Jillian touched his arm, smiled up at him, and laughed at something Knox said. I was going to jail tonight because he'd be murdered by my bare hands.

"Look who made it." Patrick threw his arm over my shoulder. "Relax, calm down, and take a deep breath," he whispered as he turned me away from the sight I was so intent on. "Want a drink, brother?" He held up two beers in his hand. "One of these is for you, as long as you promise to behave tonight and not commit murder." He tried to make it sound like he was kidding, but I saw right through him.

I grabbed the bottle and drank it all down. "Thanks," I mumbled before I glanced over at Madison who had her lips pinched together. "Let's go sit down," I suggested, but when I tried to take her hand, she pushed mine away.

That's how it went for most of the night. Madison ignored me, making sure to play nice with everyone else. She talked a lot with Belle and Claire, was polite with Knox when he stopped at the table to congratulate Jo and Pat, even nodding at me without saying anything. Madison stepped away to go speak with my parents, Brent and Joan Kelly, as well as saying a quick hello to Jillian and Jo's mother, Emily. However, she made sure to stay as far away from Jillian and Jo as possible. I think she was a little afraid of what might happen if she did, considering Jo slapped her this morning. That didn't stop Jillian from coming to me instead.

"This is adorable." She dragged her finger in the air between the two of us. "The two of you, married and all. Just sitting here looking like the perfect fucking couple." She slurred her words, which made me realize she was drunk out of her mind.

I stood up. "Where's your date?" This was bound to get ugly fast with these two. I needed to defuse this before it got worse.

"None of your business."

"Go sit down, Jills, you're embarrassing yourself." Madison rolled her eyes.

Jillian took a step forward. "What did I tell you about using that nickname, huh?" she hissed. "How does she know that nickname, Hutch?" She turned her eyes on me. "Did you tell her?"

"You're drunk." I moved quickly around the table. "You need to go sit back down."

"Don't touch me!" Jillian cried when I placed my hands on her arms. "Hey, I got one for you, Mads. Come closer so I can tell you a secret." She giggled loudly. "Hutch was a virgin until me. I took his V card," she tried to whisper, but it sounded too loud to me.

I grabbed Jillian by her hips. "You're done," I growled and carried her right outside through the back of the restaurant before she could say anything else. She flailed against me, trying to kick me any which way she could, and got me a couple of times in the shin and knee before I nearly dropped her onto the ground. "Grow up," I warned.

"Fuck you," she spat back.

I pointed a finger in Jillian's face. "You're drunk, Jilly, and you don't know what you're saying right now." I watched the way her eyes moved over me. The hurt in her greens, the way her face crumpled. I had done to Jillian exactly what she had done to me. "I'm sorry," I whispered.

"I hate you."

It was like a slap across my face. Three words that I never thought I would hear from her mouth. "You don't...Jillian, you don't mean that. That's just the alcohol talking." I wanted to hit something. I wanted to turn back the clock, and go back to that night I first told Jillian I loved her, beg her to stay, and then everything wouldn't be so messed up right now.

"Oh, but I do, Hutch. I know that I hurt you, I understand that, but what you did?" Her chin trembled as she spoke. "It's so much worse. You can't just unmarry someone. It's not a switch you turn off because you changed your mind." Jillian squared her shoulders. "We're done. We will get through the wedding tomorrow, dance together like two adults, take pictures together, and after that? I *never* want to speak to you again."

I reached for her, but she slapped me away. "I can't lose you again," I admitted.

A sob crossed with a laugh escaped her mouth. "Are you serious? Now you think about that?" she exclaimed.

"It's okay." She waved her hand at someone, and when I turned, I saw Knox standing there. "You want to hit him, Hutch? Because at least I didn't marry him behind your back. When I get married, you'll know all about it before it actually happens." She pushed past me and Knox, who stared at me with wide eyes.

"I don't need any commentary from you," I warned before I marched back into the restaurant. Jillian was gone, Madison was sitting where I left her with her arms crossed over her chest, while Pat and Jo danced together looking like the happy couple they were.

Knox made sure to knock my shoulder as he made his way past me. "Don't worry, bro, I'll take good care of Jill for you. You don't have to worry about that." He grinned at me as he went out the front door.

Chapter Twenty-Five

Jillian

I sat with my arms wrapped around my legs, my gaze fixed outside the window. I wasn't sure how long I had been sitting here, but it felt like forever. I had watched Hutch show up to his parents' place, stop and look up toward where I was, before he finally went inside. I knew he was getting dressed with Pat because Jo had told me so.

A lump formed in my throat, but I pushed it down as I thought about how I was going to have to put on a fake face today at the wedding. I'd need to stand next to Hutch, take pictures with him, and actually dance with him as if he didn't crush every single dream I had. Like my heart didn't matter. I would do it because I loved my sister and Pat enough. I just hoped that I didn't break down crying before the wedding was over.

"Sweetheart…" Mom brushed a piece of hair from my forehead. "You need to get ready." Her voice was soft, caring, and once again I had to resist the urge to break down sobbing. "I know," she whispered when I looked up at her.

I dropped my legs down so that I could wrap my arms around my mother's waist without saying anything. "I only have myself to blame," I told her. "I'm the one that left, was Hutch supposed to just wait for me? He moved on." I looked up to find her with her lips pressed together.

"Scoot over, sweetie." When I did, she sat down next to me. "I'm going to tell you something, but you cannot repeat this to anyone." She wrapped her arm around my shoulders, and I rested my head against hers. "About a year after you left, Hutch came to see me."

I sat back up. "He did what?" I knew Hutch had changed, but it couldn't have been that soon.

"He was so hurt, Jillian, he wanted to talk to you so bad, but I couldn't give him the answers that he wanted." Mom gave me a half smile. "He asked me what school you were at. He just wanted to see you, and so?" She touched my cheek. "I gave it to him."

"He never came to see me."

"Are you sure about that?"

I sat back. "Hutch came to see me?" He never reached out to me when he was in New York.

She nodded. "He said he watched you dance, how beautiful you looked up on stage, and he realized that you belonged there." She gathered me against her again. "That boy loves you. He loved you enough to come to me, ask for my help, and when he realized that you were where you belonged, he backed off."

"I hated it there," I reminded my mother.

Mom sighed. "You didn't like the city, but you still loved dancing. We really do need to get ready." She released me to stand up. "I'm sorry things didn't work out with the two of you, but Knox is a decent boy."

"I'm not with Knox, Mom, he's just a friend." I wasn't going to marry him. I wasn't sure I would ever marry anyone. Ballet was my husband now.

She held out her hand. "Come on, sweetheart." She hugged me tight again once I got to my feet. "Remember I love you," she whispered.

***

Jo was a vision in her wedding dress. It was a ball gown with sheer tulle and a V-neck bodice that had a vintage-inspired lace appliques, delicate spaghetti straps, and a cutout back. All the work my mother put into it was worth it the moment Patrick saw her walk down the aisle because his face lit up like a kid on Christmas morning, and then he nearly burst into tears. Hutch was able to calm him down, but not before we made eye contact that only caused butterflies to build inside my stomach. I quickly looked away, but I could feel Madison staring daggers into my back. I made sure to keep my eyes straight ahead for the rest of the ceremony, hoping that the ground would open up and swallow me.

The wedding was beautiful, and I couldn't have been happier for Jo and Pat. They knew the moment they shared their first kiss all those years ago that they were going to get married someday, and even though I might be a little jealous, I knew they were meant to be together.

Once the minister pronounced them husband and wife, I turned to find Hutch holding out his arm for me. I wanted to refuse, but I had no other choice. Electricity crackled as our skin touched. I hated him. I hated myself for what I did. I wish I could go back in time to change everything, but I didn't own a time machine.

"You look beautiful, Jills." Hutch's husked voice sent shivers up my spine.

I glared up at him only to trip over my dress in the sand. "Don't speak to me," I hissed back. "We talked about this."

A sly smile spread across his handsome face. "You spoke about this." He chuckled, keeping me from tripping again. "I know that weddings are all about the bride, but for me? It was all about you. Your tits look great in that dress. Thank your mom for me."

I smacked him across the chest with the bouquet. "You're an asshole," I croaked as the sunset blinded me. Did I mention they got married on the beach? Very cliché around here, but it's what my sister wanted. "Where's your wife?" I seethed.

"Probably wishing you were dead."

"That's how I feel about you." I yanked my arm away from him in time to see the hurt in his eyes. "Don't talk to me. We're here for a wedding and I promised Jo I wouldn't ruin her big day." I turned to find Knox standing there.

He looked between the two of us. "You alright, babe?" I really wish he wouldn't call me that. We weren't dating, we weren't fucking, and we certainly hadn't kissed. I think Knox just liked to push Hutch's buttons to see how far he'd take it.

I moved closer to him. "Perfect now," I assured him as Hutch stalked away. "Thanks," I added.

"He's hurting pretty bad."

I rolled my eyes. "He's married."

"You still love him, though."

I leaned my head against his shoulder. "More than ever." I felt my chin begin to quiver. "Shit, I can't mess up my makeup. We still have more pictures to take." I smiled when Knox handed me a tissue. "Thanks." I dabbed lightly at my face.

"Pretty sure that Madison wants to throttle you."

"Why? She's the big winner in all of this. She got the guy."

Knox looked like he was going to say something else, but was interrupted by the wedding planner, Stella, announcing that she needed all the members of the wedding party together for some pictures. "Remember to smile, Jillian." Hutch grinned at me, and I resisted the urge to flip him off.

Instead, I flashed a fake smile, batted my lashes, and lifted the skirt of my dress with one hand, while holding my bouquet of flowers in the other so I wouldn't trip and fall headfirst into the sand and made my way over to where the photographer and the rest of the wedding party were starting to gather.

"This is probably one of the most beautiful settings for a wedding I've been to in a long time," Brooklyn Shepard, the photographer, told Jo, and I couldn't figure out if she was telling the truth or not. I knew that Jo said she came highly recommended and she had gushed over every single one of her pictures she had looked at. "I really love the beach." She added, pushing a piece of dark hair behind her ear. "Okay, can we have the bride, groom, maid of honor, and best man first?" Brooklyn made a motion for the four of us to move out front.

I tried not to groan aloud, but from the way Jo shot me the evil eye, I was pretty sure that plan didn't work. "*Sorry,*" I mouthed as I stood awkwardly next to my now ex-boyfriend who looked like he was enjoying this more than he should.

"Jo, Pat, I want you two to stand next to one another but with your backs to me. Then I want Hutch next to Jo, and Jillian next to Hutch, also with your backs to me." Brooklyn nodded as we assembled the way she instructed. "Great, good. Okay, now the sisters hold hands behind Hutch, while the brothers fist bump over the bride." Then she snapped a few photos. "These are great, thank you." She told us. "Now, Pat, I want you to grab your wife for a kiss, and I want you to high-five your brother while Jillian looks annoyed." Brooklyn tugged at the camera strap around her neck.

I snorted. "I think I can handle that part." I smirked as Brooklyn raised her camera. I had to admit she had a lot of great ideas, although it was hard when she suggested a couple ones with just Hutch and me cuddled up together. He seemed to take it all in a smooth stride, wrapped his strong arms around me, and held me close. Hutch smelled amazing, like he had bathed in soap that was meant to cause my knees to grow weak, warmth to spread over my body, and desire to build inside my stomach.

"Everything alright, Jilly?" His lips brushed the back of my ear. "You seem tense."

I tried to ignore him. I tried to pretend that this was nothing other than a part I was playing. Dancing on the stage with an audience watching. Until I felt his hard length against my backside. "You fucking pig," I hissed. "Your wife is right over there, and you're getting off on this?" I dug my nails into Hutch's hands as he laughed.

"I get off on you."

"Let go of me."

Hutch tightened his grip around my waist. "You're going to cause a scene, right here, right now, while our siblings are so happy?" he dared.

Brooklyn brought the camera down. "Thank you all so much." She beamed happily.

"Hutch, Jillian, you two are a couple, right?"

"Yes."

"Hell no," I blurted out, only to slap my hand over my mouth.

Brooklyn's eyes went wide. "I'm sorry, I thought…Jo had said you were together." She looked so upset that I felt terrible.

I kicked my leg against Hutch's shin, and when he let go of me, I rushed to the photographer. "Brooklyn, I shouldn't have said that to you." I touched her arm. "It's… complicated with us." I flashed a quick smile, hoping I didn't offend her.

"Trust me, I understand complicated," she assured me as a smile pulled at her lips. "My husband and I had a very rocky relationship in the beginning. I thought he was the most arrogant man I had ever met, but things changed."

Hutch gasped, "I knew you looked familiar! You're married to Rand Shepard, aren't you?"

I had no idea who that was. "Who?" I looked between the two of them.

"He's a NASCAR driver, Jills, remember I had his shirt on the night of our first date?" Hutch's brows dipped.

Nope, I did not remember the shirt. The shirt he had on was stretched to its limits across his very thick and muscled chest. "Sorry, doesn't compute." I shrugged as if I could care less.

"He's my husband, yes." Brooklyn was flipping through her tablet. "He's actually back at the Ocean View Hotel right now, totally bored out of his mind. He hates weekends off, but didn't want to stay home alone so he tagged along with me." She glanced back up. "Come by tomorrow so you can meet him. I promise you he's not the dick everyone thinks he is." She grinned. "I'll catch you both later for more pictures." She wandered off to get the rest of the wedding party.

I batted my lashes. "Oh, you get to meet your idol," sarcasm dripped from my tongue.

"Knock it off, Jillian," Hutch warned.

"What time is this happening because I want to see this go down?" I wish I had my phone so I could look this guy up. Brooklyn was super gorgeous so I had to expect Rand to be equally attractive.

"You wish."

"You bringing the little lady? I'm sure that's right up her ally."

"Watch it."

"Or what?" I rolled my eyes. "Remember you started this, so make sure you can finish it, big boy. I told you to leave me alone. Not to talk to me unless you had to. So if you can't play in the big leagues, Hutch, maybe you should go back and sit at the kids' table."

Hutch stared at me for a second before he just stomped off, leaving me there by myself. What the hell was that about? He could dish it out, but couldn't take it? He had been flirting with me all day too. I decided to let it go and went to find Knox and drown my sorrows in the top shelf booze my sister and now brother-in-law had provided.

Chapter Twenty-Six

Hutch

I felt my stomach turn and wondered if the prime rib I just finished might actually make a reappearance. Shit, why did I agree to do this? Pat had actually said I could record the best man's speech if I felt more comfortable, and now I was thinking that might have been the better option. I wiped the palm of my hands over my legs. My chest was heaving with every single breath I took, and I was sure that I was going to pass out.

"I'll be right back." I bolted from the seat next to Madison, sprinting out of the tent, and tried to catch my breath. Bad idea, bad idea, fucking goddamn bad idea. I yanked at my hair just as I felt a hand on my elbow and whirled around with my teeth bared, ready to rip whoever apart until I saw it was Jillian. "What?" I growled. "Here to tease me some more about getting the chance to meet my favorite NASCAR driver?"

Her green eyes softened. "No, it just looked like you were having a panic attack, and I thought...never mind." Jillian turned to leave.

"Wait." I watched as she slowly turned back around. "I am, or I was, about to have a panic attack, but not now. I mean...shit." I ran my hand through my hair again. "Just don't go yet," I begged.

Jillian brows dipped with worry. "I thought you weren't having those anymore?" She took a step closer.

"I wasn't, but this speech has me all fucked up. Pat told me I could record it so I wouldn't have to do it in front of a crowd of people, but I thought I would be okay, but now? Now I feel like I'm going to puke, shit myself, and pass out all at once."

Jillian exploded in laughter only to slap her hand over her mouth. "I'm sorry, that isn't funny." She tried to keep herself quiet only to start giggling again. "Could you imagine?" She pressed her lips together.

I chuckled. "If I barfed all over the table, shit my pants, and then passed out, making sure to smack my head really good on the way down?" The thought had me rolling so hard I had tears streaming down my face.

"Oh Jesus, that would really ruin everything." Jillian pressed a hand to her stomach as she tried to calm herself.

I couldn't help the smile that spread across my face. "What a story though." I roared with laughter.

"My stomach, please, I can't." She snickered.

My eyes moved behind Jillian to Patrick. Shit, was it time? I froze at the thought, and even though we had just been laughing about what could happen, it might actually come true. I glanced over to Jillian who brushed the front of her dress down.

"It's time for your toast, Hutch." Pat looked between the two of us. "I hope that I'm not interrupting." A smile pulled at his lips.

Jillian lifted a shoulder. "Nope, not at all. We were just going over the toast together. I'm going to help."

Pat looked confused. "Help? I thought you weren't on speaking terms." His eyes darted between the two of us.

"Things change, brother, so deal with it." Jillian didn't let him finish. She held out her hand to me and wiggled her fingers. "The speech," she reminded.

I stared at her. "What are you talking about?" I was confused. I thought she hated me, so why would she want to help me out?

"Give me your speech, Hutch."

I took the folded-up papers from my pocket and gave them to her. When Jillian started to walk back inside, I grabbed her and pulled her back against my chest. "You're not going to make me look bad, are you, bean?" I looked down into her beautiful face.

"You trust me, don't you, Hutch?"

I trusted her more than anyone. Even now. "Yes," I answered, then relaxed my grip so that Jillian could go inside, but followed behind just enough so I could see and hear what she was going to say.

Jillian took the microphone and smiled nervously, unfolded the paper, and looked around the tent. "As most of you know, Hutch Kelly is the best man. He's the older brother of Pat, and he's an amazing guy. Since we're being honest, I'll just admit to you all that he's my best friend." My heart thumped like crazy against my ribs. Fuck, this might be worse. Maybe I shouldn't stand here and listen. "Hutch is, well, the perfect guy, no matter how you put it, but he's not one for crowds, and so I offered to read his speech today. I hope you all are okay with that."

Jillian stopped to take a drink of her champagne, and I took a deep breath. "You just need to imagine I'm Hutch now." The crowd broke into laughter, which helped me too, and Jillian smiled as she began to read my speech.

"Patrick was always the one I looked up to, even if I was the older brother. He never judged or picked on me, even at my darkest times. He helped me whenever I needed him, and looked out for me when I couldn't do the same. When Pat was born, I was so excited to have a brother because I had never liked being an only child. When we were younger, before we grew up and discovered girls, sports, and beer, we used to build forts in our rooms, and pretend that we lived in the city. That we had wives, kids, and jobs. Stupid shit like that that didn't matter, but when you're playing make-believe, it does." She paused to look over at me before she went on. "Pat always knew he wanted to marry Jo from the moment they met. Whenever we played like that, his wife was named Jo. Even if she didn't know it yet, they were destined to be together."

Jillian stopped to swipe at her eyes before she continued.

"The first date they had, Pat came home, and told me Jo was it. They were thirteen, or maybe fourteen years old. They had been going to school together for a couple of years, had been friends just as long, but that first date had sealed the deal for him. Pat knew Jo was his forever. They had gone to the carnival, which is pretty much the first date of every single couple in this town, and he had kissed her on the Ferris wheel."

Jillian stopped again, and I noticed her hands were shaking. She flashed a brief smile before she took another gulp of her drink and then started reading again. "With everything I went through, you both were always there. You always tried to make me feel included and gave me the space I needed when I wanted it. I know that it couldn't have been easy at times when I was so moody, and when my mind went to seriously dark places. I am so lucky, Patrick, that you are my brother, and now I can officially call Jo my sister. Congratulations!"

When the tent exploded into applause, I took that as my chance to catch a some fresh air. Jillian didn't need to do that for me. I was the biggest asshole in the world, and I did not deserve her.

"That was perfect, Hutch." Jo's voice drifted through my thoughts. "You need to make this right between the two of you."

My shoulders slumped forward. "How? I married Madison." I sighed as I glanced out over the water, watching the tide roll in.

"I don't know, er, maybe a divorce? Annulment? One of those should do it. You still love Jill, and she loves you. She saved your ass out there."

"Tell me something that I don't already know."

Jo moved so that she was facing me. "Why? Why did you marry Madison when Jill is the one you're meant to be with? I don't understand." She placed her hands on her hips to stare up at me with eyes that matched her sister's.

"I was furious with Jills for not giving me the answers that I had been waiting for. She was here, but not in my arms. She left without telling me goodbye. I loved her with everything I had, and my heart was broken," I admitted. "It was childish, but I had my daughter to think about."

"People have children all the time without getting married, Hutch," Jo pointed out. "You should have told Jillian the truth before you slept with her. You hurt her."

"I hurt her? What about me!" I yelled, not caring who heard. "You can't just brush that under the rug, Jo. I trusted her. I gave her everything I had, and she fucking left. I gave Jillian my heart and she promised to make it work when she left. You know what, I'm not talking about this with you anymore." I started to walk away only to have Jillian catch up with me.

"I need to talk to you before I leave."

I stopped. "What do you mean *leave*? Are you going back to New York?" The thought had my head spinning.

"No, I just meant the wedding. I'm staying." She licked her lips. "Here, in Ocean View. I bought the ballet studio. I should probably thank you for letting me know it was available."

I stared down into Jillian's face as the sound of the waves crashed behind us. "You're staying." I was going to have to see her every single day.

"Look, it doesn't have to be weird or awkward with us. We can say hello on the streets. There will be family gatherings and stuff. I'm sorry, okay? I'm sorry that I ruined what we had. I regretted it the moment I walked out your door."

"Don't do that. Not now."

Jillian threw her hands up. "I'm trying to apologize, Hutch! I fucked everything up, and I can't go back to fix it now. You're married. I want you to be happy. We can't avoid one another forever. So I just want to start over with a clean slate. Can we do that? I'm sorry for the things I said to you when I was drunk, because you know I didn't mean them." I saw the way her chin trembled. How her eyes begged me to say yes.

I shook my head.

Her eyes wet wide. "What?" She stared at me. "Why not?" Jillian asked.

"Because I love you." I grabbed the nape of her neck and brought my mouth down to hers to kiss her soft, plump lips. Jillian didn't fight me, didn't try to pull away, and I heard her moan softly when my tongue slipped between her lips. "If I can't have you, how do you expect me to be your friend, Jilly?" I pulled back. "We can never be just friends. The thought of you with someone else makes me see red," I warned.

Jillian nostrils flared. "You would rather ignore me?" She narrowed her eyes. "You would rather punish me for something I have done nothing but apologize for since I returned, then tried to make things civilized between us? I just saved your ass back there, Hutch."

A piece of my heart cracked off inside my chest. If I couldn't have Jillian, couldn't love her the way I wanted, I would rather she hate me. "Yes." My voice caught in my throat. "Thank you for everything you have done for me." I patted her shoulder. "You're a good person." I just couldn't have her near me. Not right now and probably not in my future either. "Good luck," I added before I headed back inside the tent, making sure not to turn around because I was sure if I did I would chicken out.

I grabbed Madison from her chair to drag her out onto the dance floor and danced with her the rest of the wedding. I noticed Knox a couple of times, but I didn't care to spy on him, only because I didn't want to knock him out. This wasn't my wedding after all. If Jillian wanted to date him, that wasn't my problem. I had my own demons to work out.

Later that night, when I was lying in bed with Madison, who passed out before she could try to get me to sleep with her, I choked back tears and realized what a mess my life had become. I hated myself for letting Jillian get away again, but I only had myself to blame.

Chapter Twenty-Seven

I woke up earlier than I should for someone who drank too much champagne at her sister's wedding the night before, but I was lucky if I was able to get a couple of hours of sleep once my head hit the pillow. I kept thinking about Hutch, the words he said to me, and the fact that he told me we could never be friends. How could I ignore him for the rest of my life? Tears stung my eyes, but I blinked them away.

I sat up, pulled the blanket back, and swung my legs over the side of the bed. No, I had a big day ahead of me today. I was going to get the keys to the studio, see what kind of work I really had cut out for me, and then maybe start putting some ideas together. I wasn't going to sit there and feel sorry for myself because Hutch Kelly decided he didn't even want to say hello to me.

I stood up, making my way to the bathroom, noticing how quiet the house was. Jo hadn't lived here in a couple of years, but had stayed the few days, leading up to the wedding. She and Pat were supposed to be leaving today for their honeymoon to Alaska. Mom was a notorious morning person, but after the way she was kicking up her heels on the dance floor last night, I wasn't surprised to find her still sleeping.

I stripped out of my tank top, sleep shorts, and panties, making sure to dump them in the hamper before I turned on the water and stepped into the bathtub. The water felt good rolling off my skin as I let myself wash off everything that happened last night. I scrubbed my skin until it felt clean, washed and conditioned my hair, and then finally turned off the water, afraid that I would use up all the hot before my mother had a chance to shower. I toweled off and wrapped my hair up on my head, trying not to stare at myself in the mirror.

Once I was done in the bathroom, I cleaned up after myself before I went to dig something out of my suitcase to wear. I stopped in the doorway of my childhood bedroom, realizing I needed to find my own place. Mom wouldn't care if I stayed—actually she would most likely love it—but I would do so much better if I was able to find a cute little apartment of my own. I made a mental note as I was yanking on a clean pair of underwear to look around town today and see if anything was available.

My mother was siting when I made my way downstairs, her hands wrapped around a cup of tea. "Good morning, sweetheart." She flashed me a smile. "Where are you off to this morning?" She brought the mug up to her lips to blow on the hot liquid.

"Going to check out the ballet studio. I need to see how much work actually has to be done." I opened the cabinet, grabbed a K-cup, and popped it into the Keurig. I yanked the top off a travel mug to take that with me. My mother wasn't a coffee drinker, but made sure she kept the stuff around for drinkers like myself. I leaned casually against the counter. "I thought I would look for an apartment while I was out," I added.

"You don't need to do that," she insisted.

I twisted my lips. "Mom, I'm twenty-two. I shouldn't be living here, mooching off you, and drinking your coffee." I smiled.

"I like having you here." Which was really her way of telling me she didn't want to be alone in this big house.

I took my now-full coffee cup over to where the sugar was. "You could get a dog," I suggested. "Or travel like you always talked about doing." I wasn't sure what she wanted me to tell her. After Dad passed away, Mom knew that this day was going to come. Jo and I weren't going to stay kids forever. When she didn't say anything, I turned around to find her just staring at me with a look in her eyes I didn't recognize. "Mom, are you okay?"

She nodded. "Your father and I always talked about traveling when you girls moved out and started your own family." She sighed softly. "It's just too bad he won't be here to enjoy this with me."

I moved closer so that I could hug her. "I miss Dad, too," I whispered, my voice clogged.

"Now, now, don't go getting me started again." Mom scoffed. "I cried enough last night. Go on." She pretended to push me away. "Send me some pictures of the studio," she added as I headed toward the door.

I assured her I would as I made my way down the front steps. I couldn't help but look in the direction of Hutch's apartment, even though I knew he wasn't there. The memories of everything we had hit me, and I quickly rushed down the sidewalk before I started crying. The tourists were up and out early as I made my way past the Angry Egg and the Ocean View Hotel, before I finally found myself in front of the ballet studio.

My ballet studio. When I had spoken to the realtor and explained to him I wanted to purchase the studio, he seemed surprised. After Madam had retired, no one had wanted to buy the building, so it had been sitting here empty for nearly three years. We had a quick meeting inside, where I got a quick glimpse inside, and I told him I would take it. I signed the contract, he gave me the keys, and that was it. Today was really the first day that I would have all the time in the world I would need to look around.

As I pulled my keys from my pocket, I thought I heard my name being called out, and when I turned around, I saw Brooklyn, the photographer, from the wedding, waving before she headed toward me.

"Hi." I smiled at her.

"Are you an early riser too?" She grinned happily with her covered coffee in her hand.

I nodded. "I'm pretty sure it's from the years of dance drilled into my head." I giggled. "What about you?"

"Rand." She hooked a thumb over her shoulder just as a giant man—covered in tattoos—came walking up behind her. "NASCAR is hard work. He's up early for practice, races, meetings, you name it."

I stared up into the blue eyes of her husband as he gave me a quick glance only to wrap his arms around his wife. He was at least a foot taller than I was and amazingly handsome. Rand's arms were thick and muscled, his shoulders as broad as they were wide. He planted a kiss on top of Brooklyn's head. "Darlin', this place reminds me of where I grew up."

His southern accent was thick. They seemed like complete and total opposites, but the way he looked at her was something else.

"Rand, this Jillian Robinson," Brooklyn said, adoration in her eyes for her husband before she smiled at me. "She was the maid of honor at the wedding last night."

Rand stuck out his hand. "Rand Shepard. Nice to meet you." His hand swallowed mine as he shook mine.

"We're meeting Hutch for breakfast," Brooklyn announced as Rand moved around her making sure to keep his arm around his wife's shoulders.

"Tell me he suggested the Angry Egg? They have the best breakfast in town."

"That's the place." Rand nodded. "He said something about blueberry pancakes."

I tried not to roll my eyes. "He's absolutely right." That's when I noticed Hutch slowly walking down the street toward where we were standing. He had his hands shoved into the pockets of his jeans while he had his eyes glued to the ground. Was he just nervous because he was going to meet his favorite driver, or was he struggling in general? I shouldn't be worrying about him like that. Hutch's mental wellbeing was no longer my problem.

"Wait, you're a ballet dancer." Brooklyn glanced up at the studio. "Is this yours?" she asked as she took in the massive building.

"Actually, I just bought it." I dangled the keys in my hands. "I was going to take a look at all the work that needs to be done. Get an idea of what I got myself into." I saw that

Hutch had stopped and was staring in our direction. That couldn't be good.

"Hey, Hutch." I flashed a quick smile, trying to bring him into the conversation, despite knowing he didn't want to speak with me.

Hutch's head flew up in our direction, his eyes big and round. "Hey." His expression was a combination of thankful with a side of unease.

Brooklyn introduced her husband to Hutch, and as the two men spoke, she turned back to me. "You should join us for breakfast," she suggested.

Not happening. I shook my head. "Thank you, but I don't want to intrude on—"

"That's a great idea," Hutch chimed in, cutting me off.

I stared at Hutch in shock. His brows were pinched together, his mouth tight, and as I looked at him, I wondered if he was going to have some sort of a panic attack. It was in the way his brown eyes had gone blank. "Hutch, can I talk to you?" My heart thudded in my chest. "Inside for just a moment?" I started to unlock the door to my studio. "Will you excuse us for just a second?" I asked Rand and Brooklyn.

"I know what you're going to say, Jills," he whispered when I spun around to face him once the door was shut behind us.

I narrowed my eyes. "You have no idea what I'm going to say," I spat. "You made it perfectly clear you wanted nothing to do with me last night. I'm not having breakfast with you." I folded my arms over my chest.

"I can't do this alone."

"Maybe you should have brought your wife."

Hutch bit his bottom lip. "Right, of course, my wife." He dragged his hands through his hair. "She doesn't calm me down like you do. You are the only person that makes me feel grounded. I feel like I'm...I feel like I'm falling." Hutch looked like he was going to draw blood with the way he was biting his lip so hard right now.

"Stop." I reached up to touch his arm. "Fine, but we're not pretending to be a couple or something stupid like that." I tried not to wince when Hutch laced his fingers through my hand. What did I just tell him? "Is she working today, because we're going to eat at the Egg."

Hutch shook his head. "No, she's going to visit her parents with Hazel," he told me. "Thank you, Jilly."

"Don't thank me yet, Hutch, we haven't gotten you through this." I removed my hand from his, and opened the door. "Looks like there will be four of us for breakfast." I tried to put a big smile on my face and hoped it looked genuine. I liked Brooklyn and I actually wanted to get to know her. She seemed like a cool person to hang around.

Brooklyn clapped her hands together. "Yay! I was wondering if maybe I could take some pictures of your studio afterward? It would photograph so well."

I nodded. "Sure, of course." I had no problem with that all.

She clapped her hands again before she threw her arms around me. "Thank you!" She crushed me tightly against her. "I have a feeling that you and I are going to be best friends by the end of the day." She pulled back to look at Rand.

"I thought I was your best friend, darlin'." He winked.

"I meant girlfriend, baby." Brooklyn playfully swatted at his chest.

I glanced at Hutch to find him staring at his feet again. "We should go eat." I nudged his side before I reached down for his hand. "Pancakes are my favorite at the Egg," I blurted out.

"Usually I get chocolate and Hutch gets blueberry so that we can share." His fingers tightened around mine as the four of us began walking. "But everything they serve is the best," I added as Rand stopped to hold the door for us.

"You two aren't a couple, right?" His brows dipped slightly as he caught our fingers tangled together.

I shook my head. "No, just good friends," I said.

Just friends; where one admitted he didn't want to be around me, while the other only wanted to make things right. It was going to be a long and painful morning.

Chapter Twenty-Eight

Jillian

The four of us were now seated at a booth. Rand and Brooklyn on one side with Hutch, and myself on the other. I made sure that Hutch and I were facing the door because I knew he liked to have a view of the exit in case he needed it. I didn't need to open the menu, so instead I casually looked around the restaurant to see if I recognized anyone before I brought my attention back to Brooklyn who was busy trying to decide what she wanted. I ordered my usual, Hutch got the blueberry pancakes, while the Shepards each picked Belgian waffles with strawberries—Brooklyn with a side of bacon, and Rand with a side of sausage.

"So, Hutch," Rand spoke first, "my wife told me you own your own automotive shop. Have you always enjoyed working on cars?" His giant hand curled around the handle of his mug, and I wondered how he and Brooklyn had met. She had mentioned they didn't exactly get along at first, so I had so many questions.

Hutch chewed nervously on his bottom lip. "Uh, yes, kind of." His voice was hardly a whisper, and I gently placed my hand on his thigh to try to relax him. The muscles in his leg instantly loosened as his hand sought out mine beneath the table. "In the beginning, I wanted to be a big football star." Hutch chuckled. "But...shit happens. I've always been good with my hands, and cars spoke to me, you know?"

Rand nodded. "Me too, man." A smile lit up his face. "I didn't plan on racing stock cars but my big brother was into it, and whatever he did, I had to do, so here we are." The two men shared a laugh as I turned to face Brooklyn.

"How did you meet?" I blurted out before I could stop, myself making sure to keep my voice low and my hand firmly clasped on Hutch's leg. He seemed to have calmed down now.

Brooklyn blushed. "At a race. I was there to take some pictures." She ducked her eyes before she looked over at her husband with love written all over her face. "He really pissed me off the first time we were introduced too. Rand was an egotistical, womanizer asshole, but I couldn't stop thinking about him." She gushed happily.

I tried not let my own feelings show, but when Brooklyn reached across the table to touch my hand, I realized either I couldn't stop them or she just knew. "Do you have any kids?" I didn't want to talk about me so I tried to keep the conversation about her.

"Do you want to see pictures?" Brooklyn quickly slid her phone from her purse. "This is our son, RJ." She flipped through her Instagram. RJ was the spitting image of his father with his dark hair, blue eyes, and long legs. Even the smile was a carbon copy.

"How old is he, because he looks like he's almost as tall as I am!" I teased.

Brooklyn snorted. "He's five, but since Rand is half giant, I think he's going to be seven feet by the time he's done growing." She had a happy twinkle in her eye. "Do you have an Instagram account? Can I add you?"

I told her my IG name and then pulled my phone out to accept her as my account was still private. It was something

I did when I left Hutch, and still regretted it. I followed Brooklyn back and then made my account public again just as the server came with our order. I glanced over at Hutch who gave me a half smile as our plates were put before us.

"Sharing with me, Jills?" He waved his hand over his mouthwatering pancakes.

"Do you have to ask?"

We quickly split our pancakes between us and began to cut them up before we ate them. Why did this have to feel so natural, so normal between us? Why did Hutch want to push me out of his life instead of at least trying to be my friend?

Rand finished chewing his food. "Please excuse my bluntness, but what's the deal with you two?" I saw Brooklyn's head spin as she turned to glare daggers at him. "You're not together or anything, are you? Because I see the way you're eye-fucking one another." He chuckled as he stabbed at another bite of his food.

"Rand Shepard, you can't just say that to people you just met!" Brooklyn warned.

He shrugged. "Sorry, darlin', I can't help myself. I know I'm southern and I'm supposed to be nice, but the heat coming off the two of them is hot enough to burn my face." He grinned at her.

"We broke up," Hutch answered. "I'm married with a daughter now, and it's...fucking complicated."

"Complicated is not the word, man, you two look like—"

"Stop it," Brooklyn cut him off.

Rand grimaced. "Sorry, sorry, I can be a bit much at times," he admitted.

"It's fine," Hutch muttered, but he didn't say much the rest of the meal, and when Rand tried to pay the bill, I thought Hutch might actually throw a punch. What was it they say about meeting your idols? *Never meet your heroes, because they're sure to disappoint you?*

After we finished eating, the guys went down to Zed's Automotive while Brooklyn and I went back to my studio. Hutch assured me that he would be fine now with Rand, but I told him if he needed me, all he had to do was call or text. I hoped that he wouldn't freeze up or freak out, but something told me he was comfortable now after what had happened.

"Can I be nosey?" Brooklyn placed her phone in her back pocket after texting her friend to check up on her son.

I let out a nervous laugh. "It's that obvious?" I had hoped I had kept my feelings hidden.

"He knows you still have feelings for him." She dragged her teeth across her bottom lip.

I let out a slow breath. "I left him without saying goodbye the night we confessed our love to one another, and broke his heart. Hutch is a gentle soul, and I have never met another man like him, Brooklyn." I dropped my head down so she couldn't see the tears that threatened to fall.

"First of all"—Brooklyn touched my arm—"we're friends now that you've cried in front of me, and since my friends call me Sully, I insist you call me that." She pulled a tissue from her purse, which I took to dab at my eyes. "The man I was with before Rand was a horrible, terrible person,

Jillian. I was so closed up to anyone when I met him, and I had said no to dating any more NASCAR drivers, too." She pulled me into a hug. "The whole friends thing seems to be working out alright for the two of you."

"He told me we can't be friends."

The look on Brooklyn's face was priceless when she pulled back to look at me. "Then why did he want you to come today?" She looked confused.

"Because I would do anything Hutch asked me to do." That was the truth. "Anyway, I'm glad he did because we got to spend time together."

We talked for a while as she snapped off some pictures with her camera she took out of her giant purse. She told me she had a sister named London, and how they grew up in Connecticut but now lived in North Carolina since that's where all NASCAR race shops were located. She liked it, but sometimes got homesick. I told her I grew up here, lived in New York for the past four years, but wasn't planning on going back. I hated it.

Hutch stuck his head in the door. "I'm sorry to just barge in, but Rand wanted me to ask if Brooklyn could take a few pictures?" His eyes darted nervously around the studio as he avoided looking at me.

"That's what I do best!" Brooklyn exclaimed as she waved her camera.

Hutch blushed. "This wasn't my idea."

"It's my job, and trust me when I tell you that I love taking pictures, so don't even try to apologize."

We went down to the shop where Brooklyn did just that. She took a few pictures of Rand and Hutch together, which I did too, with my phone, and then she took a few of a couple of the cars that Hutch happened to be working on in the shop for his own personal use. She took a couple of me, had Rand take some of us together, and that was right around when Madison made her appearance with Hazel.

It was the first time I had actually seen Hutch's daughter, and even though she was sleeping, I could already tell she was the most beautiful baby on the planet. Her blonde hair fell in twisted curls around her chubby baby face, and it made me realize another thing I was missing out on with Hutch.

"What's going on here?" Madison's blues eyes moved around the room before they landed on me. "Having a party without me?" A smirk spread across her face as she fussed with her baby in the stroller.

Hutch took a step forward. "I told you I was going to have breakfast this morning," he reminded her.

"You forgot to tell me that it would also include Jillian." Madison said my name as if I had run over her family's cat or something.

Hutch squared his shoulders. "No, with Rand and his wife. Jillian was—"

"Why is she here then?" Madison's nostrils flared as she placed the baby seat on the floor. "She's your ex-girlfriend, Hutch, and in case you've forgotten, I'm your wife. This is our daughter, and I don't think you should be spending any time with Jillian." She bared her teeth like an animal.

"I invited her," Brooklyn spoke up.

Madison didn't even look in her direction. "Was I talking to you, bitch?" she snapped.

"Don't talk to my wife like that." Rand took a step forward, and I saw his eyes flash with anger. I had only just met the man, but something told me he was someone you didn't piss off and get away with.

Brooklyn touched his arm. "Rand."

"You're being rude to my guests, Madison, and I think you should apologize," Hutch growled and dropped his chin.

Madison rolled her eyes. "Is this how it's going to be for the rest of our marriage? I'm going to come home every night to find her here? I thought you said you were done with her." She rolled her eyes before she looked back at me. "I want you to leave," she demanded. When I didn't move, Madison's blue eyes turned dark. "Are you deaf or something? I said I want you to leave."

"Madison!" Hutch roared. "That's enough! Take Hazel and go upstairs. We will deal with this later." At first, I thought Madison wasn't going to listen, but then she quietly picked up the car seat, and left to go upstairs to their apartment, leaving the four of us alone.

Hutch looked mortified. "I'm sorry." His eyes were on me before he looked at Brooklyn. "She never should have spoken to you like that, and I apologize." His shoulder slumped slightly.

Rand snaked his arm around his wife's waist. "You didn't do anything, man, that was all her. I'm just sorry you have to live with her." He surely didn't sugarcoat things.

"I should go now." I started toward the door only to have Hutch grab my elbow and pull me against his chest. He didn't say anything as he held me, his arms tight, and his heart beating wildly in my ear. When he released me, we stared up at one another before Hutch gave me a quick nod and then I started back toward my studio.

That's where Brooklyn found me half an hour later with color swatches, trying to figure out just what would look best. "Knock, knock," she called out. "I just wanted to say goodbye, in case I didn't see you before we left tomorrow."

"I'm glad you did," I told her. "I hope we get to hang out again soon."

Brooklyn nodded. "Rand has already invited Hutch to the next NASCAR race closest to us, but he said Madison isn't invited." She chuckled softly.

"He'll probably bring Pat. I know he'd like to come."

We exchanged numbers before Rand popped in to say goodbye too, and told me I was always welcome at a race, and to come visit them down in North Carolina if I was ever in the area. I stayed at the studio until the sun went down, planning out my next move, figuring out colors and thoughts of what I might like to do next with the place.

It wasn't until I was in bed that night that I remembered the pictures I had taken on my phone, so I uploaded them to my Instagram, and found that Hutch still had his account too, so I tagged him, figuring he would want to see them. The last picture he added was nearly four years ago from when we went to the carnival. I felt my heart stutter in my chest at the memory. I had teased him into creating his account and all the pictures were of us or things we did together that summer. A notification came up saying someone had liked my photos.

Hutch had liked the pictures I had posted, and now that I had made my account public again, he could see the pictures I had posted over the past four years. Not that there were a lot—just pictures of ballet, New York, and with Madison, my roommate. There were a few of me with Knox at the wedding, a couple with Jo at her bachelorette party, and one I took of the beach when I was walking the other morning. When my phone buzzed with a text a few seconds later, I knew it was from Hutch.

Hutch: *Thanks for the pictures, Jills.*

Hutch: *I'm sorry. You know I'll always care about you.*

I didn't respond because I didn't want to engage him in a conversation. Instead, I turned off my phone and tried to go to sleep. But the truth was I loved Hutch, and I wondered if I would ever be able to get over him.

Chapter-Twenty Nine

Hutch

Two years later

I pulled the door open of the ballet studio as Hazel clung to my side. She had been begging me for weeks to sign her up for dance classes ever since she saw the girls leaving one day, dressed in their tutus, and I had promised her I would bring her down, but I secretly had been dreading it. I didn't want to look at Jillian, never mind speak to her, and tell her the truth. That I had royally and completely fucked everything up.

"Hazel-basil, is that you!" Jillian exclaimed when she saw Hazel looking around the ballet studio with big round eyes.

"Jilly!" Hazel giggled happily when Jillian took her from my arms and tickled her little stomach. My daughter loved Jillian something fierce, and at every single family function, she sought her out, much to the horror of my wife.

Jillian hugged Hazel tightly before she finally looked at me. "Hello, Hutch, how are you?" This is usually how it went down between the two of us. Casual conversations at Pat and Jo's house at Thanksgiving or a quick nod if we happened to see one another somewhere, but for the most part, she made sure to avoid me when she could. Like I had told her to. I hurt Jillian in many ways, but this made my life easier if I was being honest.

"I've come to sign my little nugget up for dance class." I hated how lame I sounded.

Jillian nodded. "Sure, of course." She placed Hazel on the floor only to have her run toward the barre and mirrors before she stopped when she remembered the playroom full of toys. She hurried inside to get lost in the dolls, Legos, and action figures that were kept inside.

"Hazel, sweetie, be careful," I called out before I turned back to Jillian. Her dark hair was long enough for her to pull it back into a bun again, and she had put back on the weight she had lost while at school. In my eyes, Jillian was still the most beautiful woman in the world, and always would be.

She dragged her teeth across her bottom lip. "Are you okay?"

"Don't take this the wrong way, Hutch, but I always assumed when this day came, it would be Madison bringing Hazel here." She moved to flip the Closed sign over and locked the door.

"I'd rather not talk about it," I grunted.

Jillian looked hurt, but I meant what I said. My personal life was none of her business, no matter how I felt about her. "Let's go into my office." She turned and I followed behind, grateful I could see into the playroom even from inside.

Jillian's office reminded me so much of her childhood bedroom. It was painted a pastel pink, with posters of ballet on the walls, framed photos of her students, and a few of herself with her friends. I leaned against the doorframe as I watched Jillian take out the paperwork I needed to sign, and wished that I were anywhere else. "She left me," I blurted out before I could stop myself.

Jillian stopped what she was doing. "What?" She blinked at me with confusion all over her face. She placed the paperwork on her desk and sat down. "Explain." Jillian pointed to the empty chair in front of her. "Please, Hutch, I want to know what happened. Despite everything, you know that I still care about you. You're my best friend, remember?" She tried to assure me, but I felt like such a failure.

"Madison told me she didn't want to be married to me anymore because I was always so gloomy." I hung my head in shame wondering if Jillian had heard the rumors flying around town. "She also didn't want to be a mother or a wife, and didn't want to live in Ocean View."

"When?"

"A couple of weeks ago."

Jillian stood up and rounded the desk so that she could wrap her arms around me where I stood, but didn't say anything. I stiffened at first, but relaxed after a moment because it was what I wanted. For Jillian to touch me, hold me, and tell me she loved me. That she would make sure nothing bad would happen, and calm me down when I needed her to. She still smelled the same, felt the same, and I wanted to enjoy this moment, but I knew it was wrong to do so. When Jillian realized I wasn't going to return her embrace, she stepped back to look up at me.

"Maybe now isn't a good time to sign Hazel up for classes." Her green eyes were full of concern. "Maybe you can come back in a couple of weeks. I can hold a spot for her," she suggested.

I shook my head. "Hazel has been talking about this forever, Jills, and I want to give her whatever she wants. I'd give her the moon if she asked me," I told her.

Jillian looked like she wanted to object, but instead handed me the paperwork, and I read it, signed it, and gave it back. "I can give you the money up front." I yanked my wallet from my pocket.

"No." Jillian held up a hand. "It's my treat."

I narrowed my eyes. "I don't need your damn charity," I growled. "I can afford to pay for this." I dropped my card on the desk.

"It's not charity, Hutch, I want to give it as a gift. I love that little girl like she's my own despite what a piece of shit her mother turned out to be." Jillian practically threw my credit card back at me. "You can go now. Classes start next Monday at six o'clock." She held out a piece of paper. "Here is a list of things Hazel will need. If you have any questions, you can stop by or text me anytime."

I grabbed the paper from her. "Thanks," I muttered, "for this, and for trying to comfort me before."

Jillian looked up. "Despite everything, Hutch, I still care about you," she said softly.

I didn't say anything as I told Hazel it was time to leave. She said goodbye to Jillian, and then we went home where she cried when she realized that once again, Mommy wasn't there to tuck her in or read her favorite bedtime story.

I clutched at the cell phone in my hand, wondering if it was too late to text Jillian. The one person I needed to comfort me. Would she ignore me after how I treated her earlier or would she respond? She told me that she still cared about me. Wasn't that exactly what she meant?

Hutch: *Can you talk?*

Jillian: *Of course.*

I stared at my phone for what felt like forever. How was I supposed to tell Jillian what I was thinking? That I wasn't good enough to raise my daughter. That I'd been thinking about taking my life when she wasn't around, but was afraid that Hazel would be the one to find me, and I couldn't put her through something like that. I had given up on therapy because of Madison raging on me, and felt worse than ever.

Jillian: *Hutch? Do you need me to come over? Just say the word, and I'll be there.*

Hutch: *No, you don't have to do that. I'm scared, Jilly.*

Jillian: *What do you mean? Don't say things like that because now you've got me worried.*

Hutch: *I don't want to do that. I'm just having a bad night. How do you not hate me for everything?*

Jillian: *I could never hate you. You were the best thing that ever happened to me. *heart emoji**

Jillian: *Are you sure you don't want me to come over? It won't take long. I won't even pack a bag.*

Hutch: *Just knowing you're here for me right now is the only thing that matters. Good night, Jilly.*

Jillian: *Goodnight, Hutch.*

***

A week later, Hazel started ballet classes and seemed to enjoy them even though I had no idea if she had any talent at all. I just wanted to make my daughter happy. Jillian usually smiled at me when I dropped her off, and the same when I picked Hazel back up which was fine by me. Only I still felt like I was off, and that little by little, I was sinking into something I couldn't dig myself out of.

One day before work, I stopped by the ballet studio and found Jillian dancing. She was all legs and twirls as she moved around the floor, catching me off guard. I was mesmerized as she jumped and leaped before she caught me staring at her.

"Hutch!" Jillian clutched her chest as she giggled. "Is everything alright? Hazel is—"

I nodded. "Hazel is fine," I assured her, trying not to stare at the way her body looked in her leotard. Jillian still had an amazing figure. "I just...I needed someone to talk to, and, never mind." I started to leave, but she touched my arm.

"I can come by at lunch. I have class now, but I have lunch at one. I can bring egg salad sandwiches." Her eyes searched my face as she reached up to touch the scruff against my jawline. Her fingers felt like electricity against my skin.

I shrugged. "Alright." I needed her right this minute, not hours from now.

"Hutch." Jillian kept saying my name like that. Like she knew. "Are you still going to therapy?" She dropped her hand from my face as some of her students began to file in. "After you texted me last week, I was thinking about some of the things you said to me."

My eyes hardened. I knew I never should have let her back in. "That's not any of your business, Jills," I grunted. "I shouldn't have come to you. This was a bad idea." I started out the front door.

"Don't run away from me, please. I only want to help you," she insisted as she followed me outside. I didn't want to hear that shit from her.

I pushed Jillian against the wall of the studio so that I caged her in. "You think I'm crazy or something?" I clenched my teeth together. "Is that it? I don't go to therapy anymore, so there's your answer." I took a step back. "Don't bother to come for lunch. I changed my mind. I'll find someone else to talk to me who doesn't judge me." I turned to head up to the shop.

"Hutch!" Jillian called out to me, but I ignored her. How could she expect me to trust her now after that?

Back at the shop, I told Quinn and Brad, the two guys I had hired when business picked up over and I couldn't do it all myself anymore, that I was taking the day off before I went upstairs to my apartment, hoping it would help if maybe I just slept for a few hours. I grabbed a beer from the fridge, a bottle of Tylenol from the medicine cabinet for the headache that was throbbing behind my eyes, and dropped onto the bed. Hazel was staying with her grandparents for a few days, and that was hard too. Not having anyone to talk to, anyone to check on me, or anyone to just hold me, was starting to drag me down. I kicked my shoes off and laid down on the bed.

I was so tired of all of this.

I didn't want to hurt anymore.

I didn't want to be a burden either.

Maybe everything would be better if I just disappeared.

Chapter Twenty-Nine

Despite Hutch telling me not to bother to come see him or how he acted when I asked him about his therapy, I still went to visit him for lunch. I was worried about his mental health. This wasn't like when we first met; this seemed different if not worse, and I was afraid that he might be more depressed than he was letting on. As I pushed open the door on Zed's, I didn't see Hutch behind the desk, but the bell above the door announced my rival.

"Oh, hey, Jillian." Quinn Sutherland nodded at me. "You here for service?" His cheeks reddened slightly as he realized what he had said. We had gone to high school together, but didn't run in the same circle.

I flashed a brief smile. "No, I came by to see Hutch. Is he in the back?" I nodded toward his office.

Quinn shook his head. "He said he was taking the day off today." He looked confused. "He's probably just upstairs if you want to go up. I'm sure he'd love to see you though. He's been really down lately, you know? Not his normal self." That I already knew, but if his employees were picking up on it too, then he was more off than I thought. He held out a set of keys. "This is for his place. He left a spare in case he or Mads ever locked themselves out."

"Thanks." I grabbed it before I headed back outside and around the corner to hurry up the stairs. I didn't even knock, didn't care how pissed Hutch might be at me. Something about this entire situation was making my skin crawl.

I unlocked the door as fast as I could before I shoved it open to walk into a complete disaster. Hutch was normally the neatest person on the planet, but right now...there were dirty dishes in the sink, a garbage that desperately needed to be emptied, and pizza boxes stacked up on the table. As I made way into the living room, it wasn't as bad, but not much better either. Dirty clothes, empty beer bottles, and a few empty plates were stacked on the floor and coffee table. Hutch was clearly spiraling out of control. Was it Madison leaving that had done this to him or was it something more?

"Hutch!" I called his name as I moved down the hallway. The bathroom on my right was empty with dirty clothes piled in the corner next to the washer and dryer, and the pink room decorated with ballerina everything, which I assumed was Hazel's, was clean but also empty. "Hutch, it's Jillian, where are you?" Icy fear crept up my spine as I came to the last room at the end of the hall. I knocked on the door. "Hutch, honey, are you in there?" I swallowed nervously. "I'm coming in," I announced before I pulled the door open.

Hutch was face down on the bed, dressed in nothing but his boxers. "Jesus Christ." I rushed to his side. "Hutch?" I tried to turn him over, but he was too big. I tried to feel for a pulse, and when I found a faint one, I let out a sob. "Baby, tell me what you took," I begged as I let my eyes move around the room. Beer bottles were everywhere. I didn't see anything that might have made him like this, but he was so out of it he couldn't even make a complete sentence.

He only seemed to be muttering nonsense at me while his eyes rolled back. Hutch's hand came out to grab at my arm when I yanked my phone from between my boobs where I kept it when I had my leotard on. I needed to call someone. He shook his head, but couldn't make eye contact with me. I felt my stomach drop when I realized what he was trying to tell me.

"I'm sorry, Hutch," I whispered as I dialed the number.

"Nine-one-one, what's your emergency?"

"I'm at my friend's house and he took something. He won't wake up," I sobbed.

I could hear her clicking away in the background. "And you don't know what he took?" she asked.

"No! I just got here, and he's in his bed. I can't even turn him over. His eyes keep rolling around, and he's muttering about gibberish I can't understand." I let out a low moan. "Can you send someone here, please?" I gave her the address as she requested before I burst into tears and sobbed into my hands. No, I had to get myself together. I couldn't be a mess like this. I had to be...fuck. I had to call Pat. Probably Madison too, because she would need to know what was going on. I could hear the sounds of the ambulance as they grew closer amidst my own meltdown.

I pressed my lips against Hutch's cheek. "You're going to be okay, Hutch, I promise."

***

Hutch had swallowed a bottle of sleeping pills. The thought made me so angry I wanted to punch a hole in the wall, but the doctor that was treating him told me that if I hadn't gotten there when did, Hutch mostly likely wouldn't have survived. Was I happy that I saved his life? Yes, but Hutch wasn't so happy. He was refusing to see me even though I had been sitting outside in the waiting room for two days. I even canceled my classes, just hoping he would talk to me.

"I'm sorry," Pat whispered as he sat down next to me. Jo had gone home to shower, but would be back soon.

I leaned my head against his shoulder. "I should probably just go home, right? I mean, he hates me and doesn't want me to visit him. I should just go back to living my life." I just wanted to see Hutch and tell him I loved him. That he wasn't alone. I didn't want to yell at him or give him shit for what he did.

"Once he's done here, he's going to get some therapy and rehabilitation at a place our parents found for him. It's different than the so-called rehab he went to before. I hadn't realized he had stopped seeing Megan or taking his meds."

"Hutch was on medication?"

Pat grimaced. "You didn't hear that last part from me, Jill. I assumed Hutch had told you that because you two were so close. I think a lot of that had to do with Mads, you know? She gave him shit for it, which was totally unfair. She had no right to judge him like that."

I clenched my fists as I saw red. Madison had yet to come visit her husband in the hospital. She hadn't bothered to call to see if he was okay. I had an inkling that my blonde nemesis was doing more than visiting with her parents, and it was more like she was shacking up with someone new. "You don't need me to tell you how I feel about her."

"You're a much better woman than she'll ever be." Pat casually wrapped an arm around my shoulder. "Oh, I forgot to tell you that Dad said you could stop by the apartment anytime. Dad had the key changed so he's going to bring a spare by for you."

I had offered to help Hutch and Pat's parents clean up the apartment so that when he was ready to come home, it wouldn't be such a disaster.

"Why would he change the locks?" I turned to look at him. "Is there something that you're keeping from me?" I folded my arms over my chest. "Spill it, Patrick."

"Shit." He pulled his arm back to rake his hand through his hair in a move so similar to his brother, it creeped me out. "Madison served Hutch with divorce papers," he admitted.

"That conniving bitch."

"Pretty much what my mom said."

I jumped up, ready to march down to Hutch's room whether he wanted to see me or not, but Pat gabbed my elbow. "Don't, Jill." His brows dipped, and I watched the way his face fell. "He's not...he's not in a good place. I've never seen him like this before, and he hardly even looks at me or my parents when we walk in the room." His chin quivered as he spoke.

I wrapped my arms around Patrick to pull him into a hug. "That's why I should be in there. I can help him, Pat, he needs me." I swallowed back the tears that threatened to fall.

"Hutch is not the same Hutch. He's mean, he's angry, and he lashes out at everyone. The nurses, the doctors, and every one that steps into that room is a target." Pat stepped back. "I know that if he said something to you now? He'd regret it weeks from now when his meds start working again."

I chewed on my lip. "When he asks for me, you'll tell me, right?"

"Of course," Pat assured me.

Only I didn't hear from anyone asking me to come visit Hutch. Not even when he went to the Depression and Anxiety Center two hours away from Ocean View. Brent Kelly did stop by one afternoon to drop off the key for the apartment, and when I asked him about Hutch, he simply shook his head and told me that not much had changed since the day I found him. He was still angry at the world, and would probably be at the center longer than they had planned. He thanked me for my help and for teaching Hazel, as well as for bringing her home after classes on Monday evenings, but didn't give me any other chance to ask about Hutch before he rushed away.

My heart was broken. I felt like I let Hutch down, and could have saved him if I had just talked to him that morning when he had said he needed someone, but instead I had pushed him away. I knew it wasn't my fault, but I still felt tremendously guilty. It took me a few days to work up the nerve to go to Hutch's apartment, and when I did, I cried for a good fifteen minutes in the kitchen, wondering just what he was thinking when he thought he had to leave everyone behind. I dropped to the floor, sobbing and screaming, wishing that he'd talk to me or reach out, but I knew he wasn't ready for that yet. When I was done, I washed my face with a cold paper towel and began my clean up.

First, I cleaned up all the empty pizza boxes, beer bottles, and cans. Then I took all the dirty clothes, put them in the washing machine, and turned that on so Hutch would have clean clothes when he returned home. I got rid of all the garbage, the spoiled food in the fridge, and cleaned the counters, tables, and then vacuumed the entire apartment. By the time I was done, I was exhausted, but I thought I had done a good job. The clothes were folded, put away, and both beds were made. I hoped that Hutch would be proud of me.

Chapter Thirty

Jillian

Eight weeks went by, and I still hadn't heard anything from Hutch asking me to come see him. I had stopped asking Pat if he had asked for me, how he was doing because I figured Hutch didn't care about me anymore. It hurt, wondering what I had done to him other than care, but I knew he had demons that he had never showed or told me about. It still didn't stop me from thinking about him first thing in the morning, and the last thing before I went to bed.

Summer was a busy time for me with classes so I was happy that I didn't have a lot of free time. I was at the ballet studio from six in the morning until nearly ten at night most days, and dragging myself home to eat, sleep, and repeat again the next day. Wednesday was the only day I didn't have night classes, and I took the time to catch up on paperwork and anything else I hadn't had the chance to work on. I was busy stuffing my face with dinner when I heard the front door open around seven o'clock that night and cursed myself for forgetting to lock the door.

"Sorry, we're closed." I didn't even look up from my laptop as I scrolled through my schedule, didn't even hear the footsteps that moved across the floor, or notice the beautiful man leaning against the doorframe of my office.

"Even for me, Jilly?"

My eyes shot up, my sandwiched dropped onto the desk, and I stared up into the face of Hutch Kelly. His blond hair was longer than I had ever seen it, but it looked good like that. Messy from the wind we had all day today. Hutch was dressed in a plain white shirt that looked too small stretched across his broad chest, and I noticed the way his muscled biceps flexed against the fabric. Clearly, someone had been working out over the last few weeks. His warm chocolate browns begged me to forgive him while his lush red lips were set in a firm line. I let my eyes move away from his face, down his chest, and over his toned thighs, before I realized I had egg salad all over the place.

"Shit," I muttered, jumping up to grab some napkins to clean myself up.

"Jillian." Hutch's voice dripped with sadness, which brought my attention back to him. "I'm sorry." He took a small step into my office. "Stop." He grabbed my hands as I continued to make a bigger mess of myself. "I couldn't let you see me like that, and I never meant for you to find me." His fingers traced my wrists, over my pulse, and then he squatted down to look me straight in the eyes. "Tell me I'm not too late. That you don't hate me for pushing you away like that. My head was not where it needed to be, and I didn't know how to tell you." Hutch released my hands to cup my face with his big hands. "I love you, Jills, I never stopped loving you, and I need you to know that."

I opened my mouth as tears began to leak from my eyes. "I could never hate you," I assured him. My hands came up to grip his wrists. "I should have—"

"No." Hutch shook his head. "This is not on you. Don't even say that." He moved to grip the nape of my neck with one of his hands. "None of it was your fault, do you understand?" When I nodded, he tucked a finger under my chin. "No tears, bean," Hutch whispered.

Without meaning to, a sob escaped my throat, and then I threw my arms around his neck so I could cling to him as I cried. I knew that's not what he wanted after all, but I was so happy to see him and hear his voice, that I was feeling every single emotion at once. Hutch just held me against his chest, his arms strong and firm as I let it all out until I had nothing left. When I was done, he reached for the box of tissues I kept on my desk, and pulled out a few to help me get myself together.

"When did you get home?" I dabbed at my face and turned away as I blew my nose. "You look really good. Unlike me, who is leaking snot and tears all over everything." I tossed my used tissues into the garbage, only to reach for more.

Hutch chuckled softly. "I've been home since yesterday afternoon." When I turned to stare up at him, he shook his head. "Don't think I didn't want to come to you first thing." He eased himself up onto his feet, and then helped me onto mine. "I had to work up the nerve, not to mention I needed to spend time with Hazel. She was so excited to see me, and"—Hutch's face lit up like the sun when he mentioned her name—"I swear she has grown a foot since I last saw her." His voice overflowed with emotion.

"She must have been over the moon to see you." I sniffled as I sat down on the edge of my desk. I knew how important it was for Hutch to reconnect with his daughter and he needed to be with her right now, not with me.

"Hey." He pushed a piece of hair behind my ear. "What's going on inside that beautiful head of yours?"

I shook my head. "Nothing," I lied, afraid to meet his eyes.

"Jillian." His voice was soft. "Talk to me, please, if you don't want me here or if something is bothering you, I want to know." Hutch squared his shoulders and leveled me with a gaze that made goosebumps break out all over my body. "I thought about two people while I was gone, Jillian, and one of them is sitting right in front of me." His voice had dropped so low it made my stomach clench with desire. "You're my family." Fresh tears filled my eyes, but when I tried to look away, his hand flew out to grip my chin. "No, don't hide from me. We're not doing that anymore." His features softened. "Talk to me. You're the only person that has never been afraid to do that, so don't hold out on me now," he whispered.

I hadn't realized I was holding my breath until I let it out. "Are you sure you should be with me right now? I mean, Hazel is your daughter, and she needs you more than me. You're her family." My life had seemed empty without Hutch in it, but putting Hazel first was what was important. I knew that.

"You're my family, Jilly. You and Hazel are the only ones I want in my life." Hutch stroked my cheek with his thumb, causing delicious friction to build between my legs. "Go out with me Saturday night."

"Like on a date?"

"Exactly like a date."

I dragged my teeth across my bottom lip. "Okay. A date sounds nice." I wanted more than a date. I wanted Hutch to kiss me right now until I couldn't see straight and then take me home, strip off my clothes, and drag his tongue all over my pussy until I came on his mouth. Then I wanted to wrap my mouth around his cock, make him cum in my mouth before I straddled his waist and fucked him every which way into next week.

Hutch tilted his head before he dipped his head to slide his lips over mine. "Nice," he teased, but I saw the way his ears turned pink, and his eyes flashed with need.

When he went to pull back, I grabbed his face with my hands. "Hutch." My voice cracked as I said his name, but when I pulled his face back to mine and our lips met again in a soft kiss, I sighed happily. The growl that started deep in Hutch's chest got louder the longer our mouths stayed connected together, his tongue easing its way between the seam of my lips, and before I knew it, he had me caged in between his arms on my desk, panting and wanting more.

"We should stop," he warned, his brown eyes dark as they met my greens. "Before I take you right here on your desk."

"Promises, promises," I teased and wrapped my legs around his waist to pull him closer. I bit back a groan as his erection pressed against my core.

Hutch's nostrils flared as he stared down at me. "Don't think that I didn't think about you, just like this, every day while I was gone. All the things I wanted to do to you, plan on doing to you, but"—he peppered kisses against my mouth and jawline—"let me take you out first. Like I planned."

Hutch pulled back and then helped me sit up. "That doesn't mean I don't want you any less." He pointed to his crotch.

I gazed up him. "I love you," I murmured, realizing I had never returned his endearment when he told me earlier. "Every minute of every single day, Hutch, while you were gone, that's all I wanted to tell you. How much I love you, and how much you mean to me." I sucked in my breath when he turned his back to me.

"Jillian," Hutch's voice was low again. "I am so sorry for everything that I put you through." His shoulders trembled slightly. "With Madison, with—"

I touched his arm. "Don't do that," I whispered as he glanced over his shoulder. "You have nothing to apologize for, do you hear me?" I quickly slipped from the desk to wiggle between Hutch's arms. "I left you and you had every right to move on without me." I rested my chin against his chest.

"I never wanted to move on," Hutch admitted as he wrapped his arms around me. "I was lonely, and she was just a warm body." He kissed the tip of my nose. "She served me with divorce papers while I was in the hospital. Can you believe that?"

I could, because Madison was a horrible person, but I kept that part to myself. "I'm sorry." I squeezed myself closer against his frame.

"She doesn't plan on fighting for custody of Hazel."

What do you say to something like that? That woman was a horrible human being. When I looked up at Hutch again, he was looking down at me with love in his eyes. Not anger, hate, or sadness, just the love that I had missed for the past couple of weeks.

"Saturday night." He smiled, and my heart stuttered in my chest. I had never felt so many emotions at once in my life. After everything that had happened between us, he still wanted me, and I still wanted him. "Wear something comfortable," he added.

"Where are we going?" I asked.

Hutch only shook his head. "It's a surprise, but I have a feeling that you're going to like it," he added with a wink. "I'll pick you up at six if that's okay." He held me closer to his body, and I caught the scent of his soap, taking me back to the first time I slept in his bed after he kissed me under the fireworks.

"Okay," I whispered.

Chapter Thirty-One

Hutch

Saturday night seemed to take forever to get here, but when it finally rolled around, I was a nervous wreck. I felt like this was our first date all over again. It wasn't like Jillian and I hadn't seen one another during the week, but this, this felt different. She had come by a couple of times for lunch, bringing me an egg salad sandwich, an apple, and a granola bar just like the old days, but we had kept it casual. We held hands under the table, but we didn't kiss or hug or anything because we knew how fast gossip spread in town. It was bad enough how much people were talking about what had happened to me. I didn't need them dragging Jillian into the mix and thinking she was the reason for my divorce with Madison. That part was all on me.

And, of course, there were the text messages.

Jillian: *You won't tell me where we're going?*

Hutch: *Nope.*

Jillian: *Not even a little hint? Even if I send you a boob pic?*

Hutch: *Jilly, that's not fair! But a boob pic would be much appreciated because I do miss them more than you can imagine.*

Jillian: *Not if they won't get me intel on our date.* *frowny emoji*

Hutch: *I have missed you more than you know.*

Jillian: *Me too, baby.*

Hutch: *Fuck, don't call me that.*

Jillian: *Why, will it help get me information on the date?*

Hutch: *You are relentless, you know that?* *laughing emoji*

I didn't realize how much I missed her texts until the first one she sent. In fact, I missed everything about Jillian. Her texts, her scent, her laugh, and just being near her. When I stepped into my empty apartment after leaving the hospital, I realized she had been there. That she had cleaned it up, and made sure it was just the way I would want it. It was enough to break me into a meltdown until I had nothing left inside me before I packed a bag of everything I needed and left, because I couldn't be there anymore. That had never truly been my home. It was a place I had slept and eaten, but not a place I had ever truly felt comfortable. I moved back into the apartment over my parents' garage where I could be close to Hazel until I could find something else.

I was thrilled to be home with my daughter. The moment she had seen me, the day I had come home, she had dropped the dolls she had been playing with and came running at me full speed so that I could pick her up and shower her with kisses. I loved Hazel with every single ounce of my soul. When I looked at her? I saw a future, and now that the demons inside my head were no longer speaking to me, I finally felt I could give Hazel the future she deserved.

I had spent more than enough time trying to figure out what to wear tonight before I decided on faded blue jeans, and a tan short-sleeved Henley that I was sure my mother had slipped into my dresser at some point over the past week. I had never seen it before. As I walked up the steps to Jillian's apartment building, I nervously ran my hand through my hair and tugged on my shortened locks. I had gotten a haircut this morning because I couldn't stand how long it had gotten, and as I tugged on the ends, I wondered what Jillian would be wearing. Something sexy, like that lacey number when we first went out? A dress? My mind was racing as I raised my hand to knock, only to have her open the door before I had the chance.

"Hey." She beamed up at me with a shy smile. "Want to come in for a second?" She pushed the door open. "I just need to put my shoes on."

"Sure." I stepped into the apartment and shoved my hands into my pockets, keeping my eyes on Jillian as she moved into the room. She looked beautiful, like I knew she would. Dressed in a green sleeveless keyhole top and blue jean shorts, her tan, toned legs looked like they went on forever. I liked how her hair was piled up on her head in a tight ponytail, and as she glanced over her shoulder at me, I felt my ears burn. Instead of staring at her, I moved my gaze around her apartment, taking in all the little touches I knew belonged to her.

The giant couch, covered in too many pillows, with the throw blanket on the back that I recognized from her bedroom. It was decorated with tiny little ballet slippers. There were framed photos of every size all hung over every inch of the wall, and as I leaned closer to look at one, I noticed it was from Jo and Patrick's wedding, the one of us high-fiving while they had their backs to us. My heart thumped against my ribcage as I realized she had pieces of me in her home even though we had been separated.

"Are you going to tell me where we're going yet?" Jillian asked as she slipped on her sneakers. "You cut your hair." I turned around when she passed that remark.

"No, I'm not going to tell you yet," I answered. "You like it?" I ran my hand over the shortened sides and over the top. "It was driving me crazy how long it had gotten."

"I like it." She grabbed her phone to slip it into her pocket before moving toward me. Jillian reached up her hand to lightly run her fingers over my freshly cut hair, and I felt my dick instantly respond to her touch. "Kiss me, Hutch," she whispered and then dropped her hand onto my shoulder.

Who was I deny her something she wanted? I leaned down to press my mouth against her, one hand gripping the nape of her neck, the other finding her left hip to pull her closer, and when our lips met, it was like nothing else mattered. Her mouth was welcoming me, our tongues wrapped together, and soft little moans escaped Jillian's throat as our kiss deepened, her fingers digging into my skin. How could I ever think I could find this with someone else?

This...this was what I craved.

Jillian's touch.

Jillian's kiss.

Jillian's everything, all at once.

"Jills," I murmured softly. "If we don't stop, we're never leaving your apartment tonight, and as much as I want to bury myself inside your pretty little pussy again, I want to take you out and spoil the shit out of you." I tugged on her bottom lip with my teeth.

Her green eyes were dark with molten lust when she pulled back. "Can I have both?" She smirked.

Fuck, my already hard cock liked that idea even better as it strained against my jeans. "Depends on whether you're a good girl or not," I teased, cupping her head with my hands. "I missed you so much," I whispered.

A smile broke out on Jillian's beautiful face, causing her entire face to light up. "I missed you, too."

"Come on." I tilted my head. "Let's get out of here."

***

Jillian clapped her hands together as she jumped up and down before she flung herself into my arms. "I can't believe you brought me to the carnival," she gushed, peppering kisses all over my face. "I haven't been here since—"

"The last time I came with you." I finished the sentence for her as I held her against my chest. "It felt right," I added, placing her back onto her feet. "To come back where it all began."

She nudged my side before hugging me. "Technically," she said, "it started at the Egg, but I'm not sure that's our place anymore." She sounded almost sad when she said it, and I hated how I had ruined that for her because of Madison.

"Hey." I placed a finger under her chin. "This is the place where I realized I was in love with you." I searched her green eyes as she stared up at me. "We can still have the Angry Egg too. We can just set it on fire and rebuild it." Her face broke into a smile before she burst into laughter. "Trust me, Jilly, any place is ours as long as we're together."

"Let's get inside before it gets too busy." Jillian untangled herself from my grasp, only to lace her fingers through mine. When I didn't budge, her brows dropped, and I saw worry written all over her face. "Hutch?" She touched my chest lightly with her free hand.

A smile pulled at my lips. "Just trying to remember everything," I assured her. "Which reminds me." I slid my phone from my pocket. "Picture? You know, like the old days?"

Jillian instantly snuggled in close so I could take a selfie, which she immediately demanded to see before she made me send it to her, and then post to her Instagram, tag me in it, and then added the caption: "Where it all started." I'd be lying if it didn't make me happy, and maybe just a little more than greedy when I caught other guys staring at Jillian as we made our way into the carnival.

"Where to first?" She linked her arm through mine, oblivious to the stares, the gawkers, and the ogling as we walked around. How did I become the luckiest motherfucker in the world? "You feeling like taking a turn at the swings? Or maybe the rollercoaster first?" Her plump lips twisted into that smile I loved so much. "I know, baby, you want a caramel ap—"

I didn't let Jillian finish her sentence. Instead, I crushed my mouth to hers instead, wanting her to know just how much I was feeling at that exact moment. It took only a second for her to react, her slim fingers digging in the front of my shirt before she kissed me back, and when we broke apart, her eyes sparkled with something they hadn't before.

"You know what it does to me when you call me baby."

"Baby, baby, baby."

I narrowed my eyes. "Say that again, Jilly, and I'll flip you over my shoulder like a caveman and take you back to your place, and we'll never make it through this damn carnival tonight."

When she started to open her mouth, I slapped my hand over it playfully, and she giggled happily, only to lick my palm. My dick was hard in an instant. "You're being awfully bad tonight," I hissed into her ear, dropping my hand from her mouth.

"You going to punish me later?" Jillian hooked her arm around my waist.

Jesus, she was trying to kill me tonight. "Is that...is that something you're into?" I felt my face burn as I spoke.

Jillian shrugged. "No, but I'd be willing to try anything with you." She must have realized what she had said because her face immediately fell. "I didn't...Hutch, no, I don't want to do that."

"It's okay, Jills. Don't forget my therapy. If and when I'm ready to try something like that, I'll let you know. Now come on, let's go try out the swings first." I dropped my arm around her shoulders like it was the most natural thing in the world as we began to maneuver around the crowds of people. I was saving the Ferris wheel for the end of the night. I had big plans, and just the thought made me break out in a cold sweat despite the warm air that hung in the sky.

Jillian squeezed my side as we walked, and when she leaned into me while we waited in line, I realized just how happy this made me. We had a lot of things to work out, and a lot more to talk through, but I knew that we were meant for one another. Even after all this time.

Chapter Thirty-Two

"My Instagram is really blowing up." I glanced up from my phone to find Hutch dragging his tongue over his caramel apple with a smirk on his face. White-hot desire made me squeeze my thighs, and I rolled my eyes. "Really?" I twisted my lips.

His smirk only widened across his handsome face. "Don't think I didn't notice the way you watched me," he teased. "Wish it was you, Jilly?"

"Yes," I barked and lowered my eyes. "Stop it, Hutch, or I'm going to have to pull you into the ladies room to have my way with you," I warned. My phone blinked again with another Instagram notification. "People have questions," I told him, trying to change the subject.

"What people?" Hutch asked, wiping his fingers with a napkin. "What kind of questions?"

I unlocked my phone and chuckled softly. "Rand wants to know when the fuck this happened, and is this why you aren't returning his calls or texts." I glanced up to find Hutch rolling his eyes. "Brooklyn replied with the heart eye emoji; Jo said I'd better text her tomorrow because she'd end me if I don't, and Knox—"

"You're fucking friends with Knox Carson?" Hutch snarled.

I raised my brows. "Relax, baby, Knox is married now." I put my hand over his. "Last month, to a girl named Natalie he met on vacation with his parents. Small wedding that I attended solo, if you were curious." I felt him relax. "Anyway, Knox commented that it's about time." I stopped so that I could swing both legs from the picnic table and then moved next to Hutch. "Let's forget about this stupid shit," I whispered, placing my phone down. "Tonight is about you and me." I leaned my head against his shoulder.

"Knox knows we're back together."

"That's what you got out of that?"

Hutch shrugged and kept his eyes down on the table. "You know how I feel about that dick."

"Hey." I lifted his arm so I could move underneath it. "Look at me." When Hutch turned his face, I raised my hand to trail my fingers over his jaw. "I'm sorry that I brought him up." I pressed a kiss to the side of his mouth. "Want to get out of here?" My feet were killing me from this week's classes, and I was exhausted.

"What about the Ferris wheel?" Hutch twisted his entire body to face me. "That's the best part. But you look tired, Jills, so maybe we can come back another night." Something in his voice told me he would be disappointed me if we didn't go on that ride.

I shook my head. "Not yet." I stood up and grabbed his hand. "Come on, baby, let's go." I tried to pull Hutch to his feet, but that was impossible.

He grinned at me. "Where should we go for our next date?" he asked as we moved along to the Ferris Wheel, swinging our hands in the air. Now that the crowds were starting to dwindle, the line wasn't as long and we were able to get onto the ride right away.

"You're going to take me on another date?"

"Unless you don't want to."

The bar was locked in front of us now. "I'd go out on a date with you every single night if I could." I blushed when I said those words, but it wasn't a lie. If I wasn't so busy with my ballet studio, I could see us having as much fun as when we were kids.

"That could be arranged."

I glanced over at Hutch to find him watching me with an intense gaze. "What?" I asked as a smile broke out over his face, but he just shook his head and reached for my hand.

"Just enjoying this, that's all," he admitted. "It seems like a lifetime ago, doesn't it?" Hutch asked as the ride came to a stop with us at the top. "I love you so much."

"I love you, too, Hutch..." I stopped when I realized what he was doing. He had a small black box in his hand. "Are you...what are you doing?" I stared at him as goosebumps broke out over my skin despite the warm breeze that came up from the water.

"Marry me, Jills," he whispered. "I know it won't be tomorrow or next week or even next month, but I should have done this years ago because you are the only woman for me. You've always been the only woman for me." He flipped the box open to reveal a white gold diamond solitaire ring inside. I watched as it glittered under the lights. "I know I'm supposed to get down on one knee, but I can't really do that right now."

"Yes." I nodded my head. "Yes, I'll marry you," I cried as tears spilled down my cheeks.

Hutch stared at me like he couldn't believe he heard the words come out of my mouth. "Yes?" he asked before he realized I had said the word he wanted to hear. "Shit, right." He took the ring and slipped it onto my finger. "Can I confess something?" he asked as the Ferris wheel started moving.

"Kiss me first and then you can confess later," I said before I kissed him instead. Hutch's mouth was hungry when our lips met, and I whimpered as his tongue slipped and sliced against mine. It was obvious what was on our mind after this date was over tonight, and I intended to make sure he didn't leave my apartment until tomorrow morning. "Take me home, baby," I murmured as he pulled away.

***

How we ever managed to get back to my apartment without tearing each other's clothes off; I will never know. When we got to my door, I stopped and turned to look up at Hutch with boldness in my eyes. "Do you want to come in?" I asked, knowing that he wanted me as much as I wanted him. Lust stirred in my belly, and when his eyes raked over my body before they landed on my face, I had to remind myself that we were in a public place, and that I couldn't just climb the man like a tree.

"Do you need to ask me that?" He leaned closer, caging me in against the door. I licked my lips as he pressed his firm, muscular frame against mine. "I hope that you don't have big plans for tomorrow, Jills, because you won't be able to walk by the time I'm done with you," he growled into my ear.

I couldn't prevent the low moan that escaped my lips. "Promise?" I whispered, slipping my arms up his chest and locking them behind his neck.

"Let's unlock the door so I can prove it."

"Keys are in my front right pocket."

He reached into my pocket to pull out my keys, unlocked the door, and ushered me into the apartment. I heard the front door slam behind us as he lifted me up and onto the couch. "You're wearing too many clothes." His lips landed on mine before I could respond, and I got flooded with his wet kisses.

Oh, how I had missed this. Hutch's sweet mouth against mine, and the way his tongue darted between my lips. He was rougher than usual, but I was just as eager as he was, arching my hips against his as I clung to his back, and whimpering the longer the kiss went on.

"Fuck, I want you," Hutch grunted as he broke away, his mouth moving down my neck, licking and nipping the soft spot on my collarbone. "Need to get these clothes off so I can touch you." He slipped his hand up under my shirt and danced his finger across my ribcage as he flipped us over so that I was on top. "I love you, Jilly." His brown eyes glistened with tears as he stared up at me.

I swallowed the lump in my throat. "I love you too," I assured him and pressed a quick kiss to his mouth before I quickly pulled my shirt up over my head. The bra was next as I unhooked it from behind, slipping the straps down over my shoulders, and deposited it on the floor. Hutch reached up to cup my tits with his big, calloused hands, and my head instantly fell back as he tugged and pulled my nipples between my fingers. Heat and wetness flared between my thighs as I rubbed against him.

"Bring them closer, Jill," he instructed boldly.

I leaned forward, only to have Hutch latch onto the left one, and I cried out as pleasure coursed through my veins. My hands went to his hair as he sucked, and I felt like I was going to explode if he didn't stop. "Hutch, baby, it feels good, too good, but I want your mouth, your cock, your fingers, inside me." I moaned as he ran his tongue across my chest and over to my right nipple. "Fuck," I whispered.

His eyes were nearly black as we stared at each other, his free hand reaching down to unbutton my shorts so he could slide it under my underwear. "Jesus, you're so fucking wet." He flicked at my drenched clit. My eyes rolled back in my head before he removed his hand to bring it up to his mouth. "Sweet as I remembered." Once again, he flipped us back over, shimmied off my shorts and underwear, then dragged his tongue between my wet folds.

"Hutch!" I called out his name as he did it again before one finger slowly inched its way inside my needy pussy. His tongue continued to lash at my clit, pleasure rocketed through my veins, and just when I thought I couldn't take anymore, Hutch pushed a second finger which caused my body to bow, and my orgasm to hit me full force. I gripped his hair as I screamed his name while cascading waves rolled through my body. My body shook with pleasure and my toes curled against my feet, but when I was done, I thought I might never move again.

Hutch climbed up over me to pepper my lips with kisses. "You're so beautiful when you come," he murmured.

I cupped his dick with one hand. "You want something, baby?" I purred, and the groan that escaped his throat was more than enough to tell me the answer. Me. "Maybe we should get these jeans off," I teased, reaching up to undo his button, and then pulling down the zipper. His dick strained against his boxers, showing me just how right I was.

Hutch stood up to kick off his jeans, yank off his shirt, and before he could move, I wrapped my hand around his length to slowly stroke him. "So good," he whispered, his eyes watching my every move. "Stroke my cock, Jilly."

Heat flared between my legs. Jesus, I guess he'd gotten more comfortable in the bedroom. I dropped to my knees to slowly drag my tongue over the tip of his cock and then opened my mouth to take him in. His hands found my hair, wrapping my ponytail around his wrist, pushing only enough to tell me what he wanted, and when I slid him all the way to the back of my throat, he released a primal noise that I felt all the way to my toes.

"Fuck, yes, Jilly, that's it."

I whimpered at his words, and his grip tightened, tears slipping from my eyes, but I wanted this as much as Hutch. My lips moved up and down his dick, wanting to make him come, wanting to make him feel as good as he had made me. Hutch made a sensual sound, a rumble of pleasure, and then he came, filling my throat with salty lava. I sat back on my feet to gather myself together, my body once again humming with its own need.

"Jillian." Hutch's voice was gentle as he touched my face to tilt my head to look up at him. "Did I hurt you? Sometimes I get a little carried away." He searched my face.

"I guess you can say I've gotten a little more adventurous in the bedroom."

I shook my head. "No, baby, I'm fine." I wished that it had been me to be able to share in learning with him, but that was my fault. "I actually enjoyed that more than you know," I assured him as I got to my feet. I let my gaze wander down his perfectly sculpted chest, his defined abs, and that amazing V that led me right down to his cock that was already starting to grow erect again. "You look like you've been working out more than ever." I tilted my head as I met his heated gaze.

"That's something I've always enjoyed doing, Jills." He ran the back of his hand over my cheek. "Care to continue this in your bedroom?"

I nodded as I eased up onto my toes. "That sounds like a great idea, baby." I pressed a kiss to his lips when he leaned down.

Chapter Thirty-Three

Hutch

"That's it, baby, don't stop!" Jillian met my driving rhythm beat for beat as I pounded into her from above. We hadn't stopped going at it since we arrived back at her apartment last night from the carnival. I felt the way her body trembled beneath me, that tell-tale sign that she was close to the edge, and when I reached down between her legs to pinch her clit between my fingers, she cried out, coming undone beneath me.

I buried myself as far as I possibly could inside her tight pussy, wrapped my arms around her back, and pressed my mouth against her neck as my release hit me. Jillian's nails dug into my skin as she gripped my shoulders, and I grunted as every drop of cum slipped from my body.

That was it. I was done.

Spent.

Finished.

Until I rolled over to see Jillian watching me with that look in her eyes. That smile on her face was enough for my cock to spring right back to attention again. "I need a breather." I chuckled as she started to straddle my waist. "We've been at it for hours," I reminded Jillian, although her nipples looked super inviting.

Jillian placed her small hands against my cheeks. "We're making up for lost time, baby." She slid her lips over mine as a ripple of pain ran across her face.

"What's wrong? Are you okay?"

"I'm a little sore."

I gripped her hips. "Where?" I tried to move her from my body, but she shook her head.

"You did warn me that I wouldn't be able to walk today, didn't you?" She smirked.

"Are you serious right now?" I had only been kidding.

Jillian swatted my chest. "Dead serious. We haven't stopped unless you count peeing and getting something to drink." She let out a sigh of happiness. "Maybe we should take a little break. Have something to eat and get a little rest. When do you need to be home?" She slipped from my body only to snuggle next to me on the bed.

"I told my parents I would be home this afternoon." Jillian's fingers traced the contours of my chest lightly. "Want to come over? Visit with Hazel?" I eased myself onto my side. "Tell everyone the good news?" I gripped her left hand to look at the ring on her finger, admiring how perfect it looked.

Jillian swallowed nervously. "Do you...really think that's a good idea? I mean, you're still technically married to Madison, and—"

I cut her off by crushing our lips together. "Confession, baby." I wasn't sure when I started calling her that, but Jillian seemed to like it. "I've had that ring for a long time," I whispered as she stared up with me with her big, green eyes.

"How long?" Her voice came out soft and breathy.

I glanced up at the ceiling, noticing for the first time the skylight above her bed because I had been buried between her legs. "I was going to ask you before you left for New

York," I admitted. "You picked this place because of that, huh?" I jutted my chin upward.

"Don't change the subject, Hutch." Jillian gripped my chin between her index and middle finger. "When were you planning on giving this to me? Before I left for New York?" When I nodded, her face crumpled and tears filled her eyes.

I rolled over. "Don't do that." I shook my head. "Hey, Jilly, don't cry. I didn't tell you the truth to avoid upsetting you." I brushed the tears from her face. "I knew that it was a crazy idea back then because we were both in such weird places, myself being super fucked up, but I often wondered what would have happened if I had. I wasn't sure if I even had the balls to ask you." Again, Jillian's eyes grew watery. "Why are you so upset?" I whispered, gathering her into my arms.

"All the time we lost." Jillian leaned her head against my chest. "Because of me being so selfish and afraid of what would happen if I said goodbye to you instead of growing a pair." She sniffed.

"Baby..." Her eyes turned up to mine.

"We can't change the past, only work on the present." I whispered.

Jillian's lips twitched. "You're perfect, you know that?" She pressed her lips against my pec, and my dick thumped against her side. "Oh, did you like that?"

"Jills, we were taking a break."

"Were we?"

I gripped her arms before she could mount me again. "Yes, we were, and I need to give it a rest. I don't think I have anything left in me. Remember, I'm older than you,"

I teased as Jillian's plump lips turned up into a full-fledge smile. "Come with me this afternoon," I pleaded.

"Alright," she agreed with a blinding smile. "Did you just call yourself *old*, Hutch Kelly?" Laughter hung in her voice, and I'd be lying if I said I didn't like it.

"I said I was *older*. There's a difference."

Jillian giggled. "I like it when you call me baby," she admitted sheepishly. "But not as much as when you call me Jilly." Her hand slipped between my legs to wrap around my now incredibly hard-to-miss erection.

So much for taking a break.

I groaned as Jillian stroked my length, then she stopped to look up at me, adoration shining on her face. "I love you, Hutch."

I took in Jillian's flushed cheeks, her messy dark hair, and realized that after all this time, she was still *it* for me. From the moment I had saved her on the beach all those years ago, Jillian had been the one I wanted for the rest of my life. We might have taken different turns, gone on different paths, but they both had led us right back to where we belonged. With each other. I reached down to cup her face with both hands. "I love you too, Jilly," I declared before taking her mouth with mine.

Epilogue

Brooklyn and I sat knee-to-knee, with our shoulders pressed together, and hands clutched with each other as we watched Rand take the checked flag at the final race of the NASCAR season sitting up in Rand's pit box. We sprang from our seats at the same time we heard Rand and the rest of his team screaming through our headphones. Not only did he just win the race, but he also won the championship, and Hutch had helped him do that.

A couple of days after Hutch had proposed to me, Rand had called him up and asked him if he was interested in working for him. It wasn't just any job either; it was the job of crew chief since the one that Rand originally had needed to step down on short notice due to an illness. It was also the main reason that Rand had been trying so desperately hard to get a hold of Hutch while he had been in recovery. Despite having only met once, and sharing a few texts since they had met, Rand only wanted to hire Hutch.

It turns out that Rand had been so impressed with Hutch's work when he came to visit that he had been trying to get him into the business, and when the job had opened up, he wasted no time in reaching out. I had to poke Hutch a little to go check out the job, take a trip down to North Carolina since that was where the job was based and where we would be living, but once we realized what a big deal this would be for us, as a family, Hutch jumped at the opportunity.

I loved North Carolina, and so did Hazel. She took to it like a fish in water, and I think part of that had to do with RJ Shepard, Brooklyn and Rand's son, who took her under his wing, and made sure she was never left out of anything. She was instantly included with his circle of friends, and that was a big relief for both of us. I had been able to sell the ballet studio rather quickly, and even though I missed dancing, I didn't miss it enough to start up a business again. I taught a couple of classes at a local studio in North Carolina, which was honestly much easier and a lot less stressful. The kids were great, the pay wasn't too bad; and Sully told me she had been talking me up to some of the other NASCAR wives, mentioning how they should come down to check it out. One thing I quickly learned was how supportive the racing community was.

"You should go be with your husband," I told Brooklyn once we had climbed down from the pit box, nudging her playfully. "This is kind of a big deal."

Brooklyn grinned at me. "You think?" She glanced over her shoulder where Rand's team surrounded him and some of the other drivers, had started to gather, congratulating him. Then she hugged me and took off to go to her man. I chuckled as I watched, happy for my friend, my man, and Rand, who still scared the shit out of me despite giving us a fresh start, and watched as Hutch caught my eye. He was still up in the pit box, looking serious and a little nervous because there would be interviews coming his way, too. He had his headphones down around his neck, and his trucker hat that bared Rand's number on it, on backward as he scanned over the screens in front of him. Crew chief was a big deal. He had to work with the spotters, keep the driver focused on the track, analyze lap times, fuel mileage, pit-stop strategy, and everything else that went on during the race. Any mistake, no matter how small, could ruin the chance for a win; never mind a great finish.

I noticed how handsome he looked in the shirt he wore with Rand's sponsor and number decorated all over it, the tan he had acquired now that he was out in the sun so much more prominent that ever. His blond hair curled slightly under his ears and I felt my heart swell with pride. Hutch glanced around the still busy and packed track before he looked down to catch my eye, bringing his hand up to his heart to form the sign he always gestured to tell me he loved me. I blew him a kiss before he quickly climbed down so he could grab me around the waist.

"Hey," he whispered planting a kiss against my lips. He swung me around before he gently placed me back on my feet.

I stared up at him with hearts in my eyes. "Hey yourself," I teased, watching the smile spread across his perfect face. "You know, they're going to want you in the pictures, baby, you're part of the team," I reminded him.

As much fun as Hutch had helping with the cars, he didn't like being in the spotlight. He had done countless interviews since Rand had started dominating the series, and Hutch had told me how much he hated every single minute being in front of the camera or behind the microphone. The asked him questions they shouldn't, pushed too much, got too personal, but Hutch was always professional, polite, and courteous. Only once did Rand tell someone to fuck off when they tried to pry into Hutch's background, when they were being interviewed together, and I thought for sure Rand was going to lay the guy out for it. I wouldn't call them best friends, but they were close.

"I know."

"You okay?"

Hutch still had his dark days. The ones where he could hardly get out of bed, didn't want to talk to me or anyone else, but luckily, those days were few and far between. Megan had recommended a fantastic therapist whom Hutch saw in North Carolina when he could, but had Zoom meetings when he was on the road. I wasn't sure how much Rand knew about Hutch's past, if anything at all, but something told me his past was just as dark, maybe even darker.

"I'm a little overwhelmed, but otherwise really fucking good, Jilly," he assured me, pulling me into another hug. "This is insane though, right?" His voice rumbled against my face, and I could tell he was trying hard to control his emotions. "That I helped Rand Shepard win his first championship." He pulled back to look down into my eyes. "When this is over, the celebrating, everything else that comes with it"—he pressed a hand against my cheek—"we're setting a date."

Hutch's divorce with Madison was finalized just a couple of days ago as well as her giving up her any parental rights to Hazel. How someone could do that to their own flesh and blood, I would never know, but I was happy to say Hutch asked me to adopt her as my own, which I agreed to without a second thought. Hazel already started calling me mom months ago without any convincing from our sides, and I loved her like my own daughter.

"Are you sure?" I wanted to marry Hutch just as much I needed the air to breathe. "I don't want to rush you into another marriage if you're not ready."

Hutch only smiled at me. "Don't ask questions you already know the answer to." His mouth found mine as we both heard someone call his name. "I fucking love you so much, Jilly." He confessed.

"I love you too, Hutch," I said, with butterflies racing through my veins. "Hey, uh, how do you feel about more kids?" I blurted as my nerves got the best of me.

Hutch looked confused. "I don't...holy shit." His hand went to his hat before he dropped it against my stomach. "Wait, are you saying you're pregnant?" When I nodded, he asked, "How far along?"

"I don't know yet. I realized yesterday that I was late, so I took a couple of tests this morning while you were busy with Rand at the driver's meeting. They all came back positive." I was scared that Hutch wouldn't want another child. Not yet anyway. I knew how much he loved Hazel and enjoyed being a father, but he had so much going on right now.

"We're having a baby." His voice was hardly a whisper.

I couldn't tell if Hutch was happy about this or what was going on inside his head right now. "Are you okay with this? I know we hadn't really talked about having children..." I chewed nervously on my bottom lip.

"You're having my baby, Jilly, what's not to be happy about." Hutch kissed the top of my head again, and that's when I saw the giant smile on his face that lighted his entire features. "All of this?" He opened his arms wide around us. "All of this would never have happened without you. You are the light to my dark." He pulled me against his chest for a quick hug before he let me go. "Don't go anywhere because the party is going to be wild!" He jogged off to whoever was calling his name, turning to wave at me, and I watched with a full heart as he high-fived some of the crewmembers.

"Jillian!" Rand's voice boomed loud enough to wake the dead. "Get your ass over here!" he demanded, and right at that moment, I almost wished the ground would open up to swallow me whole. "Now, or I'll come get you myself. You're part of this too, so get moving." He waved me over, and I felt my face burn as I started walking with all eyes on me. As I approached the crowd, I saw my future husband waiting for me, my dearest friend smiling with her arms wrapped around her husband, and I realized one thing...

My life was perfect.

The End

A Note from Sundae

I had planned to write a standalone. This is not the book I thought it would be, but Hutch Kelly would not leave me alone. When I try to explain to people my writing, I often say that the characters speak to me. And that's just what these two did. I absolutely loved writing Hutch and Jillian's story more than I thought possible. Hutch was the sullen, gloomy, alpha just waiting to get out, and I'm pretty sure that I love him more than the others (just don't tell Easton or Rand). I started writing the story right after I finished Cakewalk, in April of 2021, and I didn't stop until it was done on June 11th, 2021. I felt like I had to get this story out.

I chose to add in Brooklyn and Rand from my first book because Sully is a photographer, and I thought it would be fun to twist them together. Who knows what I could do with their kids further down the line if I feel like it *if* they start talking to me since I made Hazel and RJ besties. Check out the first two chapters of *Picture Perfect* at the end of this book if you want to learn more about them. It is currently free on all digital platforms.

If you are waiting for more of the Knights, you don't have to worry. The third Kingston book is coming in March of 2022. That book is already turning out to be much more than I ever hoped. I can promise you it's going to be bigger, darker, and not what you're expecting. If you are a member of my Facebook group then you have seen the spoilers I've posted, and have somewhat of an idea about the book.

Once again, *thank you* for reading this. If you enjoyed this book or even if you didn't, please take the time to leave a review because it would mean the world to me if you did. Thank you from the bottom of my not so black heart for helping me achieve my dreams.

Acknowledgements

My husband— My rock, my lover, my soulmate, my *everything* in this world. Thank you for continuing to be the glue that holds me together in the good times, and the bad. *The light to my dark.* Thank you for being my biggest supporter when I doubt myself, and for loving me when I don't feel like I deserve it. I truly do not deserve you. I cannot wait to take this next step with you no matter how *FREAKING* scary it might be. This is a set—**DO NOT SEPARATE**.

Laura— Your edits are truly beautiful works of art and I can't thank you enough for taking the time to make my art into yours. I am so glad that you have enjoyed reading the Kingston High series (Cash is getting his book soon I promise), and I hope that you loved reading Hutch's story as much as I enjoyed writing it.

My readers— I have no words. You took a chance on me, an unknown indie author, and decided you liked what you read. I appreciate you all so much. Thank you for sharing my work on social media, loving my boys—*Cash*— and giving your feedback. Without you, I would not be able to continue to do what I do.

Books N Moods— The teasers, the covers, the promotions ... they mean everything to me. Your hard work is much appreciated.

Mom, Ellen, Dea, Sissy, and Debby— Yes, you're family, but you didn't need to do all the things you've done to help me along the way. Sharing my teasers is one thing, buying my books is totally way beyond what you have to do. I love you all so much for having my back.

Dad— *I miss you.* I would never let you read my books, but I hope you would be proud of me.

Serena— Reading my books, sharing with your family, and then asking me to sign them is like a dream come true. When I say thank you, I mean it sincerely. Thank you for all you do, and for your service.

Before you leave, here's an excerpt of *Picture Perfect*.
I know you're going to love Rand Shepard.

Chapter One

Sully

I have absolutely *no* business being here I thought to myself as I looked around the busy NASCAR track. This was a huge mistake and I knew it. I kept telling myself on the drive up to the track that I was doing this because I needed the money and to keep that thought in my mind while I was out there sweating my ass off today. I was lucky enough to be a freelance photographer so I could take on projects like this, for companies who would pay me for my work. I normally loved shit like this, but today? Today this felt like an actual damn *job*.

I stood in the hot New England sun and pulled my dark hair into a messy bun before snapping off a couple of pictures. The drivers were getting ready to qualify for the race on Sunday and those that already had finished were standing around talking to the press and each other. I pretty much knew all of the drivers and I knew at one point or another, I was going to run into the ones that I was trying to avoid. Isn't that usually how it worked?

I used to love NASCAR racing. In fact, I used to go to as many races as I possibly could, *when* I could, up until that fatal day that broke my heart and changed my life forever. Wait, no, scratch that. It did more than just change my life or smash my heart into a million fucking pieces, but that's at least a good place to start. My entire world was turned upside down and I had been avoiding NASCAR racing ever since that happened. I had my entire life planned out up until that day and when Cooper died? He took everything I had planned as well as my happiness with him.

"I should have stayed home," I mumbled to myself as I lifted my camera to try to get a few more pictures. Lately, I had tried to stick to babies and weddings. Again, I made a mental note to think about how I was doing this for the money and nothing more. It was nice to get out of the house for a bit and enjoy myself. Maybe I could think of this as a vacation of sorts, even if it was only a couple of hours from my house.

I spotted my friend and driver Finn Houston standing up ahead with another driver who I hadn't had the chance to meet yet. It was actually because of Finn that I heard about this job and if he hadn't pushed me to take it I most likely would be at home right now taking pictures of another *Frozen* birthday party. Nothing against Elsa or anything, but I'm just ready to *let it go*. As much as I prided myself in being a strong and independent woman, I felt a sense of relief wash over me when Finn raised his hand to wave me over.

"Hey, Sully!" Finn flashed me a big smile before he pulled me into a giant hug as soon as I got close enough. He was handsome, not as good looking as his brother Cooper had been, but close enough. He was over six feet with broad shoulders and thick dark hair. His green eyes sparkled with happiness when he pulled back to look at me. "I'm sorry I didn't get the chance to see you until now. How does it feel to be back?"

I shrugged my shoulders as I tried to think of an answer. I couldn't lie to Finn without him knowing. We knew one another too well. "It could be worse. It hasn't been as bad as

I thought it would be." I let my eyes wander a bit and they landed on the driver standing next to him which turned out to be a big mistake. *Huge* mistake. I made sure to familiarize myself with some of the newer drivers once I had been hired for the job and I recognized him immediately.

Rand Shepard was not your typical race car driver. He grew up in Georgia and was around five or six years old when the racing but bit. The guy was as big as a linebacker and looked to be seven feet tall from where I stood. This was his first season of NASCAR so he might be a rookie driver, but the rumors about him being a bad boy, heartbreaker looked to be true as I watched plenty of women walk by trying to get his attention.

There was no denying Rand was attractive. The pictures I had seen did not do him justice with the inky-black hair that curled around his ears as well as the tattoos that covered his entire body. Or at least, the ones I could see with his fire suit on which was saying a lot since it covered his entire body.

Finn put his hand on Rand's shoulder. "Sully, have you met Rand yet?" He raised his eyebrows at me with a look of concern in his eyes.

I shook my head. "No, not yet." I smiled up at Rand as I tried to ignore the alarms and bells going off in my head. Warning me to run, telling me to watch myself. I wasn't sure what it was about the young driver that had me so on edge.

"Brooklyn, right?" Rand's thick southern accent caught me off guard. His eyes were hidden behind a pair of dark sunglasses, but that didn't stop him from making me feel like he was undressing me as he slowly looked me over. A smile tugged at the corners of Rand's perfectly shaped lips and I got the feeling that he wanted to eat me alive.

I immediately hated Rand Shepard. There was no other way to describe the feeling running through my mind right now. Anger flashed through my veins as I stared up at him. Drivers like him? They thought they were every woman's dream. Cocky and so goddamn full of himself, Rand probably thought I would drop my panties for him the second he asked. Over my dead body.

"It's nice to meet you, Rand." I plastered a fake smile onto my face and turned back to Finn.

"Oh no, the pleasure is all mine, darlin'." Rand's voice shouldn't have made me feel the things I was feeling right now, but I couldn't seem to control my body. It was like it had a mind of its own right now. I could hear the teasing; the flirting behind his words and it took all I had not to slap him across the face just so I could wipe that smug smile from it.

Finn coughed softly. "Alright then." He shot Rand a look that might have killed him if this was a movie or television show and I was never happier to have him in my corner. "Sully, how about you take a few pictures? Rand and I would love to help you out with that."

I gritted my teeth. "That would be great, thanks." I avoided looking back in Rand's direction and instead, picked up my camera from around my neck as the two men tried to get into a more natural position. "Just relax, both of you." I giggled at the expression on Finn's face. "Just try to act normal." I clucked my tongue along the roof of my mouth. "If that's possible." I shot a look at Rand for a second just so he knew that yes, dickhead, I was talking to you.

"Darlin.'" Rand's smooth southern accent washed over me like butter on toast. "I couldn't be more natural if I tried." I resisted the urge to tell him to shove it up his ass and instead, plastered that fake smile back on my face. I needed this job. I needed this money. London, she needed to stay in school.

Finn shot a look over at Rand. "Dude, you're acting like a real douche. We talked about this." His eyes had gone hard. "Knock it the fuck off."

Ha-ha, I wanted to laugh at him. Finn, forever my protector and for a second I felt a wave of heartache wash over me like I hadn't felt in a very long time. Cooper and Finn, shit, they were the best bodyguards a girl could ask for until—.

"Sully?" Finn brought me back to reality.

I looked up at the sound of my name. "Sorry." I turned to face Finn and Rand but had to take a step back. Rand had removed those dark sunglasses and staring back at me now were a pair of the bluest eyes I had ever seen. They were so blue you might think you could swim in them and for a moment I swore that he could see straight into my soul. Shame and desire mingled deep in my throat as heat settled deep in my belly. Fuck me.

I gathered myself together and managed to snap off a few shots of Finn and Rand together before I got a couple of each, alone. I knew that I was working faster than I normally did and I hated myself for it. I tried to shrug it off with the excuse that I could see how tired they both were, how tired *I* was, and the fact that I wanted to try to get ahold of London tonight if possible. I wanted to make sure she was doing alright and just wanted to hear her voice. I hated having her so far away, but she was happy and doing what she loved. We both were.

The real reason I was moving so fast was because I wanted to get away from Rand Shepard as fast as I could. I didn't like him or trust him.

"Thanks." I covered the lens of my camera when I was finished. "Appreciate your help." I met Finn's gaze and he smiled at me. "Good luck this weekend," I added as an afterthought.

"Text me later, Sully." Finn pulled me into a hug again and I knew he meant well. I also knew he would try to drag me out to some party that I didn't want to be at. He let go of me and glanced over at his teammate who was unzipping his fire suit.

"Don't need luck," Rand stated and when I turned to look at him I instantly regretted it. "I could, however, use the company of a beautiful woman. Any plans tonight, darlin'?"

My mouth fell open as I stared up at him. Motherfucker, who did this guy think he was? I noticed the way his white undershirt clung to his broad, chiseled chest and the colorful tattoos that were visible now. "Excuse me?" I managed to stammer out.

"Come on, Brooklyn." Rand took a step toward me, and I took one back. ""I don't see a ring on that pretty little hand of yours, so unless you have a boyfriend back home—"

My entire body began to shake. I wasn't entirely sure if it was because I was angry or excited about the words coming out of Rand's mouth right now.

"That's enough, Shepard." Finn stepped between us before I had the chance to do something I really shouldn't. Or say something even worse.

I watched as a huge smile broke out on Rand's face. A smile so bright that it would put the Rockefeller Christmas tree to shame. "Alright, no need to get so upset." He ran a hand through his hair. "I'm sorry if I upset you, darlin'." He still had that shit-eating grin on his face that made me not want to trust him. "But, if you change your mind, you know where to find me."

"You." Finn gave Rand a little shove. "Need to chill the fuck out and go back to your RV. Take a cold shower or something. What the fuck?"

Rand didn't look one bit sorry about what he said. He shook his head at me before turning and leaving me standing there with Finn who looked absolutely madder than a wet hornet. "Sully—"

"I'm fine." I put my hand up. I'll be fine. I have a few more pictures I need to try to get before I head back to my hotel. Don't worry, I'm a survivor, remember?"

Finn looked like he wanted to say something more, but he didn't. "Text me. Just let me know you're alright."

I assured him I would and we both went our separate ways. I realized that I wanted *nothing* to do with Rand Shepard and I was going to make sure as hell I stayed away from him the rest of the weekend.

Little did I know that wasn't going to be the case.

Chapter Two

I couldn't seem to get that cute little brunette out of my mind. She wasn't the typical woman I went after. I was more of the blonde hair, big tits kind of guy, but I couldn't help but give Brooklyn a hard time. Shit, she had tried so hard to come across as *not* interested in me that I knew she had to be.

Finn had made me promise to leave her alone, told me she was off-limits and not available. I wanted to tell him I didn't see a ring on her finger, which had never stopped me before, but the look on his face was so serious I thought he might actually hit me. Sure, Finn was a good dude. But we weren't super close or anything. He wasn't my best friend.

So, when Finn came banging on my RV door forty-five minutes ago and asked me to do him a solid or rather, Brooklyn, I was kind of caught off guard. Seemed the little firecracker had gone and told Travis Kerr that she had a date with yours truly tonight.

Let me back that up a bit. Travis, a fellow NASCAR driver, was having a get-together tonight with a bunch of other guys and apparently invited Brooklyn. I guess that he had a thing for her from way back, I couldn't blame the guy, and she had had a reason to blow him off in the past. Until now. But, this time she went ahead and said she had a date with me. Which I found completely hilarious.

"Wait a second." I grinned at Finn. I couldn't believe what he had just told me. "Tell me again what she said?" I folded my arms across my chest and leaned against the door frame.

Finn shifted his weight from one foot to the other. "You heard me the first time, Shepard. Can you help Sully out or not?" The look in his eyes was hard to figure out and I hadn't had the balls to ask him what their deal was. Yet.

"I think I remember you telling me to stay away from her?" I reminded him. "She also made it pretty clear that she wasn't interested in me so why would she tell Travis she had a date with me?" I chuckled softly.

"Look." Finn narrowed his eyes at me. "I can't answer that, you'll have to ask Sully that question. Can you please help her out? Go with her to the damn party and leave after an hour. Fuck it, thirty minutes for all I care. Do it for me, man."

"Fine." I was going to say yes anyway because even though I could handpick a dozen girls, Brooklyn Sullivan was the one I couldn't seem to stop thinking about right now. "Tell her to wear something nice," I added and saw anger flare up in Finn's eyes. "I'm kidding!" Jesus, did he have a thing for her? If he did, all Finn had to do was tell me and I would back off.

"Take a damn shower and put on something clean and simple. I'll go tell Sully you'll go with her. Don't be a fucking asshole tonight." Finn glared at me. "I fucking mean it. I'll be back within an hour." He looked like he might say something else, but instead turned and stomped out of my RV.

It wasn't a date or at least a real one, but I dressed like it was anyway. After my shower, I put on a polo shirt that had my sponsors' logo on it and a fresh pair of black jeans. I liked my hair the way it was these days even though it was a little longer than most of the other drivers'. Then again, I wasn't like most of the other drivers and I liked to remind everyone of that. I was six foot five which made me taller than they were. I worked out as much as I could so I was solid muscle and I was completely covered in tattoos.

See? Different. I liked it that way, too.

I slipped my wallet into one pocket and my cell into the other before I heard Finn outside again, but I could hear Brooklyn out there, too. I squared my shoulders and opened the door. I had been kidding when I said I wanted her to look nice, but she was wearing a little green dress that made my cock swell and stand at attention so much it hurt. She looked downright sexy. I stepped outside and immediately started sweating which caused me to wonder if it was the warm summer night or the woman standing in front of me.

Brooklyn smiled up at me, her face looking fresh and clean, except for a slight tint of lip gloss on her pouty lips. "I appreciate you helping me out tonight, Rand." Her dark hair was no longer pulled back and I noticed it was so long that it almost touched her ass. Twitch. There went my cock again.

"I'll leave you two." Finn's eyes were glued to me like I was some sort of serial killer. "Have fun and *behave*." He hugged Brooklyn, but narrowed his eyes at me again like I was Ted Bundy. Like I was planning on riding off in my Volkswagen Beetle and someone would find her body on the side of the road tomorrow morning.

I hadn't even said a word yet. I was too busy ogling Brooklyn and staring at the way her dress hugged her waist and the way her small tits were pushed together just showing off enough cleavage to be classy, but not slutty. Shit, I shouldn't have agreed to this. I wasn't the type of guy to just go on a date with a woman, and not bang her.

"Listen." Brooklyn put her hand on my arm and it was like a jolt of electricity right through my veins. I'm pretty sure she felt it, too, because she pulled her hand off me faster than the babysitter's boyfriend when the parents' car pulls up. She didn't seem to miss a beat though. "We'll go to the party and stay for about a half hour or so. Then you go off and do whatever you had originally planned for your Saturday night."

I usually had a girl waiting for me, but tonight for some reason I didn't. Not for the lack of trying, because I had with Brooklyn, but she shot me down so fast I hadn't had time to try another one. I think I was going numb with her warm little hand on my arm because I couldn't even begin to think about anything else.

"Sure, no problem," I mumbled like some sort of stupid kid who was talking to his high school crush. I didn't trust myself to say anything else at this point because my brain was thinking about Brooklyn's lips wrapped around my cock or her soft skin pressed against my chest.

Shit. Fuck. Crap.

"Should, should we go?" Brooklyn glanced up at me and when she started walking I managed to start moving with her. She started talking again but I'll be damned if I could tell you about what.

Fuck, I was getting hard and I should have been focusing on what Brooklyn was saying. I might have been a playboy kind of guy, but I *was* the kind of date that liked to actually listen to what his date was saying when they were out together. I wasn't a *complete* prick. I stared at her profile as we got into her little blue Ford and thought about what her legs would feel like wrapped around my waist. Dammit. I was doing it again.

Brooklyn kept glancing at me while she was talking and I'm pretty sure she noticed the bulge in my pants. I mean, it was pretty obvious. But, she just kept on talking. Maybe she thought I was just being that asshole again from earlier, the one that had hit on her. Or maybe she was just trying to be chatty and get this whole thing over with so she could go back to her hotel room and do whatever it is she did when she wasn't taking pictures. Call her boyfriend. Or girlfriend. I don't judge.

Or, maybe I was making Brooklyn nervous. The thought made me feel a little bit more like myself and I felt a little sense of relief wash over me. Who the fuck was I right now? I watched as she pulled her car into the restaurant parking lot and we both climbed out of the car.

Brooklyn turned to me outside the door before we went inside. "Don't take this the wrong way, but Travis is a fucking asshole."

I laughed. I couldn't help it. She was right; even though I liked Travis he had this sort of arrogance about him. Some drivers got that way. Seriously, the guy rented out an entire restaurant so that he could celebrate his own fucking birthday. Who does that sort of thing?

"He annoys me sometimes. He drives great and I'm sure in time will be racing with the best of them. I thanked you before and I'll thank you again for coming here with me tonight," Brooklyn told me.

I leaned forward and opened the door letting Brooklyn go inside before me. "I'm glad I could help, darlin.'" I smiled as she walked inside. Pretend date or not, I was going to try to make the best of it.

***

Want to read more? *Picture Perfect* is free on all digital platforms.

Also by Sundae

Kingston High
Piece of Cake
Cakewalk
Triple Layer

Wide Open
Picture Perfect
Gravity

Standalone
Out of the Dark
The Lying Tree

Signed books, merchandise and more at:
http://4sund.ae/

About the Author

Sundae Leighton writes romance novels that are sweet with a dark twist.

She got her start writing fanfiction with her friends in school, but didn't take the plunge to publish her first book (Picture Perfect) until 2020. Born and raised in Connecticut, where she currently resides with her husband and their cats. She sometimes scares herself when she writes things darker than intended, considers coffee the nectar of the gods, and once ran the NYC marathon (OK - *half* marathon). When she isn't writing down what the voices in her head tell her to, she likes watching murder shows, auto racing, and reading romance books with a lot of dark angst.

Read more at https://sundaeleighton.com.

www.ingramcontent.com/pod-product-compliance
Lightning Source LLC
Chambersburg PA
CBHW071410200726
48294CB00002B/341